SAVING WASHINGTON

CHRIS FORMANT

SAVING
WASHINGTON

THE FORGOTTEN STORY OF THE MARYLAND 400
AND THE BATTLE OF BROOKLYN

A PERMUTED PRESS BOOK

Saving Washington:
The Forgotten Story of the Maryland 400 and The Battle of Brooklyn
© 2019 by Chris Formant
All Rights Reserved

ISBN: 978-1-68261-832-5
ISBN (eBook): 978-1-68261-833-2

Cover art by Cody Corcoran
Interior design and composition by Greg Johnson/Textbook Perfect

PERMUTED PRESS

Permuted Press, LLC
New York • Nashville
permutedpress.com

Published in the United States of America

To the Sons of Baltimore,
whose bravery saved America.

An hour more precious to American Liberty than any other in history.

—THOMAS W. FIELD, nineteenth-century historian

Go tell the Spartans, stranger passing by, that here,
obedient to their laws, we lie.

—SIMONIDES OF CEOS, epitaph on the site of the
300 Spartans' Battle of Thermopylae

FOREWORD

"Mike, what can you tell me about the Maryland 400 at the Battle of Brooklyn?"

This was the start of my many conversations with Chris Formant, the author of *Saving Washington*. Chris could not believe that soldiers who had sacrificed so much for our Nation would have been forgotten over time and buried under the streets of Brooklyn. He wanted to discover who they were and what motivated their service and their sacrifice at Prospect Park in August 1776. He wanted to bring to life their story: The forgotten story of America's first heroes. I did as well. So together we began this unbelievable road of discovery.

These young men from Maryland were not the first to join and fight for American independence. The first to respond hailed predominantly from the New England colonies that had long been a hotbed for the rebellion. Beginning with the Stamp Act of 1764, they had most strongly voiced their complaints of taxation without representation and the abuses of the British Parliament and King George. Their complaints, never satisfied, culminated with their resistance to the Tea Act, and in December 1773, an act of defiance that we know as the Boston Tea Party. British response to the colonist insubordination was rapid and in the summer of 1774 the Parliament voted to close the port of Boston and passed a series of Intolerable Acts aimed at ending the resistance to British law.

Adding fuel to the dissent of the New England colonists were the sermons of its Congressionalist clergy. These ministers gave religious sanction to their members' opposition and told them that revolution was justified in the eyes of God. So strong was this moral imperative that in response to the Battles of Lexington and Concord, in April 1775 more than 19,000 responded to a call to arms. They laid siege to the British in Boston and provided the core soldiers for America's first army that George Washington came to command in July 1775. With the support of cannons moved in the dead of winter from recently captured Fort Ticonderoga in New York, this young Army expelled the British troops from Boston in March 1776.

In Maryland, opposition to the British grew more slowly and the colony's response was more measured. However, by June 1775, Maryland organized two companies of backwoods riflemen, who carried the Pennsylvania Long Rifle. Sending them off to join with Washington's troops outside of Boston. In July, the colony voted to join the rebellion, and by January 1776, the Maryland Provincial assembly voted to create the Maryland Line to serve as an element of the Continental Army. Smallwood's Battalion, consisting of men from Baltimore, Annapolis and the western counties of the colony, provided the core of these troops. By the summer of 1776, they began their movement from Maryland to New York, where they would face an undetermined future.

With *Saving Washington*, Chris has crafted a very special historical fiction that transports the reader back to that moment in 1776 and deep into the emotion surrounding the escalating tension with the British. Seen through the eyes of two teenagers, the reader viscerally feels the colliding forces of personal freedom, taxation, American exceptionalism, and religious fervor, swirling the emotions of the boys and the colony as a whole.

Chris asked me one day: "Mike, teenagers are not going to sacrifice themselves for taxes. That's a rich person's problem. We need to uncover the underlying reason these boys were prepared to die for their country." It is this illumination of the boy's profound motivation, that makes *Saving Washington* so unique at this moment in history.

MIKE PERRY
Executive Director
Army Heritage Center Foundation
Army War College
Carlisle, Pennsylvania

PROLOGUE

Evening, March 3, 1776
Cambridge, Massachusetts

Washington's exhausted body sagged deeply in his chair as the full weight of the tectonic upheaval seemed to collapse on his shoulders.

"George, my love…what is troubling you?" Martha Washington asked as she stroked her husband's hand.

The commander of the Continental Army stared down at his full dinner plate of fish muddle, which he usually didn't hesitate to devour.

"Here…have some wine," she said, filling his glass. "Ambassador Franklin sent it from his personal French collection. It is divine."

He ignored the glass set in front of him. He poked a fork into the stew several times, but couldn't bring a morsel to his lips.

Martha sighed. This was *their* time. They should be focused on each other—especially after all of their weeks apart and everything he had endured thus far in service to his country. Most of all, she had to find a way to help him relax and alleviate some of his burden. She could tell from his lost gaze that he was plotting, strategizing…envisioning every angle and pitfall of numerous critical decisions that lay ahead. There was

1

so little margin for error. So many lives hung in the balance. Their very freedom and chance at building a nation were at stake.

"Please, dear…try to enjoy your dinner."

She slapped her napkin down, hoping her firmness might finally draw his attention. "George," she snapped. "Instead of all this fussing in your head, you should be counting your blessings. Who would have thought that we would have been victorious in Lexington? Or in Concord? Or in Boston? You have been repeatedly victorious against such overwhelming odds."

At last, he turned to her with an unconvincing smile. "It is only the beginning, my dear," he whispered, repeating under his breath, "Only the beginning…"

"What do you mean?"

He looked into his wife's eyes and took her hand. "England has yet to bring their full might upon us. We are but a nuisance to them right now. Once we declare our formal independence, this will all change. They will bring forth their entire armada against us with legions of professionally trained soldiers with weaponry we cannot begin to fathom. How can we defend ourselves against such forces? Our leaders cannot even agree upon minimal funding to subsidize our army."

"But George, remember: We have the Lord on our side."

Now it was George's turn to take note of his wife's deflated expression. "Yes, you are right. I'm sorry," he said. "I shouldn't have said so much. I've upset you and ruined your dinner."

"No you haven't," she said, resuming her meal. "My appetite is perfectly fine. But you have hardly touched yours."

George faithfully took a forkful of fish and swallowed it. "Indeed." He dabbed his lips. "It is most delicious, the best I've ever tasted."

"You say that every night, George," Martha chuckled.

"Yes." He grinned. "I daresay I do."

They clasped hands, and George loosened up enough to taste the wine. As he was about to compliment it, a knock came upon the dining room door. "Please, come," George called out.

The doors opened and a young courier entered with a note clenched in his hand. "I am terribly sorry, sir; this just came in."

"Thank you." George nodded, taking the scroll from the courier, who backed out of the room and closed the door.

Martha studied George's reactions as he read. She decided she should finish her wine in peace to be prepared for whatever news he had in store.

George rolled up the missive and placed it on the table. He shoved his dinner plate out of the way, signaling he had no intention of completing it.

"What, dear?" she demanded. "What is it?"

George didn't hesitate to reply. He shared everything with her. "We received some news from the south. We have lost the Battle of Rice Boats."

"Rice Boats? Whatever does that mean?"

"A dozen cargo ships carrying rice in the Savannah River have been captured by the Royal Navy," he replied. "They are no doubt en route to feed the British up north."

Martha knew from prior experience that bad news signaled the end of the meal—for both of them. She rose with George, and the couple walked arm in arm toward their bedroom.

In the hallway, Martha paused abruptly by two massive objects on the ground: finely decorated pine chests. They were both open, as if preparing for imminent military travel. The chests were well stocked with a cooking stove, folding pots, utensils, plates, platters, bottles, and other items necessary for a prolonged excursion.

She had presumed they had at least another week—if not two—before he would once again venture off to battle. These chests meant not only that he would be leaving ahead of schedule, but that he would be gone for a greater duration than anticipated.

Only one word could escape her lips: "George?"

"I had them delivered today. I must be prepared for a prolonged engagement," he explained, before adding, "Just in case the Lord hasn't yet fully committed to our cause."

ONE

Evening, Friday, May 3, 1776
Fell's Point, Baltimore, Maryland

Thomas rounded the corner so frantically that he slid on the damp cobblestones and landed on both knees with an echoing thump. The twelve-year-old boy rubbed the hot tears from his eyes and scrambled to his feet.

Where could he hope to find anyone willing to go back and help him fight? Never mind that—where could he possibly hide?

No. He must save his father. Surely those men had no qualms about murdering a colonial citizen in cold blood. What repercussions would they face? None. They were lobsterbacks, for sure—even though they wore sailors' clothing and not the traditional redcoat uniforms. *They all treat us the same*, he thought, *like we're worthless colonial trash.*

His father's last words to him rang mercilessly in his head: "Run, Thomas, run!"

He was small and agile enough to have woven under and around a couple of the British sailors to make his escape. He had managed to turn for one last look back upon his anguished father: Three British sailors had taken hold of him by his arms and yanked his hair at the back, while another repeatedly dug his finger into his chest as he shouted indiscernible taunts. It was only a matter of seconds before the finger would curl into a fist.

Run, Thomas, run!

* * * *

JOSHUA BOLTON STEPPED OUT of the Cat's Eye Pub to provide his nostrils with some relief from the rotted oyster and sweat stench of the dockworkers and sailors crammed inside. He inhaled deeply while attempting to tune out the raucous laughter and off-key singing escaping through the window.

His fingers flicked back his long, wavy brown hair as his gaze wandered up toward the sky. He had made a good week's wages that week, but struggled to envision himself as a wretched dockworker too much longer. His father wanted him to learn the merchant business from the ground up, but he now began to question whether all the toil learning the ropes was worth it. What would serve as his reward—cats trailing after him for his fish scent? Trolling the pubs like the sullied drunks within? How would this kind of labor ever lead to his finding a respectable woman? Was his life's dream really to become a merchant like his father?

A finger jabbed him in the ribs and remained there. "Gimme all your tax money, mate, or I'll toss you in the King's tower!"

The assault jolted him at first, but he would recognize that disguised voice anywhere. He shoved the man aside and said, "Knock it off, you runt!"

"Aw, how'd you know it was me so fast?"

Josh turned to face the grinning Ben Wright, his best friend since childhood. Ben was short but stocky and could outwrestle pretty much any other nineteen-year-old, but it took a great deal to rile him up. Born free while many other Negroes served as slaves, Ben was well aware of his comparative good fortune. He had a contagious smile and had no issues being on the receiving end of a good ribbing from his friend. "Your voice and accent were pathetic. And it felt like I was being poked by a pansy."

Ben could give as well as take. "You *wish* you were being poked by a pansy," he said, slapping his friend's shoulder.

Josh couldn't contain his laughter. Ben always had that knack for helping him let loose—even when they were little mischievous boys putting "kick me" signs on the bottom of their feckless neighbor, Abner Higbee.

"Well…are we out here staring at the moon, or are we ready to celebrate?" Ben asked with a closed-mouth grin, on the verge of laughing. "I'm ready to spend some hard-earned coin on a few pints."

"Ben," Josh began, turning serious. "Do you think we'll be in Baltimore our entire lives?"

Ben looked blankly at his friend. "What?"

"Do you think this city is the only one we'll ever see?"

"I don't know," Ben said, considering. "What's wrong with Baltimore?"

"Nothing," he replied. "But don't you ever think about seeing the rest of this land? There is an entire world of opportunity within these colonies."

"I doubt there would be such opportunity elsewhere for me."

Josh realized his friend had a point. There were colonies, such as New York, where a freed Negro could get by, but that didn't mean he would be well-received there, either. "Never mind," Josh said, ushering Ben toward the door. "Let's go inside and lighten our pockets."

As they turned to enter the Cat's Eye, Josh discerned a faint voice in the darkness: "Help me…"

"Did you hear that?" Josh asked.

Ben paused to look around; he saw nothing. "Hear what? I think maybe you already had one too many. Come inside—maybe having another will stop you from imagining things."

Ben lured his friend halfway inside when the voice called out again, this time much stronger. "Help me, help!"

The young men returned to the railing, beyond which they could see a little boy with his cap in hand, tears falling down his cheeks. His knees wobbled, barely able to support his slight frame. "Please…help…"

"Are you all right, boy?" Josh asked as he examined Thomas for signs of injury.

The boy wheezed, trying to compose himself enough to speak. "Never…mind me…. Please, sir…my father…he needs help."

Josh knelt down and held the boy by the shoulders.

"Where is he? What's happening?"

The boy pointed toward the other end of the street.

He could hardly spit out the words. "Back there…sailors."

Josh nudged the boy toward the door. "Go inside the pub. Tell them you're with Joshua Bolton. You'll be safe in there," he said. He glanced up at Ben, but his friend had already started off in the direction of the scuffle.

"Hey, wait for me!" Josh called out, following his friend down the street.

Within moments they heard the shouts. In the shadows, three men were huddled over a broken figure pleading feebly for his life.

Josh and Ben exchanged troubled glances; they knew this could end badly for them. Should they really get involved in a stranger's plight? They read each other's minds and shrugged: *Why not?*

"Hey! He's had enough," Josh ordered the sailors.

They ignored him. One sent a high, arcing kick into the prostrate man's chest. Josh could see that his face was bloodied and he was on the verge of unconsciousness.

"Leave him alone—I said he's had enough!" Josh exclaimed.

A scruffy sailor with glassy eyes snapped his head toward Josh. "Fuck off!" he growled in a guttural Welsh tone. "All you colonial whores owe the crown money."

The group showered a new rain of kicks onto the man's back. The victim stopped moving.

Josh had originally hoped these sailors were colonials. But by now it was clear they were British, which complicated things.

"Gentlemen, please," Josh continued, giving it one last try. "He has a son."

"Yeah? And that little bugger is next!" the Welshman cackled back. He hoisted up the victim's bloodied head by his hair. "You hear that? Your son's head is going to be split open, you Yankee Doodle bastard. He'll be crying blood and pissing himself for the rest of his days."

So much for diplomacy, Josh thought. He unleashed a devastating kick into the Welshman's groin, sending him sprawling backward in agony.

Ben wedged himself between the victim and the remaining two sailors. One chuckled as he sized Ben up as a shrimp.

"This should be fun!" When he drunkenly lunged toward him, Ben sent a well-timed uppercut into his chin and a roundhouse left into the side of his nose.

The third sailor raised his fists toward Ben, but thought otherwise as he saw Josh coming toward him.

The Welshman and his compatriot—whose nose was gushing blood—both stumbled to their feet and gurgled curses under their breaths.

Josh grabbed the ringleader by his jacket and tossed him forward onto his knees.

"We owe you nothing!" Josh shouted. "Get out of here—*now!*"

The three men retreated down the alley. Josh watched them disappear before helping the victim to his feet. One eye was swollen completely shut, and the front of his white tunic was soaked with blood. He could barely stand, much less speak. "My...boy...Thomas."

"Don't worry. He's safe," Ben answered, helping the man stand up. "We left your son at the Cat's Eye Pub."

"God...bless you," he choked, as tears ran down from his one good eye. His head slumped downward. "They took all my money...and beat me...in front of my boy," he said. "What kind of animals...are these?"

Ben took the man's bruised hand and inserted a few coins into his palm. It was the money he had allotted for the night, but this was a far better way to spend it.

"I...can't accept this," the man protested.

"We take care of each other here," Ben said. "Come. We'll bring you to your son."

As Ben assisted the man toward the Cat's Eye, he noticed that Josh remained and was staring down the alley. His friend's hands were shaking, unable to release the surge of adrenaline from the fight.

"Goddamn British bastards!" Josh yelled into the darkness.

It was the first time Ben had ever heard his friend say anything like that. Perhaps it had been welling up inside him—like it had in the rest of the city, ready to explode.

TWO

Saturday, May 4, 1776
Curley Hill, Pennsylvania

Levi Doan crouched beneath the saturated branches of a towering oak tree. It was a hot, humid evening and the leaves continuously dripped rainwater onto his hat, although the storm had cleared a few hours earlier. It was now well past midnight, his scheduled rendezvous time with his brother. He remained unconcerned, however; Moses always showed—eventually.

Besides, Levi was patient man. He had been born a Quaker—a faith that instilled a certain amount of righteous patience from the onset. He had been taught that good things come to those who wait, and that philosophy had become particularly useful to him in his line of work. Long periods alone blessed him with time to sink deep into thought. Even as a boy, while his fellow worshippers sat in stoic silence during their morning meeting to commune with God, Levi's mind would be working overtime on worldlier pursuits…mainly scheming.

Levi heard sloshing footsteps approaching and ventured out from under the oak tree toward a lit lantern. He stood up to his full six-foot-two, broad-shouldered frame. He removed his hat to shake off the water, revealing jet black hair speckled with gray strands. "Next time, Moses, mind your feet—lame jackass," Levi said in a low tone, replacing his hat. "We won't get far if you slip and slide and make a racket around the forest all night."

Moses Doan was used to being on the receiving end of his younger brother's relentless teasing. But it was past midnight and he was in no mood for nonsense. "Howdy to you too, brother," he grunted as he spat on his brother's boot.

The response was not only welcome—it was expected. The two embraced and clasped forearms. Together the pair made an imposing sight dressed in black, visible only by muted lantern light. They were equally imposing in size and stature and had matching blanched, wrinkled skin with deep crevices on their faces from the scorching Pennsylvania sun.

The pair formed the center of the notorious Doan Gang who roamed the hinterland between Baltimore and Philadelphia. The newspapers had sensationalized their exploits and given them fanciful nicknames with bloody backstories. But the truth was far simpler: They were good old Quaker boys who had turned to robbing the obscenely rich colonial elite of wealth those people would never use.

Moses, the gang's leader, released his brother, spat again—off to the side, this time—and flashed the lantern by his side. "The fence lies about twenty yards beyond. I'd reckon there are a good ten corralled inside, unprotected. Should be an easy night."

Levi tipped his hat to his brother and pulled a double-edged hunting knife from his trousers.

"Grab that rope," Moses instructed his brother, who followed the command. "We'll fetch the horses."

The brothers ducked beneath the heavy limbs of the forest's oak and pine trees and weaved through the wet foliage. At the edge of the forest clearing, they extinguished the lantern and exchanged nods.

Click.

They froze, instantly recognizing the telltale thunk of a hammer's cocking back on a Brown Bess musket. Levi drew his knife and spun outward to the dark forest, preparing for a fight. He was unaccustomed to being trapped, and bristled at the sensation. "Who's there?" he demanded.

"Drop the blade, mate," a plummy British voice called out from the darkness.

Levi stood firm with the knife as his eyes scanned for any sign of their attacker.

"Don't fuck with me," the Brit ordered. "I have no qualms about blowing the head off a Yankee rapscallion."

Levi tossed the knife into the wet underbrush.

"The rope, too."

Levi grimaced as he tossed the rope into a puddle of mud with a *splunk*.

A flicker of light emerged from behind a grove of apple trees. The Doans tensed, trying to size up their pursuer as he gradually came into view.

The brothers squinted in the direction of an approaching tall, thin man in a dark wool coat and with a black tricorn on his head. He had a narrow patrician face that seemed prematurely worn. He presented a musket, flicking it between the two of them, with a double pistol holder across his hips and a twelve-inch military blade pasted to his left leg.

This was no farmer: He was clearly someone who knew his way around weapons.

And no, they wouldn't fuck with him.

"Sit," the man commanded.

The Doan brothers sunk their rumps into the sopping leaves.

He leveled his musket into Levi's temple as he spoke. "You know what happens to horse thieves in this county, yes?"

Levi's head went up and down.

"Who are you—some hired gun from the governor?" Moses intervened.

The musket swerved into Moses' temple.

"Did I grant you permission to speak?" he asked.

Moses closed his eyes and lowered his head.

"I thought not. Now, get back on your feet and walk straight ahead with your arms over your heads where I can see them."

Levi and Moses did as they were told, all the while astonished that they—the legendary outlaws of Bucks County—were being marched through the damp forest at gunpoint. Both men envisioned which part of the Englishman's body they intended to slash off first—as soon as an opportunity presented itself.

"Keep walking," he commanded from behind, making sure both men felt the weapon tickle the back of their necks.

They proceeded about fifty yards further through the forest when they came across a guarded tent. "Go inside," he directed. "You may slowly remove your hats, if you like."

The hats came off as they made their way into the tent.

Levi and Moses had a funny feeling about this. They could understand being beaten or even shot as interlopers, but this was something else…something quite different. Three armed men awaited them, as if their arrival had been anticipated all along. They weren't dressed as redcoats, but the brothers sniffed out right away that they were the next closest to be found hidden in these parts: loyalist colonials, if not actual disguised British advisors.

"Your legend precedes you, Moses and Levi Doan," their attacker said, passing them on his way to stand beside the other men.

Fear overtook both brothers: *They are the enemy. And they know who we are.*

"I hope that your reputations are everything we had imagined," the man said, filling a glass of wine for himself. "We are looking for astute businessmen. People who are seeking, shall we say—lucrative opportunities."

The brothers didn't know what to make of this. Should they respond? They hadn't been granted permission to speak.

"Oh, forgive me, I have been rude. My name is David Brown," he introduced himself. "Would you gentlemen care for a glass of wine?

THREE

Josh and Ben fidgeted and slumped in one of the front pews of St. Peter's. They were each nearly twenty years of age, but continued to act like bored teenagers when it came to sitting still in church.

Mary Bolton, Josh's mother, turned her head to them and hissed, "Boys—straighten up. *The sermon.*"

Josh sat up and ran his hands through his hair to try to wake himself up, as Father Fischer addressed the congregation. He tried his best to focus on the numbing monotone words coming from the pulpit during the early-Sunday-morning mass. He had been distracted and was having a difficult time concentrating on anything since Friday evening's run-in with the British sailors in the alley. The stifling hot summer air trapped indoors wasn't helping any.

Josh was pleasantly relieved to find that the Father's usual raspy recitations and admonitions were cut short this week. He was already starting to wrap things up. "Blessed be those among us those who have gathered here today…"

Josh knew he shouldn't question his good fortune, but wondered why Father Fischer wasn't quite as rambling as usual. The answer was unexpected. "As we near the end of our service, I would like to introduce a special guest speaker to our congregation this morning. We have with us Colonel Smallwood of the Maryland Militia, who has asked to address us on an important matter of community interest."

All heads turned at once in the direction of the man who rose and headed toward the pulpit; he was a round-faced, barrel-chested soldier with a cleft chin, dressed in a crisply tailored military uniform. Josh was mesmerized by his polished brass buttons, which glinted in the morning sunlight pouring through the windows, as well as his three-foot-long sword dangling from his hip. Colonel Smallwood had his complete attention.

"Thank you, Father Fischer, and good morning to all of you," Colonel Smallwood said.

"As you are no doubt aware, the tension between London and some of the colonies has been increasing at an alarming rate..."

The congregants murmured and nodded affirmatively.

"As a result, the colonial leadership here in Maryland is convinced we must expand our militia in order to better self-police our citizens."

Whispers of the word "militia" spread throughout the church. Josh and Ben exchanged curious glances.

"We believe that this is a far less antagonistic approach to maintaining order than allowing British soldiers to enter Baltimore," the colonel said. "We all know full well what transpired in Boston and in other colonies..."

Josh studied the surprised reactions of the congregants. The colonel's words were generally not something people talked about in the open. Maryland's ruling class had eyes and ears everywhere—well-paid informants—who wouldn't hesitate to report this back to the ruling powers in London.

"I hereby extend an open welcome to any able-bodied man to enlist and assist this cause," Colonel Smallwood said, scanning the crowd. Josh swore the colonel's eyes homed in on him, and he felt a buzz of energy surge throughout his body. *Imagine*, he thought, *being singled out by a soldier of such honor and glory who was a native of his own colony*. He had heard that the colonel had served with distinction in the French and Indian War and was even held in high esteem by General George Washington himself.

"I cannot understate how vital this effort is to the future peace and security of our colony..."

Josh shot an expectant look at his mother to get a read on her reactions to the speech. He had his answer as she rolled her eyes and turned away. Colonel Smallwood's words were not at all what she wanted to hear at Sunday church Mass. She had heard about the colonial skirmishes with the British and thus far had managed to keep a firm lid on such conversations in the Bolton home and around the dinner table. Mary was keenly aware that her son knew even more about current affairs than she from working on the docks. She had overheard Josh go on and on to Ben about the heroes at Bunker Hill and playfully repeat the phrase, "Don't fire until you see the whites of their eyes!"

The moment she dreaded most might soon be upon them: The revolution was heading toward Baltimore. At some point the reality of the ragtag northern farmers battling the might of the world's greatest army was bound to become a *southern* reality. What if her son were to serve this cause and put his life at risk? It was conceivable that this was a possibility when such talk now suddenly intruded on their Sunday church sermon, of all things.

"I will be available outside to speak with any interested parties," Colonel Smallwood announced. "We begin training in two weeks. Time is of the utmost importance..."

* * * *

STANDING OUTSIDE THE CHURCH, Josh and Ben watched a frenzied crowd of young men surround the colonel and barrage him with questions: *How much does the militia pay? Where do we sleep? Will we get to fire guns in battle?*

Front and center was Christopher Smithson, Josh and Ben's anxious redheaded former schoolmate, whom they last heard had been studying to become a lawyer. He caught their eye and helped usher them in closer to the colonel. "Bolton, Wright—you must hear what the colonel has to say," he said.

"Sir, I'd like to introduce you to my old schoolmates, Joshua Bolton and Benjamin Wright," Christopher said.

The Colonel sized them up while keeping one hand on his sword hilt. "Ah yes, I noticed you boys in the front pews," he said.

It is *true*, Josh confirmed; the Colonel had been studying him during the speech.

"The two of you are *friends*?"

They instantly knew what he was getting at: Was Ben accompanying him as a friend or as property?

"Friends," Ben cut in.

The colonel didn't flinch. "Good. We want men who are *willing* to serve, not those who are coerced," he stated. He came to a realization as he turned his attention to Josh. "You're Samuel Bolton's son, are you not?"

"Yes, how did you—"

The Colonel overlapped Josh before he could complete his question. "Your father is a good man—a patriot, in fact, no matter what he might say about himself."

An awkward silence lingered in the air as Josh was taken by surprise at the comment. His father kept his points of view to himself and, to his knowledge, didn't take sides.

Breaking the silence didn't seem to bother Colonel Smallwood in the least. "We need more men like you both. I hope you will consider what I said today. This is a chance to serve your colony and keep your families safe. It will be *increasingly* important work."

His emphasis on "increasingly" didn't go unnoticed by the young men. *What, exactly, did that imply?* they wondered.

A familiar voice interrupted the discussion. "Colonel, please excuse these boys," Mary Bolton said, encircling Josh and Ben in her arms and guiding them away. Josh wanted to remain longer, but his mother could be quite forceful. "They have an important engagement to attend."

"I understand, my dear," the Colonel said with a slight bow.

Christopher jogged up behind the trio as Mary hastened them away from the church.

"Bolton, you *must* join—the colonel seems to want you," he breathlessly pleaded. When that failed to slow them down he added, "We can keep the city safe and the British out at the same time! We might become heroes—like the men at Fort Ticonderoga!"

Mary saw that the young man's garrulous assault was having a motivational impact on her son, and immediately cut it off. "That will be all for now, Mr. Smithson," she snapped at Christopher. "Enjoy the rest of your Sunday."

Christopher stopped in his tracks, his efforts rebuked. He'd find some other time and place to recruit his old mates—when Mrs. Bolton wasn't around, of course. He took his cue and retreated back into the crowd with the colonel.

As the three wordlessly headed through the streets, Christopher's enthusiasm and the colonel's words sank deeper. *A chance to serve. Increasingly important work.* If Christopher was willing to defer his legal studies to sign up for the militia, maybe Josh's merchant training could be put on hold as well?

One thing he knew for certain: If he were to volunteer, he would have quite a sizable hill to climb convincing his mother and father. But first and foremost, the militia wouldn't be a remote possibility if Ben didn't agree to join with him. Since they were seven years old they'd done everything together, side by side. It would be unthinkable for one to head off to service without the other.

When his mother wasn't looking, Josh turned to his buddy to discern any sign of what he might be thinking. Ben's head bob was all the confirmation he needed.

FOUR

Tuesday, May 7, 1776
Half Moon Inn, Newtown, Pennsylvania

Moses Doan swigged down the remains of his lukewarm beer and squinted into the sunlight streaming through the windows of the Half Moon Inn, his gang's favorite watering hole among the many rustic Pennsylvania towns they roamed.

In the light of day, with his curly, dirty blond hair exposed, he didn't behave anything like the newspaper accounts portraying him as a bloodthirsty bandit. He seemed relaxed and at home in this establishment—like any other Pennsylvania good ol' farm boy just passing the time.

Moses slid his empty mug across the wooden table to signal a refill needed just as the tavern door swung open. David Brown, the tall, thin man who had held Moses and his brother at gunpoint a few days earlier, entered the pub—again dressed in black.

This time Moses was able to get a good look at Brown as he approached his table with a stiff gait. Moses surmised he suffered from an old leg or hip injury. He was clean-shaven with pale blue eyes and a tidy, close-cropped hairstyle. His clothes were considerably finer than those of most of the patrons who staggered into the Half Moon. Peeking out of the folds of his black coat were those familiar twin pistols he'd carried the other night. *Likely these are loaded*, Moses thought. Brown's expression seemed to be set in a permanent grimace, which made Moses sense there was something sinister about him. While the man had let him and his brother go the other night, he didn't exactly seem the altruistic type. What was his game?

As Brown took the seat opposite Moses, he folded a pair of black riding gloves in a neat pile and positioned his hands at the edge of the table. "I see you have begun," he said, glancing at the empty mug. "Permit me to buy you another."

Moses nodded and the man flashed two fingers toward the barkeep, who hustled over a set of frothy mugs.

Brown drank half his beer in one swallow and then set it down. "Much better," he said with a wan smile. "I've looked forward to that since Princeton."

Moses sipped his own fresh beer and hazarded a guess. "You've ridden a long way, then?"

"Indeed," he replied. "But we are not here to talk about me. We have business matters."

"Fine with me," Moses retorted.

"Let's start with the matter of the other evening," Brown said in a singsong manner, like a diplomat or politician. Moses pegged him right away as high-class.

"We don't appreciate our work being interrupted," Moses said. "You cost us an expensive haul."

"Consider yourself lucky I let you go," he shot back.

Moses shrugged. "It wouldn't have been the first time we've fought our way out of a corner."

Brown folded his arms and smirked. "I sincerely doubt you would have been able to fight your way free the other night…. In any respect, it was good of you to hold up your end of the bargain and show up here— in your favorite establishment."

Moses shifted. He didn't feel comfortable with Brown's knowing so much about him.

"I don't care much for negotiating at night," Brown mused. "Much better during the day—when I can completely see my counterpart."

"Let's stop with the sideways talk," Moses said sharply. "What do you want and how much will you pay?"

"Your reputation and unique skills precede you," he said with an inscrutable grin. "My colleagues and I intend to make good use of them."

Moses studied Brown as he paused to complete his beer in one more gulp. He dabbed his lips with a napkin before resuming, "I think it's clear whom I represent, and you know we have the resources to pay. We hear whispers and must find out if they are true."

"You mean rebellion activities?" Moses probed.

"Indeed. Clearly, men like myself can't be seen asking questions. But you know people deep in the ranks, and you know where pressure may be applied."

"Why should I trust you?"

Brown leaned back in his chair. "Because I know you do the things you do for more than just money. I know precisely *why* you chose this life—why you are not a farmer like your father."

Moses was struck silent by the statement. The man had done his research. Though the press painted the Doan brothers as daring thieves after a colonial fortune, there was another side to their fight. Moses had seen his father—a reserved and devout farmer—physically harassed for money and goods by the patriot forces massing in Philadelphia. The old man stood his ground but, like a good Quaker, never took up arms. For his beliefs, he was ostracized and the family farm had been sacked more than once.

Moses had no such qualms about violence—or retaliation. His nighttime horse raids and robberies were as much for vengeance against the haughty colonial elite as they were for the money.

There was no doubt in Moses' mind that he was being recruited to perform subterfuge for the British. Why not agree? He considered. Brown understood him, appreciated his talents, and seemed willing to shell out compensation. He extended his hand and said, "Name me a price."

Brown's smile widened as he shook Moses' hand.

FIVE

Josh hurried inside the imposing brick building on Courthouse Square as the plaza began to fill with people eager to catch a glimpse inside.

Heading uptown away from the docks wasn't a typical part of Josh's evening routine. He felt a lot more comfortable tossing back a beer among the dockworkers or rubbing elbows with the city's well-traveled sailors. But tonight he was doing a favor for a friend, putting on his best attire and joining an elite group of Baltimoreans for a debate that had sent the whole town into a flurry of gossip and activity.

He caught Christopher's eye as he made his way through the crowd toward the towering oak courthouse doors. Christopher flashed his trademark smile and gestured for Josh to join him through a side entrance, away from the crush of people.

"I've never seen this many people in town!" Josh marveled. "What's all the excitement about?"

Christopher ushered him inside the courthouse as he shouted, "Come on, Bolton—don't you pay attention? Tonight is the debate!"

"I know, Christopher," he said sarcastically. "I just don't understand why everyone is so excited to listen to two old men talk."

Christopher scoffed in mock indignation as they made their way into the dark hallways of the courthouse toward the central courtroom. They ventured past several men in finely tailored regalia and women in enormous flowing summery dresses.

"You've never seen Samuel Chase in person, then?" Christopher asked, shoving Josh toward a leather-bound seat in the back row of the courtroom. He didn't wait for an answer as he blurted, "They say he was kicked out of his debate society in school for being so wild. And his letters in the *Gazette*? They're legendary!"

Josh hadn't a clue what Christopher was babbling on about—he knew nothing about Samuel Chase—but couldn't resist his friend's giddy enthusiasm. He also looked forward to another taste of the revolution. It was all he could think about since he'd spoken to Colonel Smallwood in the flesh a few days earlier. His mother forbade him to even mention the colonel, the revolution, or the militia around the house and yet...it was all Ben, Christopher, his mates, and coworkers around the dock seemed to want to talk about.

Josh scanned his fellow Baltimoreans as they settled down. The room was filled to capacity; many attendees clutched pamphlets and leaflets from the street preachers circling outside. Some used them as fans, but many more read the literature as if it were biblical in origin. It struck him how powerful it was that all of these people had come from far and wide for one shared purpose—to become privy to more facts about the cause, whichever side they were on.

After a few moments, the verbal adversaries appeared. Samuel Chase, a massive man with a mane of coiled graying hair, strode into the center of the courtroom with a scowl. His opponent, Michael MacNamara—a wiry Irishman who had once been the mayor of Annapolis—stood opposite, eying him with equal contempt.

Chase wasted no time setting the tone with his opening remarks. "Gentlemen and ladies, your attention please!" his voice boomed. "Those of you who know my past history with Mr. MacNamara know that we are fond friends."

Laughter filled the room. MacNamara's face turned a fiery red.

"That Chase, what a wit!" Christopher said. He leaned into Josh to whisper, "A few years ago, he called MacNamara a corrupt drunk in the *Gazette*. It didn't go over well."

"Tonight, we are gathered here to debate the cause of freedom for these colonies," Chase continued. "Mr. MacNamara believes in using the power of wealth and influence to become a favorite of the ruling class.... I say we have had enough with wealth and influence in our land. What has wealth and influence brought us, except more taxes and less opportunity?"

Half the crowd erupted in a cheer, while the other half leapt to their feet with boos and hisses.

MacNamara held up his hand to beckon the crowd to simmer down. He fired back with equal venom in his Irish brogue, "What Mr. Chase means to say is that he hates wealth and influence because he doesn't have any! He's nothing but a foul-mouthed mob ringleader!"

Chase raised an eyebrow and stomped toward the Irishman in fake outrage. He gestured his beefy finger at MacNamara. "Listen to corruption speak! Is this the type of leadership we desire for the future?"

The heated exchange of jibes and attacks continued for several minutes, creating grand entertainment for everyone—no matter where the allegiances resided. Christopher elbowed Josh with a wide smile plastered across his face. "Isn't this exciting, Bolton? What a thrill to see Chase standing up for the cause of freedom!"

Josh wasn't sure how persuasive either of their arguments were— it struck him that they were merely trading insults—but it was rather exciting for him to see two such dignified men disagree so openly and passionately. It felt as though an unspoken secret had spilled out into the open for all to see.

At the end of the debate, attendees from both sides rose to their feet claiming their respective champion had been victorious. MacNamara urged his supporters to gather at a local pub, where he would continue to make his case. Chase, for his part, seemed satisfied with his performance as he dabbed his forehead with a handkerchief. Before he could catch his breath, he was surrounded by supporters, who peppered him with questions.

Christopher tugged Josh toward the throng surrounding Chase. "Come on, Bolton—now is the chance to meet the great man in person!"

Josh gestured toward the exit. "I'm sorry, mate," he said. "I have to go."

"What are you talking about, Bolton? Your mother isn't here."

Josh grinned as he shook his friend's hand. "I have to wake up early in the morning. I have a hectic day at the docks."

"Always checking out early, eh Bolton?" Christopher asked. "It's all right. I'm just glad you came."

"So am I," Josh admitted.

Christopher wished him well and then rushed headlong into the crowd swarming Chase.

Josh headed in the opposite direction and slipped outside into the now empty square. As he made his way home, he soon became lost in thought. First about the fight in the alley to aid the man and his boy. Then about Smallwood. Now Chase. His future somehow seemed wrapped up in this swirl of events—but what did it all mean?

A sheet of paper whirled past his face. Curious, he gave it chase for a few steps and then snagged it. He unfurled the leaflet and read the words of a preacher he had never heard of, Isaac Backus:

> Whereas in ecclesiastical affairs we are most solemnly warned not to be subject to ordinances, after the doctrines and commandments of men…. And it is evident that he who is the only worthy object of worship, has always claimed it as his sole prerogative, to determine by express laws, what his worship shall be, who shall minister in it, and how they shall be supported…

Josh stared at the paper as the words resonated in his head: "warned not to be subject to ordinances." He folded it up into his pocket and resumed his walk home, suddenly regretting not joining Christopher to chat with Samuel Chase.

SIX

Monday, May 13, 1776
Fell's Point, Baltimore, Maryland

Sam Bolton had absentmindedly left one of the merchant ship's contracts buried somewhere among the stacks on his writing desk. This was not the first—or even the second—time he had been this absentminded, and his son half-expected it.

Josh shook his head as yet again he had to explain to an impatient group of sailors waiting to be paid that he would return in an instant. The sailors cursed at his back as he dashed toward his father's office.

Josh was familiar with all of the shortcuts along the cobblestone back alleys of Fell's Point. He deftly maneuvered through manicured gardens and hopped over several fences as he made his way down a narrow street leading up to the business district.

He wiped his sweaty palms on his loose tunic and muttered under his breath, "How can such a smart man be so addle-brained?"

Josh breathlessly stormed into his father's dim office, shoving the door so hard that it swung open and smacked against the wall. He rifled through the stacks of papers on his father's desk—almost tipping over an inkwell but righting it in time—when he heard muffled voices from the sitting room next door.

He inched closer to the door to get a better listen. "It's just too much," rattled an agitated voice.

Josh knew he should grab what he needed and return straight away. The sailors wouldn't be patient for too long. But his boyish curiosity had been aroused enough for him to edge even closer to the door and open it a crack. *What's another minute?* he mused to himself; *the sailors have already waited this long.*

He peered into his father's wood-paneled sitting room. Sam was slumped back in his favorite leather wing chair, puffing on his pipe; his brows were furrowed. Next to him sat Horace Greenwood—a wealthy merchant friend—and, at the head of the table, Father Fischer. His father respected the reverend and had turned to him for counsel at difficult times.

Greenwood, who held up a crumpled piece of parchment, spoke up first. "Did you read the latest dictate from the Crown? First a tobacco tax. Then a sugar tax. Now the threat of an embargo that would shut down our port—just like they did in Boston. This is hell for the farmers and even worse for us. How are we supposed to make a living if half of it goes across the sea with nothing in return?"

Sam took a slow puff on his pipe then set it down gingerly in the ashtray. "Yes, but the Crown isn't so foolish," he said. "We are, after all, British subjects and we are obligated to pay British taxes."

"Are you serious?" Greenwood spluttered. "I'd expect to hear that from the rich families of Annapolis who have their noses up the governor's ass—but most certainly not from you. You feel the sting of this tax more than anyone in this city!"

"What do you suggest, Horace? Shall I become a Frenchman? Or run off and join the natives? I'm a British subject, just as you are."

"Don't count on that for much longer," Greenwood said. "If they keep up these insidious, demeaning insults, we'll be forced to boot out the bastards—like in Boston."

"I'd like to see the taxes lifted as much as anyone else in this city, Horace," Sam stated. "But do we really want bloodshed on our streets?"

"Of course not," Greenwood replied, his face darkening. "But it doesn't matter what we want. It matters what we *need*. And you and I and all the other working people in this town need to be done with this. We can't allow these leeches to suck the life out of us any longer."

Father Fischer shifted nervously in his corner chair. "Gentlemen," he said, almost as a whisper. "You speak of money as though it is the only means of deciding this dilemma. But this is not simply a business transaction. It is far more."

"With respect, Father, your church stays open because of our business transactions," Greenwood snapped.

"Indeed, you're very generous with the collection plate," Father Fischer conceded. "But there are matters on this earth larger than taxes and, yes, even larger than the Crown—"

"The Crown that forces us to pay these absurd taxes—ha!" Greenwood blustered, holding up the paper again.

"Let the Father finish," Sam said, relighting his pipe.

"Do you recall when the Puritans ruled over us and we Catholics could not vote? We could not worship. We could not even gather together in the same room," Fischer said in the same low tone. "But we had faith, even then, that God would never forsake us."

Greenwood shook his head. He seemed eager for the sermon to be over—but the reverend pressed on and commanded the conversation, in spite of his soft tenor.

"How do we know this to be true? Because the Puritans, like us, were only of this earth. Over a brief span of time, their numbers diminished and their ideologies began to fade. But God is constant. God never changes. And God has told us that we are free men with free will. Free men to rule ourselves—sent to this new world to be free."

Father Fischer paused for a moment but was not yet finished. He leaned forward and added, "We are all on this magnificent land to found a *new Jerusalem*. A better way of living. That is far more significant than taxes, kings, and crowns—don't you think?"

The door creaked; Josh realized he had leaned on it too heavily. Father Fischer eyed Josh eavesdropping on the conversation. He shot Josh a knowing look to indicate that he didn't mind being spied on and wouldn't expose him.

Josh realized that he had kept the sailors waiting long enough. He slipped out of the house with papers in hand and retraced his path back to the main pier, hoping the sailors hadn't mutinied in his absence.

* * * *

Josh completed his business with the irritated sailors without incident. As dusk settled in and the harbor's frenetic pace began to wind down, he leisurely made his way back to his father's office.

He'd hoped he might catch his father during an unguarded moment and ask about what he had overheard. Sam Bolton was an insular man of few words, more content to let others do the arguing and blustering. But the office was dark and empty: His father, Greenwood, and Father Fischer had left. He guessed that his father was likely out inspecting the last of his shipments for the day or negotiating a deal; he was always wrapped up in some business matter or other.

Josh had so many questions for him...so many things spinning inside his head that needed answers. How long had his father been having these private discussions with Greenwood, Fischer, and maybe even others? Were they, too, part of the rebellion in some way? Did they know its secret leaders, hidden amongst the merchant class of Baltimore? What did rebellion mean for the future of Baltimore—not to mention their family?

Out of habit, Josh started straightening out the scattered papers on his father's desk when a brown, well-worn Bible caught his eye. As he lifted it and rubbed the thick, worn cover, he knew right away it couldn't belong to his father. He cracked it open to the inside page and saw Father Fischer's looping signature.

A priest without his Bible? he thought. *That's not good. I must return it to him before it gets dark.*

He sprinted eleven blocks up Charles Street to St. Peter's Church. After catching his breath, he entered through the open doors and made his way through the corridor, which was lit only by the glow of a single oil lamp hanging in the narthex. He could make out the heads of a few devout worshippers who were seated in the front pews, solemnly reciting their evening vespers.

He wound his way past the altar to the back of the church and to the cramped cell where Father Fischer read, prayed, slept, and kept his office. The reverend, wearing his spectacles, was preparing the next day's sermon at his desk. He peered down through the lenses to regard Josh in the doorway. "I thought you might be coming by, young man," Fischer said, gesturing for Josh to sit at the edge of his made bed.

"I found this in my father's office," Josh said, presenting the Bible to the reverend and then perching where he had been directed. It took a lot to intimidate Josh, but Father Fischer's reserved and strict authority gave him pause—especially in this confined space. He'd known him only through his Sunday sermons and certainly had never personally spoken to him before. He was hoping this would be the same impassioned man who had challenged Greenwood back at his father's office.

"Thank you, son," he said, taking the Bible. "Is that all?"

Josh gulped and froze: The words weren't coming out of his mouth, and he couldn't get himself to rise and leave.

Father Fischer decided to put the young man at ease and help him out a bit. "Is there something you wish to ask?"

"Yes...I have more than a few questions," he sheepishly replied. "I heard what you said in response to Mr. Greenwood, and I was confused. Why do you never talk about these things during Sunday Mass?"

Father Fischer set the Bible aside and leaned in closer to Josh. "That, my son, is because most people aren't ready to hear it," he whispered. "We are living in a changing world—yet so many people refuse to see what is staring them right in their faces."

Josh had hoped the reverend would be a lot less cryptic. He gave the old man a chance to elaborate without interrupting him.

"So many of our founding families came to the new world for a fresh start—a new beginning," Father Fischer said. "Yet when there is the chance for a true break with the past, they hesitate. They see only the small lives they have built here for themselves, and they miss what is written in this very book."

He hoisted the Bible dramatically. "You know the story of the Israelites?"

"Of course," Josh answered.

"You'll recall that when Moses commanded the people to flee Egypt, many of them hesitated. They had all manner of excuses to avoid heading into the desert. 'If only you had let us stay in Egypt,' they argued, 'we could have been simple servants of the Egyptians forever. We could have been safe instead of alone, lost in the desert to die.' And do you know what Moses told them?"

Father Fischer didn't give Josh a chance to answer as he quipped, "He told them to not be afraid and to believe in God, for the Lord would fight on their behalf. And so Moses raised up his staff and the waters parted and the Egyptians—well, you know the ending to this passage."

Josh grinned. When he was a little boy, he had always loved the scenes of the Egyptian chariots washed away by the Red Sea.

"I think many of us today are like the Israelites who had doubt and were content to be servants to the pharaoh forever. But God has other plans. God delivered us here not to be servants but to be *free*."

Father Fischer's words echoed the sentiments of what Josh had read in many of the circulating leaflets and pamphlets. But one question nagged at him. "If we're intended to be free, where is our desert? Where are we supposed to go? We can't simply pick up and leave or march out into the forest."

Father Fischer opened the Bible and ran his finger along the verses. "You forget your scripture, young man," he said. "What did Moses say to the Israelites in the desert? He did not say, 'Run away.' He told them: 'Stand firm and you will see the deliverance of the Lord.'"

He rustled through some items on his desk and produced a leaflet, which he handed to Josh. "This may help clarify things a bit more for you," he said.

Josh glanced down at the leaflet; it was marked with the stamp of a prominent Boston church. "Was this…written by a revolutionary?"

"The population here is not yet ready for something quite that radical," Father Fischer admitted. "But the times are changing quickly. This particular work comes courtesy of a dear friend of mine—a congregationalist pastor who led the charge against the British in New England. I think you will find it most illuminating."

Josh tucked the leaflet into his pocket—the same exact spot where he had been keeping the passage from Isaac Backus. It occurred to him that even though he was not a true revolutionary, he now had officially become a *collector* of such literature. If he were found with such documents, there could be hell to pay; he might even face imprisonment.

"Thank you, Father," he said as he stood up and moved toward the door. He hesitated for one last question.

"Do you truly believe we have God on our side in this fight against the British?"

Father Fischer removed his spectacles and clasped his hands together. "That is between you and God," the Father answered. "*You and God.*"

SEVEN

Evening, Monday, May 13, 1776
Fell's Point, Baltimore, Maryland

The new barmaid at the Cat's Eye Pub was well aware of the incessant ogling and catcalling by the male patrons. She was more than accustomed to men acting childishly around her and used it to her advantage as often as possible.

Although she was a few years into her thirties, she could have passed for a much younger woman. Her Irish features—cascading strawberry-blond hair, fair skin, faded blue eyes—and tight, revealing corset ensured constant attention and generous tips from the patrons without the need for any overt flirtation. A smile and a beer in hand were more than enough to help her get what she desired.

She found herself intrigued by one young man who wasn't taking notice of her. *Why isn't he looking my way like all the others?* she wondered. It made him stand out even more.

On closer inspection, she found him pleasing to look at, with wavy hair and a strong physique. The fact that he was on the boyish side and several years her junior didn't faze her in the least. To her, this meant he might be considering becoming a cadet—a uniform that held great attraction for her—and that he could be easily drawn in by her charms. He wasn't brooding, exactly; more accurately, he seemed to be lost in deep thought, which made him all the more interesting. Certainly he seemed more attractive and polite than the typical grimy, sunburnt dockworkers at the pub who groped at her.

The young man had a friend with him, a black fellow, who was unsuccessfully prodding him into having a good time. The barmaid realized he had caught her gazing upon his friend and gave her a suspicious look. When she turned her head away as a reflex, he tapped his friend's shoulder. She could imagine what he was saying to him: "Hey, mate, look—the barmaid has eyes on you!"

She felt a tinge of embarrassment as the young man lifted his head and shot a look at her. She wasn't certain why she reacted that way—it was unlike her to be shy—but this was not necessarily a bad thing. She noticed that his beer mug had been drained and took this as a cue.

As she made her way toward the young man with fresh mugs of beer for him and his friend, the patrons began to stir. The pub instantaneously filled with music, singing, and raucous laughter. She had to spin around carefully to avoid spilling the frothy mugs as a fiddler darted in front of her.

She paused at the sight of a foolish-looking man in a redcoat jacket two sizes too large staggering into the empty space. Next to him appeared a taller, lanky man in a luxurious silk jacket. Behind them a tipsy fiddler and another man with a fife played a jaunty tune.

"For your entertainment this evening, we give you the tale of the redcoat and the vice admiral—brought to you by your favorite freshwater mariners!" shouted the redcoat.

The barmaid saw the handsome young man laugh and couldn't resist offering him her trademark smile. She took her small window of opportunity to flit past the performers toward him.

The redcoat warbled, "*Oh tell me, oh king, to thee I do sing, I have arrived in this faraway land.... And, just as you say, I am here to obey, I am at your total command.*"

To which the admiral mocked, "*Come hither, my friend, your money to spend, I'm afraid I must thee entreat. We've got stronger drink in these parts, it will help with your smarts, but never lead you to retreat!*"

* * * *

Josh was startled by the barmaid's bold approach, maneuvering her way across the pub to deliver a beer he hadn't requested. He had already downed several pints—so many he'd already lost count—and was feeling sufficiently inebriated. He tried to regain his composure, keeping his eyes on the performers instead of her lovely form as she placed the beer on the pockmarked wood table. He'd been wrong before while trying to determine a woman's interest and didn't want to again be played for a fool—especially not here and not with respect to such a beautiful, older woman.

Josh felt her lingering beside him, enjoying the show. The silence between them made his head feel numb. Why had she stopped there? Earlier he had been trying to process everything Father Fischer had said to him. But now this beautiful woman was standing right next to him, brushing against his side...wasn't it what he wanted? *Say something*, he pressed himself.

"*The king has too many pence and not enough sense....*

"*Not enough sense! Not enough sense! Not enough sense!*

"*Now my friends, please respect and show your class—and come on over and kiss my ass!*"

The two men dropped their pants and bent over.

"*Kiss my ass! Kiss my ass! Kiss my ass!*"

The crowd ignited in hysterics and roars of "Kiss my ass!" No one laughed harder than the barmaid, which somehow made Josh feel more at ease.

The performers and musicians bowed to a lengthy ovation. The barmaid placed her fingers between her teeth and unleashed an impressive whistle, the likes of which Josh had never heard from a woman. Over the applause she shouted to Josh, "Didn't mean to scare you before—you seemed thirsty."

Josh raised the mug and blurted, "Yes, I was. Thank you."

The clapping subsided and Josh was now face-to-face with this beauty. "I'm Joshua Bolton," he managed, extending his hand. He didn't know what intimidated him more: the reverend's spirituality or the barmaid's stunning magnificence. "Please, call me Josh."

"Tessa," she replied, placing her hand in his. She brushed her fingers on his knuckles before shifting them away.

"You're new to the Cat's Eye?" Josh asked.

"I am," she answered. "And I can tell that you most certainly are not."

"Forgive me...I'm being rude. I should introduce you," Josh said, pulling back on his stool to make Ben more visible. "This is Ben, my best mate. Ben—this is Tessa."

Ben smirked at his friend before he put out his hand to her. "A pleasure, Tessa."

"Nice to meet you, Ben," she said, shaking his hand. Josh was thankful that she didn't tease his friend with her fingers in the same way she had done to him. Surely that had been a sign of interest—wasn't it?

"Where are you from, Tessa?" Ben asked.

"Here. There. Everywhere," she joked. "And you?"

"Just here."

If Josh wasn't mistaken, he swore he had picked up on a slight tone in Ben's words. "Well then," Josh intervened. "Since I've done the proper thing and introduced you, perhaps you can now"—he added a subtle wink—"go somewhere *over there*."

Ben stood up, getting the hint. "Ah yes," he said. "I do have business over there...with my friend Aleister, the cobbler. We have important, er—*cobblering* talk to discuss. Charmed meeting you, Miss Tessa."

Tessa seemed pleased as Ben slinked off to give them privacy. "Tell me, Mr. Joshua Bolton," she leered. "What were you thinking about earlier? You seemed completely lost in your thoughts. I haven't served in this pub for very long, but from what I've seen so far around here, men don't seem to do much in the way of thinking."

"I was thinking about a conversation I had with a reverend..."

"Here?"

"No, of course not." He laughed. "In church before I arrived here."

"Oh," she said, pulling back a trifle. "You're a religious one. That's not exactly my—"

"Don't be silly, I'm no fanatic," he interrupted her. "I was returning a Bible the reverend left at my father's office. We talked about things…"

She leaned in further. "Things such as?"

Tessa had a way of getting words to flow out of his lips. "Independence," he whispered.

"Independence?" she asked, feigning ignorance. "Do you mean like independence from home? I did that a long time ago."

"No," he said, lowering his voice further. "From England."

"I see," Tessa said, planting herself on the stool Ben had occupied. "Tell me more about this reverend."

Ben, who had shifted across the room to start up a separate conversation, wasn't listening to Aleister, a cobbler who babbled on about stylish new boots that had come in from France or someplace. He couldn't help but look at the barmaid—Tessa. She was beautiful, for certain, and he didn't for an instant fault his friend for being receptive to her flirtations. There was something wrong about her, but he couldn't point his finger at what it was. Not to diminish or insult his friend, but, of all the men in this establishment, why had she chosen him? How is it a woman like this suddenly appeared at the Cat's Eye? What secrets might she be hiding?

Finally, something Aleister said in a loud voice about shoe buckles brought Ben back to his senses. *Damn, what kind of friend am I?* he thought. *I should be* pleased *for my friend's good fortune.*

He chalked it up to a bit of jealousy and faced the cobbler with greater focus. "Yes, French black boots with a buckle," he said. "I've always fancied having a pair myself."

* * * *

After Josh and Tessa finished their brief, intimate conversation, she kissed him on the cheek and excused herself. "I have to go back to work. Maybe we can talk more later? A drink?"

"Sure," he responded, unable to breathe as he spun in his seat to soak in every inch of Tessa as she stepped away.

The slap against his back served its intended purpose. "Well, mate! Having a grand time tonight in the Cat's Eye, I see! Quite an impression you're making."

Josh swiveled around to see that Ben had returned to his stool and was beaming slyly at him. When Josh didn't say anything, he chimed in, "Oh please, don't kiss and tell—not even to your best friend."

Josh blushed; obviously Ben had witnessed the exchange. "There's nothing to tell…we hit it off, that's all."

"Uh-huh," Ben skeptically said. Josh realized he could avoid going any further into this conversation by burying himself in his beer.

"That's right, drink up," Ben teased. "You'll need all the courage you can get with that one."

Josh dreamily filled his friend in on his time with Tessa. *Oh Lord*, Ben thought, *she's already reeled him in and he's flopping all over the deck.*

Ben was about to offer a brotherly word of caution when a voice near the bar broke in, "I know you two boys."

It was a fresh-faced man in a tailored brown patterned jacket and royal blue silk shirt. He leaned against the bar, sipping from a small liqueur glass. "I've seen you work the docks."

The man raised a toast to their health.

"We work with the Bolton company. Are you a sailor yourself?"

The man laughed and took another sip of his drink. "Me? Oh no, I stick to the land. I'm afraid I'd be of no use on a clipper ship."

He placed his glass down to extend his hand. "The name is Mordecai Gist. I'm a merchant myself…. I'm familiar with Mr. Bolton, the owner."

"As am I," Josh mused. "Since he is my father."

"The young master Bolton—this is indeed a pleasure," he said, crushing Josh's hand in his grip. "Your father is a good man. How is his business faring?"

"All right…but not if the taxes continue piling up."

Gist downed the remainder of his drink in one gulp. "Ah, so you're no fan of our colonial wardens either, then?"

Ben felt he had remained silent too long and blurted, "Are you? I can't imagine you'd be laughing at songs like we heard before if you were. My name is Ben Wright."

"Indeed, Mr. Wright," Gist said, shaking Ben's hand, adding proudly, "I'm actually a cadet."

Josh couldn't believe what he was hearing. Somehow he hadn't pegged a man at the pub in a fancy jacket as a member of the city's highest-ranking volunteer military force. If Colonel Smallwood's militia were to be the policemen of the colony, the Independent Cadets were its elite corps.

Josh bowed his head. He hoped his movements looked purposeful and not drunken. "This is truly an honor, sir.... If you don't mind...may we ask a few questions?"

Gist agreeably waved his hand.

"Colonel Smallwood said he was recruiting his own troops.... Do you know anything about that?"

"Do you think the fight will come to Baltimore?" Ben followed.

Gist raised his hands in mock surrender. "Easy now, boys," he said. "I will answer all of your questions.... I'm sure you've heard rumblings from Boston."

Josh was fine that Ben was managing the questions at this point. He had started to doubt his own coherency. "We know that General Washington has taken command of an army outside the city."

"Correct—but even General Washington can't fight the British with New Englanders alone."

"He's in need of more soldiers," Ben said.

"Yes, badly." He caught the boys regarding each other with slight confusion and added, "We can't throw off British rule with only half the colonies at war."

"War?" Ben blinked. "You believe we all need to go on the battle-field? Including Baltimoreans?"

"If I had to predict what lies ahead in the coming months," Gist stated, "I would say that there is no household in the colonies that will not have family members on a battlefield. We are all going to have to choose sides and contribute to our chosen cause."

Josh's head swirled. Was it the beers—or all of this escalating revolution talk from Colonel Smallwood, Samuel Chase, Father Fischer, and now this gentleman—Mordecai Gist? He had only read about the exploits of the cadets in the newspapers and pamphlets around town; this was his first conversation with one in the flesh.

Ben was about to ask Gist another round of important questions when the cadet noticed someone across the pub. "I am terribly sorry, gentlemen. There is another cadet here I must speak to," he said. "But mark what I've told you: My words will be of vital importance in the weeks to come."

He bowed slightly to Josh and Ben and disappeared into the crowd.

"That conversation was intense," Ben said, wiping his forehead with a handkerchief. "I think I'm done for the night. And I can see you are as drunk as a wheelbarrow."

Josh wanted to argue and remain for a nightcap with Tessa, but deep down he recognized he was in no condition to stay a moment longer. He had never thrown up or passed out in a pub, like he'd seen happen to so many others, and he didn't wish this evening to be the first time for either event—especially in view of Tessa. The room tilted on its axis, and his mind raced as he lagged behind his friend. His drink with the beautiful barmaid would have to wait for another evening.

The friends supported each other as they staggered toward the door. Josh's eyes were barely open as they trudged into the night. But Ben was sober enough to catch a glimpse of Tessa—giggling while draping her body against Mordecai Gist's silk-jacketed shoulder.

EIGHT

The oars of the rowboat gently dipped into the warm middle reaches of the Chesapeake as David Brown took in a lungful of the salty air. The faint tinge of mud, silt, and sand reminded him of his childhood along the Cornwall coast; he pictured himself running barefoot on the beaches in a gentler time.

Brown shook away the daydream and frowned, flicking a sand fly from his jacket collar. This was no time for reverie. He spotted an anchored merchant ship wallowing in the middle of the bay; it didn't fly any colors. *Everything is as planned*, he thought. He gestured his arm at the ship to help guide the oarsmen, who angled their paddling accordingly.

The rowboat saddled up against the vessel's starboard side as the oars were raised upward. Brown took a deep breath and climbed aboard the dark ship.

A figure emerged from seemingly nowhere to greet him. "Welcome back, sir," said a uniformed guard, snapping to attention in his gleaming red dress coat with a long musket.

Brown shrugged off his black cloak and headed for the hold. "Ensign, remove that uniform," he barked. "We don't want you shot, after all."

The soldier blanched and hurried away with a mumbled, "Yes, sir."

Brown shifted past a dim oil lamp that swayed on a single iron chain as he made his way into the smoky hold. Beneath glowing candlelight sat three men around a table. He instantly recognized all of them, although they were in plain clothes: Gibson, a light infantry commander; Harrison, a cavalry tactician; and a tall gentleman whose countenance and bearing strangely resembled General Washington's, although no one would dare tell him so—General William Howe, the legendary parliamentarian and soldier.

The general spoke up first in a deep voice from his barrel chest. "Good evening, Colonel."

"Good evening, sir," Brown said, removing his hat. "I must admit I was unaware you would be joining us tonight. It is always an honor, sir."

Gibson directed a withering look toward Brown. "Don't bother yourself with formalities," he said. He pointed down at the parchment map stretched across the table. "This is where you should be focusing your attention."

The general rose from his seat and paced behind Brown with his arms behind his back. "I am afraid this is as close to New York as the command feels comfortable sending us right now," he informed him. "Hiding us in the marshes, it seems, far from prying eyes."

Brown bent over the map and inched the candle closer to the location Gibson had marked. The colonies were sketched out in black ink: Lines and squiggles represented British troop placements in blue; assumed patriot forces were in red. When Brown regarded the map from a further distance, the picture turned into a sea of red with some scattered dots of blue.

"A trifle overwhelming, wouldn't you say?" Harrison asked.

General Howe stabbed at the blue dots on the map with a finger that appeared permanently bent from an old battle injury. "This is not even the half of it."

"Quite," Harrison volunteered. "Militias are being formed left and right throughout the colonies—we do not know where or how many."

"I have a strong distaste for vagaries," General Howe said. "These rebels must be exposed and swept away."

Brown looked the general in the eye. "I'm confident we will know a great deal more about their movements and intentions by week's end."

Gibson rolled his eyes. "Playing those spy games again, eh Brown?"

"I have already recruited the finest at cloak and dagger."

"And this will deliver results?" Gibson guffawed.

"If you have doubts, my friend, perhaps you would like to go behind enemy lines and take a look around for yourself."

Gibson pushed himself back from the table. "General, I beg your pardon," he said. "I will leave Colonel Brown to his spy adventures. If you require me, I shall be in my cabin devising genuine military strategy."

Harrison stumbled to his feet after Gibson. "I beg your pardon as well, General." He bowed.

Brown covered his mouth to conceal a chortle. *These two men are nothing but desk lackeys*, he thought. *They know nothing of warfare on this new continent.*

But he was well aware that failure was not an option. If his spy network was unable to produce usable intelligence, Brown was certain he would be sidelined to train cadets back home at Warley. His reputation would be ruined, and his war would be over before it even started. He refused to head anywhere near his father's disgraced path.

"I expect to hear progress within a fortnight," the general proclaimed. "I've entrusted you with an imperative mission, Colonel. You shall not disappoint the Crown."

Brown indicated that he understood the stakes, and the general disappeared into his quarters. Left alone in the main cabin, Brown took a seat to focus on the map. He focused his concentration with such intensity that the red and blue marks blurred into magenta.

General Howe was right, of course. The Crown had taken a chance on him; he was, after all, the son of a high-flying commander who had been court-martialed and stripped of his titles in the Seven Years' War.

The Brown family name may have been tainted in military circles—yet there he sat, on the eve of another campaign.

There were only two possible outcomes here for him: redeem his family's reputation or die trying.

NINE

Ben dumped his barely conscious friend on the bed with a thud. He panted heavily from exhaustion, amazed that he had been able to make it all this way from the pub in this condition with another man in tow.

He watched Josh roll over under the covers and murmur, "Tessa…"

Ben chuckled to himself and found himself unable to resist bending down to Josh's ear to whisper in a falsetto female voice, "Joshua…I love you, my Joshua darling."

"I love you, too," Josh responded.

"And I love *you*, Benjamin," came a familiar voice from the shadows.

Ben shuddered to his feet. He turned to face his mother, Lydia Wright, leaning against the doorway. Without missing a beat, she cut in, "But I would prefer it if you weren't out drinking and doing who knows what other shenanigans all hours of the night."

"Josh and I were letting off some steam at the pub, that's all," Ben defended himself as he approached his mother. As drunk as he was, he could still discern worry and crease lines across her face. Was all of this caused by just one night of fun?

"Is everything all right, Ma?"

"Mary told me she knows what you and Josh have been up to," she said.

Ben's mind raced to what this could possibly be and drew a blank. His mother and Josh's mother, Mary, often confided in each other; it could have been about anything.

"You've been going to all these talks," she said, adding with severity, "About the white man's revolution."

He could not lie to her. "Yes, Ma, that's right."

She shot a look back at Josh on the bed. "If he enlisted, would you join him?"

Ben was too drunk, wiped out, and intimidated for this conversation. He felt envious of his friend's slumber and wished he could escape headfirst into his own bed. "I…don't know."

"Let me ask you this, Benjamin," she said, softening a bit with her hand on his cheek. "If you were to sign up, what would you be fighting over? Taxes?"

"Well," he pondered. "Freedom, I guess." This was the best he could venture given the circumstances, but the words felt feeble as soon as they left his mouth.

"You guess?"

"I mean, we'd be trying to fight for our freedom—from the British."

"I know a thing or two about freedom," she said, as Ben braced for the worst. "*Trying* to be free left you without a father. *Trying* to be free left us living in another woman's home—though God bless the Boltons for sharing theirs with us for all these years…. *Trying* by itself don't do nothing. You must believe with all your heart in what you're fighting for. Do you believe that the white man's war will free *our* people?"

"I don't know that, Ma—but I do believe in the cause of freedom for all of us," he said with conviction.

She tugged his cheeks close to her own. "Ben, if you choose to fight for freedom, you've got to do more than *try*. You must *win*—and come back *alive*."

This took Ben by surprise. What had begun as something of a reprimand had turned into something entirely different. His mother recognized the cold, hard reality of the situation around them: The colonies were inexorably heading for war.

"I will, Ma. I promise," he said, embracing her.

They held each other tight before she patted him in the rump. "Now you go right to bed—you reek like a drunken old fool."

Ben obeyed his mother and stumbled toward his room with one question in his mind: *Are Josh and I really ready to fight and win?*

TEN

Josh was lost in a fog somewhere far away from Baltimore. Out of nowhere Tessa appeared, her smile brimming as she approached with widened arms. As they embraced, he heard drums...patriotic whistles... the screams of men in combat...cannons in the distance.

"I must go," he heard himself say.

"Don't," she whispered, kissing him.

She disappeared as soon as their lips met. Josh was certain he saw something in the haze: redcoats with muskets and bayonets. The *rat-a-tat-tat* of gunfire drew closer and closer.... He discerned voices calling to him. Oddly, they were familiar and seemed to know his name.

"Bolton...Bolton!"

Josh stumbled out of bed and landed crouched at his feet, unable to stand upright. His head ached. The sun barely peeked through the corner of his window; it was way too early for him to be awake.

He heard rattling against the window. "Bolton, wake up!"

Josh rubbed his eyes and moved toward the window. He saw Christopher and another man tossing pebbles against the closed tinted glass.

"Bolton—good, you're awake," Christopher said, sounding muffled through the glass.

Josh waved them off. "Go away."

"Come on, open up," Christopher implored.

"Not now, come back later," he hissed.

"Bolton, this is important."

Josh knew Christopher meant business; his usual lightheartedness was gone. His face already shone with sweat, and his red hair was tucked beneath a black watch cap. He noticed what could only be a musket behind his shoulder.

Josh gestured with his hand. "Come around front."

"Got it."

Josh hoisted on a fresh pair of trousers as he moved through the house and out the front door to the porch, where Christopher awaited him. The other man, with a moustache, whom Josh didn't recognize, stoically stood beside him. Both leaned on their muskets; Josh couldn't take his eyes off them.

Christopher was unaccustomed to seeing his friend in this condition: unzipped trousers, wrinkled shirt, mussed hair, reddened eyes. "Long night, eh Bolton?"

"You might say," Josh said, rubbing his forehead. After a slight pause, he gestured at the weapon. "What's that about?"

"Heading out."

Josh's eyebrows raised. "Where?"

"Off to Charleston—to fight the British," Christopher replied. "If Baltimore isn't ready to fight, then we will bring the fight to the enemy."

He had known the day would come, but couldn't believe it was happening on this morning. "You're joining General Washington's army?"

"It's time for Maryland to join the fight, and we're leading the charge."

The conversation lapsed into awkward silence. Christopher reached into his jacket and extracted a neatly folded, sealed envelope, which he presented to his friend. "Josh, I have a favor."

Josh studied the envelope. "What's this?"

"In case I don't come back from Charleston…please make sure my parents receive this."

Josh held the envelope outward, as if he had no intention of ever accepting it. "Nonsense," he dismissed. "Of course you're coming back. You'll probably end up bored silly from months of guard duty."

He waited for the usual jovial response, but it didn't come. The man with the moustache spit.

"Josh—this soldier here is Robert Buchanan. There are twenty just like him from Baltimore who have vowed to face the enemy head-on, understanding full well that we all might die for the cause of freedom…"

Josh hardly recognized his old friend underneath his new façade as he continued, "The revolution is everywhere. Our friends, our neighbors, our families, our church—we are all tired of the king and his tyranny and are united against him. The solution is not through talk but action— through a bayonet and a bullet."

Josh now stared at the envelope in his hand, unable to look at the muskets that continued to hold such fascination for him. *Am I willing to die for this cause?* he wondered.

"There is no other choice, Josh. We settled these colonies to be free, to create a new world. But every day the king's boot grows stronger on our necks. We've tried compromise, and you saw where that got us— dead bodies of innocent people on the streets of Boston…. It's not too late to join us, Josh."

"I don't think it's such a good idea to make decisions the morning after a night of intemperance," Josh said, using a mock sophisticated air he hoped would bring some of his old friend back.

"The cause will be there when your head is clear," Christopher sternly said, hoisting his musket back over his shoulder. "In the meantime— don't forget what I said about the letter. Goodbye, my friend."

"Goodbye…and good luck," Josh said, watching the men march toward the sun as its beams now spread over the city of Baltimore.

Josh longed to go back to bed, but knew he couldn't with this letter burning a hole in his hand. He stepped into the house and entered his bedroom, where he placed Christopher's envelope under his mattress; he didn't feel there was any need for this to be discovered by his mother or anyone else.

He lay down on his bed, but instead of going back to sleep he read Father Fischer's leaflet. As he scanned the words he began to wonder: *What would mother think? What would father think?* And…perhaps even more important: *Would Ben be willing to take on this cause with me?*

ELEVEN

Mordecai Gist leveled the pistol at the brick wall, shut one eye, and squeezed the trigger.

The gun recoiled into his palm, but he knew his aim was true. A hot metal musket ball tore through a glass jar propped up against the wall in an explosion of noise and shards. He lowered the pistol. *Not bad*, he thought.

He heard polite clapping and turned around to see the regal Captain Samuel Smith leaning against a tree. "You're improving," Smith remarked.

Gist pocketed the pistol and clapped Smith by his free arm. "We aren't all as naturally gifted with firearms as you, Sam."

The gentlemen had known each other for years, and their sarcastic banter had become legendary. Both from privileged families, they were the young vanguard of the revolution in Baltimore. But battle-tested soldiers they were not—at least not yet.

Gist wiped the perspiration off his forehead with a handkerchief and gestured Smith inside his townhouse, where Sarah, his cook, awaited them in the foyer with two cups of tea.

Gist handed Smith a cup as Sarah disappeared into the kitchen.

"What brings you here today, Sam?" Gist asked as he sipped the tea with pleasure. It was the perfect combination of black tea, fresh mint, and sugar.

Smith reclined in Gist's parlor chair. "Nothing good, I'm afraid," he said, resting the teacup in his lap. "I've received word from Washington's men to the north that it's eerily quiet in New York. We know the British will counterattack after Boston, but we don't know where and when. We are clueless."

"And Washington's troops in New York number how many?"

"A garrison force but no more," he replied. "Hardly enough to defend against an assault by sea."

Gist set the teacup on the wood end table. "Has he called in reinforcements?"

Smith shrugged. "My contacts tell me that he has troops on the way, but it could take months to muster an army large enough to defend all the islands."

"It would seem we are outnumbered any way you look at it."

Smith gazed out the window into the backyard, where the remnants of the broken jar glinted in the sun. "There remains one possibility…but I doubt you will like it."

Gist knew exactly where he was headed and volunteered the answer. "The Maryland Regiment."

"We could certainly use seven hundred more well-equipped soldiers on the front," Smith explained.

"You do know how to bargain, my friend," he said, raising a smile. "But these local recruits are largely untrained. Undisciplined. Most of them have never even held a firearm before."

"Let's not forget the fact that these poor boys still believe they are signing up for a police force—at least that's what Smallwood has been telling them at the churches and taverns."

Smith shrugged and rose to his feet. "I don't care one iota how they are recruited; just get me every last one of those men…. We haven't any time to waste."

Gist placed his hands on Smith's shoulders and refused to blink as he pledged, "Sam—you are my dear friend and a true patriot. You shall have your seven hundred men."

"Excellent," he said, heading toward the door. "Thank you for the delightful tea."

As Smith was halfway out, he heard Gist add, "Just don't expect them to shoot straight."

"Then you had best figure out how to become an even better teacher than you are a marksman," Smith said, ensuring he had taken the final swipe along with the last word.

TWELVE

Tuesday, May 28, and Wednesday, May 29, 1776
Fell's Point, Baltimore, Maryland

The week was a continuous blur of activity at Baltimore's ports. A steady stream of ships arrived and departed day and night, as merchants took full advantage of the clear weather and smooth seas to unload bursting loads of cargo. The unrest in Boston and rumors swirling in New York were at least good for one thing—the thriving Baltimore economy—although every boom seemed to be accompanied by increased taxes with less time to pay them.

Josh reflected long and hard about his future in the days that followed Christopher's departure. *If my friend volunteered to serve our country, shouldn't I do the same?* he wondered, his mind racing to all sides. *I'm not a soldier—at least not yet, anyway. What good would I be? My father needs me on the docks; perhaps my contributions to my family are just as valuable. But…if I don't join and others like me think the same, who would stand up to the British? How would General Washington ever win?*

Josh had hoped work would be a welcome distraction from these pervasive thoughts and from deciding his next steps, but his responsibilities and workload at the docks had piled up and weighed heavily on him, creating even more anxiety. Throughout his daily grind of managing waterfront logistics and pitching in with loading and unloading, he caught unpleasant glimpses of his father grappling with belligerent ship captains over the increasing taxes and transit restrictions. He would find his father at his desk murmuring to himself—his face flushed from another day of negotiations and his hands rippling through his thinning strands of straw-white hair. "First sugar…then stamps…now it's *everything*…a tax on paying taxes…are we still funding the French and Indian War?"

Josh became uncharacteristically distant from his dockworker friends and colleagues. He even averted Ben's gaze, feeling guilty knowing that his friend was puzzled by his aloofness. Each evening, as darkness fell and work subsided, Josh raced home and plowed through his accumulated array of patriotic pamphlets and leaflets, which had become almost shredded from all of the folding, hiding, and constant rereading. He had them virtually memorized anyway, but felt an unusually strong connection to them; they were almost sacred.

Every fiber of his soul directed him on what he had to do. Yet how would his mother and father react? How would *Ben* respond—could he convince him to join the cause alongside him and, if not, would he be strong enough to head off without him?

Then there was Tessa: He had spent only a brief time with her, but had felt an immediate connection with her and was torn about the prospect of leaving her before anything had a chance to begin. He longed to share his thoughts and confide in her—the revolution, his work…his feelings toward her, as naïve as they might be. He became tinged with fear and embarrassment wondering how she would respond and if she would reciprocate. He envisioned her smile and her comely figure in revealing barmaid's clothes and apron, and found himself unable to hold off a moment longer. He tucked away the literature and, with his heart pounding, made his way toward the Cat's Eye Pub—alone.

* * * *

Arriving at the Cat's Eye, Josh was pleased by three things: The pub wasn't nearly as crowded as usual; the patrons didn't include anyone in his immediate circle of friends and acquaintances; and, of course, *she* was there. Tessa looked exactly the same as when he had last seen her; she was just as stunning to him when he was sober as when inebriated. He trembled at the thought that she might not remember him—or worse, felt snubbed that he had left early the last time they met and hadn't even said farewell.

He sat on a bar stool in close proximity to her as she finished settling up a tab with a customer. She turned around to wipe off the counter with a dishrag when her arm stopped at Josh's. "Oh, hello. It's you," she said in a cool tone. Had he just been imagining all her flirtations and interest? "I wasn't sure if you ever planned to come back."

Josh felt his voice crack as he responded, "Of course I came back. This is my place. I'm here all the time."

"You don't tend to stay long when you do," she said.

"Yes…right…about the other night," he began. "I…errr…I had a bit too much…not that I can't handle a lot…but, well, my friend saw my condition, carried me off, and—"

Tessa's eyes scouted around. "Your friend. I don't see him here. Did you come alone?"

He hesitated before blurting, "Why y-yes."

"Did you come for a beer?"

"Yes, please," he said.

She nodded icily and started off to fill his order when he held her back by the forearm. He didn't want their relationship to be about just beer. "Actually, I came here for you, Tessa…. The beer is a side benefit."

She swiveled back toward him. Her eyes fixed on him for a moment until the familiar smile extended across her lips. She filled the seat beside him and beamed. "I suppose that side benefit can wait a few minutes."

"I'm not that thirsty yet," he said.

"Tell me, Mr. Joshua Bolton," she began. "That is your name, if I remember correctly—"

"Yes…but please, call me Josh," he said, immensely thankful she had remembered his name. If she had said George, Thomas, or Alexander he probably would have just gone along with it and pretended she was correct.

"Well, Mr. Josh," she teased. "You always seem to be so lost in thought. Are you a philosopher? A student?"

"No, nothing like that. I'm training as a merchant. Like my father."

"I see," she said. "So all of that talk the other evening about the reverend and his philosophies about the revolution. They meant nothing to you?"

"To be honest," he said, moving in closer to her to avoid being overheard. "It's all I think about…when I'm not thinking about you, I mean."

"I see," she said.

"I've actually made a decision…I think," he stated.

"You *think* you've made a decision? That doesn't make much sense. It's not a decision if you're still thinking about it."

"I've made up my mind to enlist in the militia. A few weeks of training and then I'm back at work."

Tessa lit up as she squeezed his arm. "A militiaman—how wonderful! But what are you still thinking about?"

"Honestly…how to talk to my mother and father about it. My mother doesn't want me to have anything to do with the cause. My father doesn't want anything to interfere with my merchant training, especially since this has been the busiest time ever. Then there is Ben—my friend, whom you met the other night. I don't know if he'll join me or not."

"And if he doesn't?"

"I don't know what I'll do."

"You will do as your heart tells you to do. And he will do the same," she said. "If he shares the same patriotic thoughts and values as you, he'll come around."

Josh relished her optimism. "We've spent enough time talking about me. What about you? I don't know anything about you. I only know you aren't from Baltimore."

"That will take a bit of time, which I don't have right now. I am working, you know," she teasingly responded.

"Maybe later we can go someplace private and talk. When do you get off? Perhaps we can go for a walk? I don't mind waiting…"

"I can probably sneak out in a couple of hours—it's a slow night. Let me help you pass the time with some drink—if you can handle it," she teased. "And promise not to run off this time?"

He grinned back at her, which was ample reply.

Josh watched her slink off behind the wooden counter. She returned with two frothy beers, which she slid in front of him. "I brought you two. Like I said, it will be a while."

"I'll be fine, thank you," he said, kissing her hand.

She blushed slightly, enjoying his fawning as he gulped some beer. While stepping away she said, "Pace yourself, Mr. Josh…pace yourself. You don't want *me* to have to carry you home this time."

* * * *

Josh's eyes remained transfixed on her for the next two hours as she served other patrons. He tried desperately to avoid feeling jealous, but he couldn't help it. Men of all ages salivated in her presence and seemed one pinch away from pouncing on her. But what could he do? This was her job—and she hardly even knew him. He went through the two beers in less than fifteen minutes, shrugging innocently when she replaced them with two more. "I know, I know…pace myself."

This time he was true to his word and slowed down, nursing the beers and stretching out their contents for the duration. At 11:30, Tessa folded up her apron, took Josh's arm, and escorted him down the block.

The night air was perfect: The temperature had cooled and a soft wind slipped through. Josh prodded her to talk about herself, which she did in elaborate detail: how her parents had died in a fire when she was a young girl; how she had dressed in rags and was a homeless urchin until she was scooped up and placed in a Pennsylvania orphanage; how she had been tormented by the other orphans and molested by the caretakers; and how she had hopped for years from job to job looking for a comfortable town to forget all the men who had taken advantage of her. Josh held her hand as he listened intently, and offered his handkerchief at the right moments for her to dab her eyes while recalling the painful memories.

"I'm so sorry you went through all of those things," Josh said. "And here I've been stewing and moping and complaining to you. I've had nothing but lucky good fortune by comparison—a good family, a good career, good friends. There must be something positive in your life—a dream you've had?"

"It's not about being a barmaid, I can tell you that!" she snapped. "Actually, I've been saving most of my wages. Someday I'd like to open a business. Maybe a perfume shop."

"Perfume?"

"Why not perfume? Something wrong with perfume, Mr. Josh?"

"Oh, it's perfectly fine. I like perfume—on women. I mean—on you. Not on the dockworkers and fishermen I see all day, although Lord knows they could use it!"

She laughed: How he loved to make her laugh.

They walked hand in hand for some time in what at first seemed haphazard fashion, until she stopped abruptly and pointed out a worn cottage with doors for multiple tenants. "This is my home."

"It's lovely," he said.

"No it's not," she said, playfully shoving him. "It's cramped, dirty, smelly, and temporary until I can find something better."

"Any place where you live is lovely," he countered.

"Stop, please, I don't deserve such flattery," she said, not in any way meaning it. "But…perhaps I do deserve a kiss?"

"Oh?" he said, his knees starting to quake. "Oh—of course."

When he leaned in to kiss her on the cheek, she shifted for their lips to meet and wrapped her arms around him. When she released him, she found herself as surprised as he was to be so stirred by it. "Will I see you tomorrow night—Mr. Josh, the militiaman?"

"Y-yes, of course," he stammered. "Tomorrow, for certain.... Goodnight, Tessa." He wanted to add "my darling" or some such romantic-sounding thing, but couldn't get the words out.

She waved to him as she stepped toward her door, unlocked it, and entered. He waited until the door was closed, a lock was bolted, and a candle flickered on.

Josh nearly kicked his heels together as he spun around for the long walk home. "Tomorrow," he murmured. Teeming with excitement and anticipation, he now confidently looked forward to the next day. He knew what he had to do.

THIRTEEN

Thursday, May 30, 1776
Fell's Point, Baltimore, Maryland

Josh waited for Ben to finish loading the last crate before pulling him aside. He had an entire speech memorized, but now that the time had come, the words were lodged in his throat.

"What is it, Josh? Has that barmaid bitten off your tongue?"

Josh laughed. "You wish! I know, I've been acting strangely lately…. I have something important to tell you."

Ben didn't blink. "You're enlisting for the militia."

"How…how did you—"

"Come on, mate," Ben said. "We've known each other for years. You can't keep anything from me. I see you've been slipping away to read all of those pamphlets. You've been leaning in this direction all along—it was just a matter of time. Christopher's signing up pushed you over the edge."

Josh chortled with relief. "Whew—I'm glad I got all that off my chest!"

"You didn't have to say a word, mate—I said it all for you."

"Still, it does feel better that it's out in the open," Josh said. "What about you? Will you join me?"

"Are you joking? Come on," Ben said, feigning being offended.

"I'm sorry, I…I know it isn't really your cause."

"*Not my cause?* Of *course* it's my cause. *Now* I'm offended," Ben said, folding his arms. "I decided to join up the moment Smallwood opened his mouth. Already told my ma, in fact."

Josh was dumbstruck. "You told Lydia?"

"Yep. I was just waiting to see what you were going to do," Ben explained. "It sure took you long enough."

"Imagine, the two of us: protecting our people—side by side!"

Josh and Ben embraced, laughing. He was relieved to find that his friend was three steps ahead of him.

"What about your mother and father…when will you tell them?"

"Tonight," he replied. "It won't be an easy conversation."

"You're right about that one, mate."

* * * *

Sam and Mary Bolton gazed at their son—their only child—as he told them he was heeding Smallwood's call to arms. Once Josh was done speaking, they watched him flick the peas back and forth on his dinner plate with his fork.

Mary broke the uncomfortable silence. "You are doing nothing of the sort," she said. "You have your father's business to consider; have you not thought of that? By no means are you joining the army to lose a limb or get killed."

Josh was prepared for this response. "Mother, you were there. You heard Colonel Smallwood. It is the *militia*, not the army. It is simply a volunteer police force to protect the colony. I'll be back at work in just a few weeks, right after training."

Everyone remained frozen around the dinner table. Mary turned to her husband, who stared down at his cold dinner plate. "Sam, please explain to your son that you won't permit him to do this. He's too young and you need him at the wharf."

When Sam failed to respond, Josh intervened, "Mother, the business will survive a few weeks without me."

She snorted in disgust—mainly, it seemed, at her husband's lack of engagement in the conversation and support for her position.

Josh took his mother's hand, attempting a gentler approach. "I understand how you feel, Mother, but please understand: I am now nineteen years old. I need to be my own man and make my own decisions. More than anything in the world I want to help serve the colony and keep us safe."

"Safe? Safe from what, Joshua?" she snapped. "We are perfectly safe. We don't have any of that Boston nonsense here. The Crown takes care of us in Baltimore."

Josh's chair screeched as he pulled a few inches back from the table and raised his voice. "*Takes care of us? The British?* The people who levy inflated taxes on everything we make? The captains who continuously badger father? The ruthless harassing of our people? We aren't British citizens, we're British slaves. They treat us like *shit.*"

"Watch your mouth, young man! We didn't raise you to speak like a peasant. No wonder the Crown intervenes when we have such rudeness from our youth. You might stand to learn some manners from the British."

"Mother, please, stop!"

Sam's fist landed on the table with a thump. "Enough!" he shouted.

It was unusual for Sam to raise his voice or act out in any way, so his demand had an immediate effect in gaining their full attention. "Mary, you must listen to me," he said, his voice becoming more soothing. "Our son will only be gone for a few weeks. The docks will survive without him."

Mary tossed her napkin onto her plate and stormed out of the room without having eaten a single morsel.

Josh and his father exchanged glances. "I didn't mean to upset her," Josh said.

65

"She has strong opinions—but she will recover."

"I won't let her change my mind."

"I know, son," Sam said. "But she does have a right to worry. You've seen the mood on the street and the docks. This could turn dangerous very quickly."

"Yes, Father, but—"

Sam held up a finger. "I am giving you my full blessing. You are a grown man and I respect your decision. I can see you've given this a great deal of thought and haven't taken the matter lightly. But also recognize that we are at a precipice. Our people are angry—and with anger comes violence."

"I am aware of that, Father," Josh said. Sensing a lecture was forthcoming, he rose from the table and added, "Thank you for your blessing."

"We aren't done here. Sit back down," Sam ordered.

Josh obeyed the instruction, but refused to look his father in the eye. He had already given him his blessing and acknowledged his right to be his own man. *What does he want from me?* he wondered.

"If our colonies fall off this precipice, what will you do when a musket is placed in your hands?"

"I will fire at the redcoats and I won't miss. Is that what you wish to hear?" Josh responded with a hint of sarcasm.

"Damn it all, Son!" Sam roared. "This is not a childhood game or some meaningless sport. Please: Listen carefully to what I am about to tell you. Everything we know is all about to change. Years ago, your grandfather and great-grandfather battled vicious natives in the woods. To survive, they had to create crops in mosquito-infested swamps, build their own homes, and defend against wild animals. They paved the way for everything we have and the many freedoms we now enjoy. We have had peace in this land for generations, and suddenly everything our forefathers achieved is at risk. By volunteering for the militia, you are placing yourself directly in the middle of a conflict that has hardly even begun. I have no doubt that this training will ultimately lead to army service and battle. It's inevitable. But you have led a pampered life. You have never had to scrounge for survival. You have never fired a musket. You have never had to face down a charging bayonet or duck for cover when cannon fire is blasting around your feet. You have never seen your comrades and mates spurt blood and have their arms and legs dismembered."

Josh sat back as his father took a gulp of wine for a recharge. He had never heard him speak this way before. "I admire what you are doing, Son, and I do give you my blessing. At some point you will march against the loyalists, which means you must be completely aware of what you are risking and are willing to do. You must believe in this cause and train to be a soldier with all your heart and all your spirit. You must revel in our freedoms. You must protect yourself at all costs—but also be willing to sacrifice yourself for your compatriots and leaders, including General Washington himself."

"I understand, Father," Josh said, rising to hug him.

"You take care of yourself, Son—now and always," Sam said, patting Josh on the back.

"I will," he said. "I promise."

Josh pulse raced as he stepped out of the dining room and into the warm night air. He was relieved to find Ben waiting for him.

"I overheard some raised voices," Ben said, clapping his friend's shoulder. "How did it go?"

"I could use a drink," Josh replied.

As the pair headed down the dark, empty street, Josh glanced back and caught a glimpse at the window: His mother was crying, while Lydia consoled her.

"What have we done?" he whispered under his breath.

Josh played back his father's words in his head, as if to reconvince himself that he had made the right decision. "...including General Washington," he muttered, not meaning to have said it aloud.

"What did you say?" Ben asked.

"Nothing," Josh replied. "I was just wondering how tall General Washington is."

"You're thinking about that now?" Ben chuckled. "I have no idea—but from what I heard he's a lot taller than the two of us, especially me!"

FOURTEEN

Josh and Ben downed several beers as if they were in a competition. The time passed quickly as they ribbed each other and relived some of their old antics and pranks. It seemed like it had been forever since they'd laughed so hard. For Josh, this was a welcome relief from his emotional family discussion. For Ben, he was just glad to have his old friend back.

Ben was startled when Tessa appeared. "I'm off a bit early tonight," she said, shifting in between the men on the stools to plant a kiss on Josh's cheek. Ben had an awkward view of her backside as she leaned in to his friend. "Tell me…how did it go…with your mother and father?"

"My father surprised me—he was pretty supportive," Josh reported. "As for my mother—well, let's just say that she's still digesting things, and it's not her dinner."

Tessa yanked Josh off the stool by his left hand as if he were a little boy. "Come, you'll tell me all about it." She gestured. "Let's go for a stroll."

"Hold on," Josh said, eyeing the remains of his beer. He snatched the mug and chugged down its remaining contents before addressing Ben. "You'll be all right?"

"Sure," he cheerfully said with a leer. "Have some fun. I believe it's a full moon tonight."

As Josh patted his friend on the shoulder, Tessa lured him away with a giggle. When the pair disappeared into the crowd, Ben hunched over the table with his head in his hands while he mulled his thoughts. He couldn't get his suspicions about that barmaid out of his head.

The hefty, unshaven barkeep nudged his shoulders. "You all right, mister?"

"Sure," he said, gesturing to his empty mug, "I'll have another." After a second's thought he called out, "Wait. Something a little stronger this time…"

* * * *

The couple admired the full moon illuminating the sky as they walked arm in arm along the water's edge and up to Federal Hill. Josh became a bit emotional as he played back the conversation with his parents. He felt a pang of guilt that he was sharing more of his innermost feelings with her than he had with Ben, his sole confidant to that point. But there was something about Tessa…something he couldn't resist that made him comfortable opening up about things that might have been embarrassing with anyone else.

"My mother doesn't understand at all," he went on. "After all they've done to my father and to our people, she actually *admires* the British."

"Does she?"

"Yes," Josh continued. "Their so-called good manners and elegance. Like how they use fancy monogrammed handkerchiefs to dab perspiration off their brows after a day of counting our tax money."

Tessa didn't flinch. "She's just worried about you. Give her some time; I'm sure she'll eventually accept your decision."

"I doubt it. She can be pretty stubborn." Josh shrugged, stopping to hold her and look into her eyes. "But at least I have you."

He instantly realized it was a foolish thing to have said to her and was embarrassed that he looked like an eager, inexperienced child. *I've been trying so hard to look and act like a man to this beautiful woman*, he thought, *and here I am whining to her about my mother—how pathetic.*

Her response gave him ample reassurance. "Yes. You *do* have me."

She leaned forward and kissed him lightly. His face flushed and he summoned the courage to lean in and kiss her on the lips. She responded warmly and encouraged him to wrap his arms around her body. He didn't quite know what to do with his hands once they landed there, and simply let them hang loosely.

"It's all right," she whispered. "You may touch me…I'm not exactly British royalty."

His hands twitched at first and then rested on her hips. He maneuvered to pull her closer, and their lips met. They held each other for several seconds, and Josh opened his eyes and whispered, "I love you so much, Tessa."

Tessa blinked; his admission had caught her off guard. He couldn't tell if he had overstepped, or if she felt the same way and was too emotional to express it. "Tessa, did I…say something I shouldn't have?"

"No," she said, clasping her hands over her chest. "It was wonderful of you; it's just that—"

"Josh!" an agitated voice bellowed out in the distance. "Josh—is that you?"

Josh turned away from Tessa to see who was calling him in such a panic. "Josh! It's me!"

He squinted into the darkness and saw Ben haphazardly ambling toward them. He could tell from the swinging arms and wobbly stature that his friend had consumed quite a bit more alcohol after his departure from the Cat's Eye. *This had better be pretty darn important to be bothering me when I'm…involved*, he thought.

Ben was breathless by the time he reached Josh. "Thank heaven…I found you," he said, bending over to catch his breath.

"What is it?" Josh demanded.

"So sorry…to interrupt…. Come with me, now. It's *urgent.*"

Although Josh was convinced his friend was thoroughly soused, he knew him well enough to tell this wasn't a foolhardy, drunken joke. Something must be terribly wrong.

Tessa clutched back Josh's elbow as he turned to leave.

"I have to go," Josh said.

"I know," Tessa reluctantly admitted, touching her hand to his chest. "Go with your friend."

"But…I should at least take you home."

"Don't worry." She shooed him. "You go on. I can handle myself."

Josh gave her one last look and desperately wanted to say something—but couldn't with Ben wheezing so close to him, beckoning for him to go. By the same token, how could he leave her like this with his words dangling in the summer moonlight?

She tilted her head to coax him into leaving. "It's all right, Josh. I'll see you tomorrow. You know where I'll be."

Josh bowed his head to her as he sought some appropriate parting words. Before anything could leave his lips, Ben grabbed him by the arm to drag him down the winding path toward the docks.

* * * *

Josh sprinted toward the main pier, struggling to catch up with his friend, who was surprisingly fleet-footed for someone who could hardly stand up straight and had been gasping for air a few minutes earlier. "Ben, would you please slow down and tell me what's going on?!" he demanded.

Ben turned on his heel and pointed toward the swaying mast of a newly arrived schooner in the distance. "You see that boat?" he said. "It's just arrived from the Carolinas—something's gone wrong. Come on!"

They rushed up alongside the docking boat to join a rapidly growing crowd, including several people who had been at the Cat's Eye when the news broke. It was almost unheard of for a ship this large to arrive so late in the evening. It would have been a risky navigation through the sandbars and shoals of the bay to reach Baltimore—which meant its arrival was an emergency.

Josh squeezed his way through the crowd toward a familiar mustachioed dockworker steadying a ramp into position. "What happened?" Josh asked.

"The schooner's just arrived from Charleston Harbor," he explained, leaning in closer for effect. "Carrying fifteen dead men from Maryland."

"Dead?"

The dockworker shrugged. "Something about fighting down south. I haven't a clue."

The dockworker straightened the gangplank and waved toward the sailors on deck to begin unloading. Sailors aboard the ship began to winch six-foot wooden crates into the air one by one and then lower them onto the ramp, where Baltimore dockworkers adjusted them into position.

Josh had loaded and unloaded all kinds of cargo over the last couple of years, but had never seen crates of these sizes and dimensions before. He joined Ben and the other onlookers as they studied the exteriors of the makeshift crates. Ben elbowed Josh. "Look—on the sides."

Josh curiously leaned in to see what his friend was referring to: initials smeared in black paint on the crates. The first had "T.R.," the second, "R.M.," the third, "GK".... None seemed familiar until they reached the fourth: "C.S."

Josh, feeling nauseous and lightheaded, bent over and clutched his stomach. He turned to Ben for acknowledgement, but all he could muster was the words, "I'm going to be sick…"

Yet Ben was no longer beside him, as he was leaning over the far side of the dock. A few moments later, the sounds of him regurgitating the evening's libations echoed throughout the night air.

Josh was struck by a realization: The war had come to Baltimore.

FIFTEEN

That night and into the following day were a blur for Josh: a mix of sights and sounds he had never before witnessed on the streets of his hometown. Growing up over the years, he had seen the corpse of a street dog on the corner, a rat crushed beneath a wagon wheel, and even the body of an accidentally drowned sailor that had washed ashore at the dock. But never had he known anything nearly as horrific as this…

It was past midnight when he first heard a guttural scream that cascaded out of the dockmaster's office window and reverberated down the docks. As it faded away, another equally wrenching one took its place. The pattern continued several times, causing the teary crowd that surrounded the docks and stared at the open window to clutch their chests and pray for relief. When the office's front door creaked open, Henrietta Smithson emerged; her face was smothered with tear-soaked handkerchiefs, which muted her pained groans and sniffles. Propping her up from behind was her redheaded husband, Charles, who barely seemed able to keep his own body upright.

Charles directed his wife toward Josh and Ben, who were among the onlookers.

"Thank you, boys, for bringing us," he croaked. "It was the right thing to do."

The young men lowered their heads. Josh and Mrs. Smithson exchanged glances. He didn't know her as well as the parents of some of his other friends, but he had an affinity for her and wanted to reach out and console her in some way—possibly a hug. Instead, he focused on an obligation that pressed him. On his return to the dock from having personally summoned the Smithsons, he'd had the presence of mind to stop at his home and retrieve an important document.

Was this the right time? he wondered. *Then again, is there ever a right time?* He figured it was far better to just get it over with and not risk procrastinating to the point of not being able to hand it over. He extracted the sealed envelope from his breast pocket and presented it to the couple.

"Christopher asked me to give this to you…if anything were to happen."

Mrs. Smithson was not prepared to face this, not yet. Her eyes burned on the document as she burst into sobs. "He was going to be a lawyer…he was always fired up about things. He always knew what was right…but had that wonderful sense of humor too…"

Mr. Smithson snatched the envelope from Josh's hand and murmured, "Thank you, son," before stuffing it in his own coat pocket and directing his wife away from the docks.

Ben patted Josh's arm—code to indicate that he had done the right thing. But Josh remained unconvinced.

* * * *

Josh and Ben lingered with the others for some time, unsure of what to do with themselves until daybreak when John, the leathery old dockmaster, shuffled out of his office. The young men, who knew him well, tentatively made their approach. He greeted them with a grunt accompanied by a salt-stained hand to prevent them from moving any further.

"Can we go in?" Josh asked.

"We'd like to pay our respects," Ben added.

"Sorry, boys," he said. "Family only."

"John, please—he was our friend," Josh persisted.

John stood rigid and almost fully upright with folded arms. "Nothing doing."

As Josh and Ben considered protesting further, the office door squeaked open and the head of a weather-beaten young soldier poked out. "It's all right, John," he said. "Let them in."

John shook his head in disapproval but allowed the two to pass. They followed the soldier into the dank, stifling office confines and into a dingy back room, where the body had been laid on a spare cot and covered with frayed bedding.

"I'm Gregory," the soldier said. "How'd you know Christopher?"

"Josh attended school with him." Ben gestured.

Gregory ushered them closer to the cot as he volunteered, "He was a good man."

"How did it happen?" Josh asked.

Gregory acted out the scene with his hands while he spoke. "We were stationed in Fort Sullivan, just outside Charleston in the marshes, at a small guard post. We heard rumors the British were planning an attack to try to seize the city. We readied our defenses.

"One day we saw the ships coming in on the tide and let loose our cannons. We nearly took down one British ship altogether, but there were three more still—all returning cannon fire. The pounding was merciless—we were no match for it.

"Our fort was really just logs lashed together, and could only take so much. A British round broke through one wall, and it exploded everywhere. Christopher was taken down when the wall collapsed on his company."

Gregory paused as if to register the impact of his own words. He could barely withhold a tear as he added, "We believe it was over rather quick."

Ben stepped forward. "Can we see him?"

"I must warn you, it's been several days."

Ben and Josh indicated they were fine with it.

"Suit yourselves," Gregory mumbled. When he peeled back the blankets, a sweet, sickly odor filled the room.

Christopher's remains weren't anything like the body Josh had seen in the water, which had barely looked human after days at sea. The only recognizable feature was Christopher's cascade of red hair, which was streaked with dirt and ash. His formerly youthful, pale face was coated with grit, puffy, and distended. A raw, tomato-red wound snaked down the left side of his head; his blackened eyes were swollen shut. His mouth was misshapen in a grimace, forever capturing his final moments of suffering—however "quick" they might have been.

Josh turned away, staving off the vomit in the back of his throat.

"You should know that your friend did not die in vain," Gregory said, rolling the covers back over the corpse. "Thanks to the service of volunteers like him, we were able to hold off the British. Charleston remains in patriot hands."

Unable to utter a word, Josh hastened out of the room.

Ben noticed his friend hadn't been himself and extended his hand to the soldier. "Thank you for this. We appreciate it." They shook hands before he retraced his steps outside.

Ben scanned around and found his friend catching his breath beside a shrub. He stood by him for a few seconds to allow the stench of decay in his nostrils to subside. "You all right?" he asked Josh.

Josh's pallor seemed to return as he pronounced, "I'm not just all right, I'm one hundred percent ready."

Ben, exhausted from his night of drinking and lack of sleep, gave his friend a quizzical look. "Ready?"

"To kill some British."

Josh slapped his friend's shoulder and added, "Come, let's start making plans. Right now."

Ben was hoping they might at least get a couple of hours' shut-eye first, but Josh seemed more determined than ever. Ben didn't know why, but he had an image stuck in his head of Tessa by Josh's side before he had abandoned her. Somehow Ben felt grateful that Josh didn't seem to have any need to check in with her to make sure she was all right—or to fill her in on everything that had transpired. *She might even be out of the picture entirely*, he thought, *which is probably all for the best.*

SIXTEEN

Evening, Friday, May 31, 1776
Fell's Point, Baltimore, Maryland

Moses Doan was more accustomed to spending his evenings on sleepy country lanes or by a fireside at a quiet tavern than at this god-awful place. The briny, sweaty bustle of Baltimore's port disgusted him. He shoved his way past a group of drunks pissing wherever they happened to be standing and gazed out over the creaking masts and groaning docks until he found the alley leading to his destination—a musty watering hole he'd heard was frequented by lowbrow colonials who were too provincial and inebriated to take notice of him: the Cat's Eye Pub.

It was more crowded than he had anticipated, but he managed to make his way to the well-worn bar, slide onto a wobbly stool, and order a pint of mead from a voluptuous barmaid with strawberry blond hair. He was tempted to make an effort to seduce her—these local colonial barmaids were easy pickings—but he had work to do.

While feigning an elongated yawn and stretch, he surveyed the crowd of ragtag sailors and merchants for possibilities. He had come to this inauspicious location on a specific mission from his new boss, and had a bulging satchel of freshly minted coin on his hip to show for it. He would not leave Baltimore and face his employer empty-handed; he'd sooner get pummeled in the chest by a bayonet.

The barmaid grinned as she paraded a beer in his direction. An idea flicked at him like a horse whip snapping at the side of his head. If he wasn't mistaken, this tart's expression wasn't mere flirtation. He'd seen this knowing look before. There could be something behind it…something sly…genuine *potential*.

She intentionally brushed her arm against his while placing his pint on the counter. Seduction would no doubt have been a most pleasurable endeavor, but he had much bigger plans in store for this barmaid and wasn't about to spoil them with an impulsive roll in the hay. He maintained sharp eye contact with her as he kicked back his pint in one swallow and smeared his lips with the back of his hand.

* * * *

Tessa had homed in on the good-looking blond man the moment he stepped in the door. For one thing, he was a new patron—judging by his outdoorsy appearance, an out-of-towner—and certainly not a dockworker or merchant, which might be an indicator that an extra drop of innocent flirtation would elicit a generous tip. As she went to fetch his pint of mead, she caught him pretending to conceal that he was sizing everyone up. He was looking for someone or something…but what? She had to find out…maybe there was something in it for her?

She felt a pang of guilt when she brushed her shoulder against the stranger, enabling him to get a whiff of her perfume and a full view of her bosom. *What would* Josh *think?* she wondered, feeling conflicted. *I do feel for him—but he isn't even here. Who knows if he's even coming tonight? I heard through the grapevine that a friend of his had been one of the victims unloaded at the docks. But he hasn't made any effort to see me at all. If this is how he is treating me now, what about our future in the long run? He's joining the militia, and then who knows what? Maybe he'll end up serving in the army, only to get gunned down in combat. Or…what if*

*he comes back, takes on his father's merchant business, and decides he wants
someone more "upstanding" than a barmaid already planted in her thirties?
I have to look out for myself like I always have. I've scrounged and lived out
of a trunk long enough.*

She refused to flinch as he stared at her with piercing eyes and made
quick work of his drink. He seemed to be looking right through her.
"My, my, my," she said, impressed. "I hope we have enough left in the
keg…. I'll get you a replacement right away."

He held her back by the hips the moment she started to move off.
Her mind lit up with danger signs and raced to the unconscionable
things he might have in store for her. All of the violations she'd had to
withstand from odious men over the years returned…things she would
never tell a soul, not even Josh. There was still time to get away from this
stranger…

He smiled at her when she swiveled around. "Not just yet; I can
hold off for a few minutes," he said, patting the empty stool beside him.
"Take a seat."

She hesitated, clearly suspicious of him.

"Please. I promise I won't bite—*unless* you bite me first."

She chuckled nervously and sat on the stool. As it happened, she'd
been on her feet for hours and needed the break anyway.

"My name's Moses," he said in a lowered voice as he grasped her
hand with his well-worn palm. "And you are?"

She didn't know what this was all about, but immediately recognized
the value of matching his softened tone. "I'm Tessa," she said, her hand
firming against his tight grip.

"I've never been to this part of the city before," he said. "Is it always
this busy?"

Tessa gestured out the front windows. "The port never seems to slow
down, so we have nonstop action."

"Do you enjoy being a barmaid here?"

She thought the question had entered the conversation far too soon,
but was at least thankful that she would soon find out his game—whatever

it might be. "I don't know yet," she answered. "I haven't worked here long enough."

"How much do you earn a week?"

"I don't think that's any of your business—Moses whomever you are," she said, holding firm. "But not nearly enough, I assure you."

"Whatever it is, I will compensate you three times that amount."

Tessa slid down the stool and started to get up. "We're done here. That's one game I don't play."

Again he held her back by the hips. It crossed her mind that perhaps she should strike him on the head with the beer mug before things went too far. "No, no, no," he insisted. "You have it wrong.... What I'm about to ask of you only involves your wit and your charm—nothing more."

Tessa narrowed her eyes and flicked one of his hands away from her hip. "Not interested."

He slid four heavy coins into her palm with the dexterity of a magician. "Did I neglect to mention that I will pay you a large portion in advance?" She felt the weight of the change in her hand. She couldn't resist taking a peek at the glistening metal. This was *even more* than three times what she made in a week—and it was only an advance. She dropped the coins into a hidden pocket in her uniform.

Tessa slinked back onto the stool and leaned her hand on her fist. "So, what are you asking me to do, Mr. Moses—wander the desert?"

SEVENTEEN

Saturday: June 1, 1776-Friday June 7, 1776
Federal Hill, Baltimore

It was a bright, cloudless morning as Josh and Ben rounded a corner up to Federal Hill. Lookout posts dotted the green hillside on the edge of Baltimore's harbor, and the boys took in the sweeping view—the highest in the city. In the distance were the long piers of Fell's Point, where only a few days earlier the young men had helped unload merchant ships from Europe and beyond. Today, there were just a few fishing boats on the edge of the harbor, trailed by raucous flocks of hungry seagulls—which could be heard even from this great distance.

As they gazed out over their city, Josh thought of Christopher, whom they had buried only a day earlier. The bells of Christopher's home church had rung for nearly an hour in honor of the city's fallen native son.

Some thirty men showed up for the final early-morning enlistment with the Maryland Militia recruiters. Josh sized them up; they looked to be men mostly in his age range—some as young as sixteen, others perhaps as old as twenty-five. He recognized several old schoolmates among the group—a few of whom seemed winded just from the walk to the top of the hill—as well as a couple of able-bodied dockworkers.

Proudly standing alongside one of the lookout posts in his finest uniform was Colonel Smallwood. The morning sunlight cast his stern shadow over the crowd. After assembling the volunteers into a rough line, he cleared his throat and addressed them.

"Welcome, gentlemen. In the coming days, we will have much to teach you. You will learn to march as a disciplined unit. You will learn to eat and sleep as a disciplined unit. And yes, you will learn *to fight* as a disciplined unit."

Josh and Ben exchanged furtive glances as they thought the same thing. Despite the pretense expressed in the church that their role would be to serve as peacekeepers, there was no mistaking their real purpose: train to fight on the battlefield.

Amidst all of the chaos of Christopher's death, the ensuing funeral, and then the preparations for signing up, Josh realized too late that he had overlooked visiting Tessa and explaining to her the feelings he had awkwardly begun to express. He hadn't even said goodbye to her. How he longed to embrace her one more time...

Then he felt a pang of guilt over having intentionally skipped out on his parents without having said farewell to them. Mainly, he had hoped to avoid any conflicts with his mother about going, especially since his mind was already made up. His father had simply been collateral damage from the avoidance. *But what kind of son am I?* he wondered. *What if I end up in a crate like Christopher? I didn't even have the foresight to write them a letter, as Christopher had done.*

"Attention, Marylanders!"

* * * *

The Westminster training camp was spread throughout a tree-shaded field to the south of the mountain town. The vast area bustled with army tents, smoldering campfires, overloaded wagons, and two fully stocked horse corrals.

Josh climbed down from the creaking wagon that had transported him and the other enlistees down the meandering, rutted roads from Baltimore to northwestern Maryland. In a far corner of the field, a group of men in gray jackets were fixing bayonets on their muskets and charging full force into straw dummies. In another, men were saddling their horses with light combat gear. Everywhere else he looked men were marching, positioning themselves, attacking, firing their weapons, and realigning through pillars of smoke.

Ben whistled as he joined Josh. "This is something, eh mate?"

"Bolton—take a look at this!" shouted Jim, a dockworker Josh recognized from Baltimore. He waved him toward a canvas tent near the wagons.

Jim opened the flap and invited Josh and Ben inside, although none of them knew if he had any authority to do so. Inside it was stifling hot and dim, but the young men could easily make out what the dockworker had found: Splayed along the top of a table was a cornucopia of weapons—from long, rusted knives and gentlemen's pistols to a set of muskets with elaborate silver filigree running along the barrels.

Josh raised a hefty blade almost eighteen inches long that was spotted with flecks of rust and possibly even dried blood.

"Put that down, boy!" a voice thundered.

The weapon slipped out of his hands, struck the table, and spun around. The three interlopers glared at the tent opening, where a rugged, massive man held open the flaps with both arms. Josh couldn't tell if it would be more appropriate to describe the figure as one capable of killing a bear with his bare hands, or to compare him to the bear himself.

The hulking man was deceptively quick and leapt in front of Josh, where he reached out his callused hand to adjust the knife on the table before it could topple over and land on the boy's foot.

"What the hell are you doing?" he shouted in a strange accent. With only the slightest effort of each hand, he thrust both Josh and Ben across the room.

Josh knew he was no match for this man, but he wasn't about to let anyone get the better of him—certainly not on his first day. He recovered, lunged for one of the knives on the table, and went at him.

His opponent shrank back in mock terror. "Oh no, please don't hurt me, dear boy…please don't," he whined in a high-pitched voice. He smacked the knife out of Josh's hand and clutched his chest in hearty laughter. "*That* is how you expect to fight?" He guffawed. "They really are sending us piss-minded fuckers!"

Josh was glad, at least, that the tent was too dark for anyone to see his cheeks, which he could tell were flushed red. "Who are you?" he asked.

The man drew in so close to him, he could discern the fetid odor of a fresh kill emanating from either his furry, mismatched clothes or his skin. A knife even larger than the one Josh had first handled hung from his tattered leather belt. His dark eyes peered out from a sunburnt face covered in thick black scruff.

"Name's Paddy. I hail from the western peaks."

When Josh failed to respond, Paddy asked, "What's the trouble? You never met a man from the west before?"

Josh shrugged.

"The west is where I rule the hills," he proclaimed. "The whole western chunk of Maryland, deep in the mountains—all mine."

Josh couldn't figure out if this was bluster or not; either way, he wasn't about to challenge him again.

"You children ever skin a bear? Chase a deer for three days? Wrestle a big cat with your bare hands?"

When no one responded, Paddy continued, "Obviously not. I can tell you the west ain't made up of sand and seagull shit, like where you little boys probably come from."

Outside the tent, an officer bellowed, "Attention, recruits—fall in line! It's time for training to commence!"

"That would mean us, I s'pose," Paddy said. He opened one of the tent flaps for the three men to exit. "After you, toddlers."

When Ben, Jim, and Josh were outside, they were greeted by a scraggly pack of men: One was smoking an unusual form of tobacco, while another spit a lump of black goop onto the ground.

Paddy stepped in front of them. "These are my men."

Josh tipped his head—barely. He didn't want to appear too eager or friendly. He deduced that doing so would be a sign of weakness to these gruff outdoorsmen.

"Come on, boy!" Paddy barked, shoving him forward. "We're only half as mean as we look!"

* * * *

Under the scorching summer sun, the recruits stood in protracted lines snaking through the grassy campsite in order to allow the local country doctors to take turns poking their chests and examining their eyes. The doctors moved aside anyone too ill or otherwise physically unfit to continue.

Those remaining were directed to sprint several times around the perimeter. A few winded stragglers on the verge of collapse excused themselves, determining that they were not suited for the realities of military exertion.

In the days that followed, they worked from sunrise to sunset: They endlessly practiced taking formation, loading their weapons, aiming at targets, and fighting in hand-to-hand combat. Josh and Ben fared well throughout training, having been accustomed to long hours from their labor on the docks. A significant portion of the inexperienced recruits, who had lazy or privileged lifestyles, fumbled with their pistols, stumbled over their boots, and often collapsed at the end of a drill, gasping for water like beached fish. Josh wondered if any amount of training could possibly develop this clumsy, ragtag group into a worthy adversary against the mighty, accomplished British army.

At the end of a particularly grueling drill session, Josh joined a group of sweat-soaked men under a tree. He recognized a few dockworkers: Sullivan, who spent his days hauling cargo and his evenings on a fiddle in the pub; Morrison, who planned to become a preacher; and Walter, a Negro deckhand on a clipper ship. Several other recruits also collapsed in the shade, including a fellow named Conway, who said his parents farmed along the edge of the Potomac; and a bearded, taciturn western Marylander who didn't offer his name.

For several minutes their throats were too parched too speak, and the only sounds they made were gulping water from their canteens. Rejuvenated, Conway smacked his lips and rose to his feet. "Come on, men—we've been marching alongside each other all day. How 'bout we make a friendly wager? Have a little fun."

"Wager about what—how far you can pee?" Sullivan remarked. "I think you'd win any pissing contest!"

The men laughed on cue, thankful for a moment of levity.

Conway took it in stride. He gestured toward a row of thin maple trees on the edge of camp, each one with a few narrow branches jutting from its trunk. "Whoever can take a branch off their tree with a single clean shot gets a shilling from each of us. What do you say?"

The group murmured in agreement as Conway withdrew a pistol from his satchel. "This was my father's," he said with a touch of pride. "Gave it to me to shoot lobsters."

He measured out a dram of gunpowder and handed it to Sullivan first, who nervously squared up and squeezed off a shot that thudded into the tree trunk. He passed the pistol to Morrison, who loaded, fired, and clipped off the edge of his branch. It wobbled but didn't fall.

"Not bad," Conway said, poking Morrison in the ribs. "But it won't win you any shillings."

He reloaded the pistol and handed it to Josh.

Josh felt the heft of the pistol in his palm and squinted into the blazing orange sun. His clothes were soaked through and his muscles ached. He struggled to concentrate as sweat stung his eyes and shadows from the trees filtered in front of his view of the target. He wiped his face on his sleeve, closed one eye, and leveled the pistol. He squeezed the trigger, and the weapon fired with explosive force. The gunshot sheared off a tiny branch, missing his larger target entirely.

"Let me show you how it's done," Conway taunted him, yanking the gun from his hand. He reloaded and brandished the pistol with a flourish and aimed at his branch. The gun roared. The branch shook violently on impact but held firm.

"Damn old thing isn't accurate," he murmured. "Well, I guess no winners today."

He began to shove it into his trousers when a hand touched his on the weapon—a black hand. He froze, too stunned by the sight and feel of it to react.

"The contest isn't over, mate," Ben said, holding his hand firmly in place.

"*What did you say, boy?*"

"I said we're not done here," Ben asserted. "Walter and I haven't had our chance to shoot."

"I think you're confused," Conway spat. "No nigger is ever going to use my father's pistol. I advise you to get your filthy hand off it *now*."

Ben gritted his teeth and yielded, stepping back. *Maybe this isn't worth it*, he thought.

Conway circled him, his hand still on the gun. "Where I come from, nigger, you would be working for me. You're just lucky we're here and not anywhere near my farm. Either I'd horsewhip you or use this weapon here on you." "Good thing we're here," Ben said, refusing to flinch. "And fighting on the same side."

"We ain't on the same side, nigger. Not now, not ever."

Ben became resigned and stood in front of Conway, blocking the much taller man. "I suggest you hand that pistol over and let Walter and me take our turns," he threatened.

"Or what? What will you do, nigger?"

Ben's bluff was being called. Josh inched closer to him, readying himself in case others became involved.

The two men eyed each other with burning hatred. Ben knew he was being baited into making the first move. No commander would ever take his side in a court martial; of that much he was certain.

"If you want this pistol so much, try to take it from me."

Conway shoved his chest into Ben, pushing him several inches back.

"Come on, nigger, take it!"

He thrust his chest into him again with the same result. Ben curled his fists.

Josh prayed: *Don't do it, Ben, don't do it…*

Ben was about to strike when a blade soared into the grass just a couple of inches in front of Conway's foot.

Paddy appeared, another knife at the ready. "You best clear off," he said to Conway. "The next one will be at your crotch. And trust me, I won't miss."

Conway spat at Ben's feet and stomped toward the campground.

Paddy slid the knives back into the leather sheath on his belt and whistled.

"Time for dinner? I'm hungry enough to eat a possum."

* * * *

As it happened, dinner was vile—except according to Paddy's palate. Whereas Josh could barely coax himself into nibbling at a piece of dry, salted pork and Ben poked at a hardtack, Paddy devoured a slab of meat down to the bone, licking his fingers with pleasure.

"How can you eat this stuff?" Josh asked him, tossing his uneaten food into the fire pit blazing in the middle of the group.

Paddy wiped his greasy fingers on his furry vest. "In the woods, you never turn down food."

Paddy's compatriots grunted in agreement, savagely gnawing their meat.

After a pause, Ben spoke up to Paddy. "I wanted to thank you…for earlier. You didn't have to…you know. I can fend for myself."

"Sure you can," Paddy said while picking a blob of fat from between his teeth with his fingernail. "But either way you'd be dead. If that moron didn't shoot you, the courts would lynch you…and that would be a shame. We need every fit man we can get in this fight, especially since you seem more able than most for someone your size. Better you die serving the Lord and your country on the battlefield."

Ben nodded in agreement: Paddy's logic made sense, but he still struggled with one thing. "How do I deal with people like Conway? We're all supposed to be on the same side."

"Realize this," Paddy said, leaning forward. "We may be God's children and will be delivered to freedom—but that doesn't mean that *we're all* the chosen people…. All sides have at least a few arseholes."

The group laughed on cue.

"Do you mind if I ask you something?" Josh blurted when the chuckling subsided.

"Anything except where I bury my shillings."

"You and your friends were fine living off the land, free in the forests. Why risk everything to join the militia?"

"I'll tell you this," Paddy replied with a scratch of his beard. "I couldn't give a rat's ass about tea and taxes and all that shit you city boys worry about. I ain't paid a tax in all my life and I don't never intend to. The British look down on you and all the colonists as inferior. They look down on the likes of me and my boys even more. It's only a matter of time before they really take over and make us all their servants. I ain't no servant: I'm a free man.

"Look at the deer," he continued. "Finest running animal God put on this land. Can keep a hunter on his feet for days. But you coop him up in a pen and he just dies away. That's the way we are in the mountains. If the Crown wants to put us in a pen and force us to pay to hunt and fish, we die too."

Paddy softened a bit as he shifted closer to Josh. "You're a brave kid to be here," he said. "You got a family back home? A girl?"

"My father is a merchant back in Baltimore," he answered. After a pause he added, "I think I have girl…. I'm not sure. I might have blown it."

Paddy chomped on another piece of meat and spoke with his mouth full, "I s'pose not knowing is a good thing. You've got something to live for and something unfinished—those things are pretty important if you hope to stay aboveground while fighting a war."

EIGHTEEN

The pale, stubbly man in a patterned green vest navigated his mare through a back alley and slid off the saddle. Sore from a long ride, he rubbed his buttocks with both hands and then hitched his horse to a wooden post. A half door swung wide open, and he slipped inside a well-hidden secret entrance to the Beaver Hat that was known only to a select group of smugglers.

He shut the door tight behind himself as his eyes adjusted to the dim basement lighting. He looked upward in reaction to the intermittent footsteps on the floorboards from the bar patrons.

"Come inside, love," said the hefty, buxom woman who had opened the door for him and now solidified it by inserting a slab of wood. She led him to a curtained room in the far corner. "He'll be expecting you."

She shifted away, appearing visibly jilted by his silent treatment. His focus was solely directed on the man revealed behind the curtain: David Brown. He was dressed in black, his expression locked in a perpetual frown as he sat on a folding chair.

"Have a seat, Mitchell," Brown said, gesturing toward a filthy wooden stool opposite him.

Mitchell settled on the wobbly stool, uncomfortably—especially since his rear had already just finished taking a beating.

"I take it your ride was satisfactory?" Brown asked.

"It was," Mitchell lied, knowing that Brown didn't care one way or the other about his answer. They both loathed small talk.

Brown reached into a leather case for a sheaf of papers. "I have been quite busy since we last spoke. Our network is growing and has eyes everywhere."

He handed the papers to Mitchell, who folded them and slid them inside his pocket without giving them a single glance.

Brown continued, "We have reason to believe that local rebellion leaders will be attending a rally in three days' time here—in the capital. You will have all the information you need in the documents there. Many of these traitors may be armed, so be prepared."

Mitchell flicked his coat ends to their sides, revealing pistols on both hips. "When am I not?"

"It appears we are all set, then," Brown said, rising from his chair.

"We're not," Mitchell said, also on his feet. "There's the matter of my compensation."

Brown placed a pouch full of coins in his palm. "This should hold you for now. If you complete your assignment to my satisfaction, you have the guarantee of the Crown for your full payment."

Mitchell tipped his hand up and down as if he could weigh the pouch with this method to determine the value of its contents. He stuffed it in his coat pocket, indicating it was good enough, and left as wordlessly as he had come.

Brown flopped into the chair with a sigh. He was taking a great risk running his own operation in a restive city—but he was confident in his information, as it was derived from a reliable source cultivated by the Doans. If his plan were to succeed, it would change the course of the entire fight to come. He leaned back with his eyes closed and imagined what it would be like: a victory, a glorious victory for the Crown. His frown lifted, almost resembling a smile.

NINETEEN

Sam Bolton had always despised being in the state capital, Annapolis. As far as he was concerned, it was crawling with rich folks who preferred their seaside retreats over governing for the benefit of the rest of the colony. He felt far more at home in the bustling cobblestone alleyways of the Baltimore port—where people actually *worked* for a living—than among the refined townhomes of the state's upper crust.

Once or twice a year commerce won out over personal taste, and Sam rode in his carriage to the stuffy capital to meet with wealthy traders who wanted the latest news on the commodities passing through his business. These days, the trip would consist mainly of airing grievances over drinks—especially to exchange tales of how the steep British taxes were undercutting farmers and merchants alike.

This year was already a little different, he thought, as his fellow passenger was the irrepressible Horace Greenwood, who nagged at him throughout the bumpy trip to address a group of protestors before his meetings with traders. "Just say a few words, Sam, that's all I'm asking," he persisted. "*Please*—there will only be a few people there."

"Why me?"

"You underestimate yourself, my friend," Horace said. "You are highly respected in the capital by both rich and poor alike. And you have a cool head."

"Horace, if I had been in the shoes of James Dick and Anthony Stewart, I'm not sure what I might have done. Sometimes right and wrong become blurred when you are in the center of the storm…"

"That proves my point exactly as to why you should speak. You see all sides in the matter."

Greenwood was referring to a situation that had begun two years earlier in which businessmen Dick and Stewart had docked their merchant ship, the *Peggy Stewart*, in the Annapolis harbor to unload indentured servants and tea. Their unforgivable mistake had been to pay the dreaded import tax imposed by the British—which most Annapolitan merchants openly ignored. Outraged that merchants in their own town had succumbed to this loathsome tax and set a precedent, residents had burnt the men's ship to the waterline.

Now, as the British prepared to impose yet another bevy of taxes on the merchants as a result, Greenwood had organized a protest outside Dick and Stewart's office to speak out against this increasingly heavy burden.

Sam reluctantly caved—just to silence Greenwood for the rest of the journey. "Fine," he conceded. "I suppose a few words wouldn't hurt."

"Good. It's settled then," Greenwood said.

Sam leaned back and closed his eyes for a quick nap, but Greenwood wasn't about to let a silent moment lie. "I hear your boy signed up…for the militia."

Sam partially opened one eye with a grunt. He didn't mind so much that Josh had signed up—he had already granted his blessing—it was *how* he had gone about it that annoyed him. First, there was the matter of the Smithson boy. Sam had heard about the untimely death of his son's friend thirdhand. How could Josh not have shared such news right away? Not only had he known the redheaded boy since he'd been a skinny rascal hanging from his backyard tree, but he was friendly with the boy's parents.

Next Josh had gone off to enlist in the militia without a word to anyone. No tearful goodbye or "I love you". Not even a note. *Poof*—one morning he was gone. This was so unlike the son he knew and had raised since birth and worked alongside day in and day out.

True, Josh's mother disapproved of his decision and would have caused immeasurable drama in reaction to his departure, but that would have been a far preferable scenario than running away altogether. Sam's wife was devastated—worsened by the fact that he too was now leaving her for a few days.

"What's it to you?" he grumbled.

"Nothing, nothing, my friend. I think it's admirable that he volunteered for this noble effort," Greenwood said. "But…I have heard something that may be of interest to you…"

"Oh?"

"Rumor has it that the colonial troops are ragged and thin. They need men. *Desperately*. Many people are saying the militia enlistees will imminently become fighting soldiers. I don't wish to alarm you, but I think you should know that your boy may end up playing a bigger role in this sooner than expected."

Sam shut his open eye with an "mm-hmm" to put an end to the conversation. He didn't want to be involved in any further chitchat, especially when it came to the well-being of his only son. Imagine, he thought, how his wife would react if she were aware that Joshua was already heading into harm's way. Even he had doubts about it being possible for Josh to be suitably trained and prepared as a soldier in such a brief span of time.

* * * *

Sam was jolted from his deep sleep by shouts and claps from a rowdy group of people, accompanied by the hard stop of the carriage against a curb. "What the…?"

Greenwood tapped his friend and gestured out the window. Sam rubbed his eyes and looked out into the street, where at least three dozen people had gathered in front of Dick and Stewart's shuttered office. He recognized a few Annapolitan merchants scattered among the crowd.

The pair was greeted with raucous cheers and applause as they stepped out of the carriage. Sam turned to Greenwood and snorted. "Only a few people, eh?"

Greenwood shrugged in feigned ignorance.

The group settled down into a cubed mass as a raised podium was erected on the curb. The speakers droned on one by one. First was a local maritime lawyer, who read an excerpt from a legal textbook, arguing that the new set of tea and tobacco taxes was one-sided and improper. The second speaker, a local reverend, led the group in a prayer, after which he exhorted the British to consider the unholiness of their actions. Both men stepped off the podium to tepid applause.

The crowd became animated when a jaunty journalist from the *Maryland Gazette* took the forefront. Sam had periodically read his inflammatory column and dismissed him as something of a showboat, in it for his own glory.

"I call upon all of you, loyal patriots!" the journalist shouted, shoving a wrinkled newspaper into the air with his article prominently on top. "Follow me as we cast off the yoke of slavery and show these cretins that we are free men! We are entitled to the freedom to write and print our views! My column in the *Maryland Gazette* is a symbol of all the freedoms we hold dear in our hearts! We shall be heard!"

The majority of the crowd yelped and whooped.

Sam shot Greenwood a sideways look to let him know that he was unimpressed. His friend responded with a glance that begged him to be patient.

They became distracted by something behind them. They swiveled around to see a vocal entourage in ratty clothes lofting an oversized effigy of King George with the head of the Devil and a crown made of chicken bones; they shouted some garbled words about the "hellish ways" of the British Crown.

Greenwood indicated to Sam that it was his turn to speak. He shoved his way toward the podium, repeating some points in his head that he had considered during the long carriage ride before his nap had taken precedence. He held up his arms to quiet the swelling and now rowdy crowd that had begun to toss bottles into the cobblestone streets, in reaction to the previous speaker and the parading effigy.

Sam thought it would be only a matter of time until the constables would arrive. He didn't view this as entirely negative, for it meant he could escape this spectacle and move on to his business with the city's merchants. Now, while standing on the podium, he felt an obligation to do something to maintain order. "Please, everyone, let us settle down! We can protest taxes without turning violent!"

His words had little impact, as they were drowned out by the chanting crowd. Even the passive rubberneckers became engaged in the commotion and joined in tossing bottles and rubbish and screaming obscenities against the king and Crown.

Sam's curiosity was piqued when he saw an unshaven, determined man in an odd greenish uniform boring a hole through the crowd. The disturbance simmered, and people shifted a distance away from him as he reached Greenwood in the front row of the curb. Sam became dumbstruck as the menacing fellow anchored himself dead center, his hands measured against his pistols.

Sam was surprised that Greenwood not only was familiar with the ominous stranger but was attempting to garner his attention. "Constable Mitchell—truly, there is no need for your presence here. Everything is under control. We have simply gathered together for a peaceful protest, which is allowed by law. We are merely exchanging thoughts and ideas."

Mitchell's eyes scanned the crowd and the slovenly protestors who continued to disrespectfully wave the king's grotesque effigy. He turned sharply to Greenwood, revealing two drawn pistols. "What a perfect coincidence, sir. The Crown would also like to exchange a thought and an idea."

His right hand squeezed the trigger and blasted a shot through Greenwood's shoulder. The merchant crumpled to his knees. The crowd scattered in terror.

Mitchell swiveled, took aim with his left pistol, and shot a fleeing Annapolis merchant in the leg. Amid the ensuing chaos, he nonchalantly reloaded each pistol as if taking target practice.

Sam hurtled toward Mitchell, staring wildly into his face. "What in hell's name are you doing?! Have you lost your mind? You are shooting innocent, unarmed men!"

"Innocent? They are traitors, old man—and so are you," he mused. "*That* is why."

Mitchell pointed both pistols into Sam's chest, exploding a torrent of crimson onto the pavement. Sam staggered backward, clinging to his gaping wound. He tried to speak but couldn't as he teetered forward and toppled facedown onto the pavement.

Mitchell hovered over his victim, his pistols still at the ready. He allowed Greenwood—who nursed his bloody shoulder as best he could—to crawl to his friend and flip him over and confirm he was dead. Greenwood looked up at Mitchell, his teeth gritting with such fury to hold his tongue that he bit it and drew blood.

"What is wrong, sir?" Mitchell asked with mock sympathy. "No thoughts and ideas left to exchange? A pity."

Mitchell stuffed the pistols back into their respective holsters and meandered into the chaos and devastation he had created. He smirked while heading through the maze of narrow portside streets crisscrossing the capital. *A job well done*, he assessed. *No doubt I will be handsomely rewarded for it.*

"I'm sorry, Sam," Greenwood cried to the lifeless body. "I'm so sorry..."

Greenwood remained in that position for so long, he barely noticed the strong arms of the town watchmen hoisting him to his feet. His only thought was that soon he would be returning with Sam in a carriage for their journey back home—except this time his friend's sleep was permanent.

TWENTY

Thursday, June 20, 1776
Westminster, Maryland

The drills seemed endless under the blistering Westminster sun. The soldiers endured hours of mind-numbing marches in formation, followed by firing at makeshift targets and bayoneting straw opponents until they were piles of splinters.

As each day of training bled into another, Josh and Ben could at least admit one thing: The Maryland Militia was starting to bear at least some resemblance to a professional fighting force. No longer were they hapless, out-of-shape recruits fumbling over their weapons and collapsing after a march. They had become a finely honed group, marching in unison and snapping to attention as their commanders assessed them on horseback.

They spent most of their nights around campfires, comparing stories from the day's drills and daring each other to climb trees, throw knives, and play card games. These interactions brought them closer together and began to create bonds of trust.

At first light on the second week, as the drummers tapped out a marching rhythm, an unfamiliar figure dismounted from his horse at the edge of their marching field. Unlike the Maryland commanders—mostly wealthy men in fancy uniforms who had gained their experience from European instructional manuals rather than on the battlefield—this new arrival had a pronounced limp, a three-day-old beard, and the rumpled clothes of a man who had been long in the saddle. He hobbled to the front of the assembled men and shook the dirt off his worn clothes. He removed his battered tricorn hat and wiped the sweat off his forehead.

Colonel Smallwood introduced the new arrival in a booming voice. "Soldiers, at attention for Lieutenant Richard Cary of the Massachusetts 3rd Regiment from Boston!"

The line rippled as the soldiers stood at attention.

"At ease, soldiers," Cary said in a Boston accent. "I have been asked to join you here to pass along important news and advice from the front in the north."

Smallwood strode past the militiamen with his staff in hand, prepared to whack any recruit found daydreaming. Satisfied, he gave the all-clear to Cary.

"As many of you know, the patriot cause is strong in New England, where I hail from," he proclaimed. "And I'm proud to say Boston is once again in patriot hands. But the fight against our oppressors is far from over. They will return—with forces stronger than we have yet seen, and we must be prepared.

"I am here to tell you that it's likely you will face the British in open battle. Many of you are eager for that day to come, I'm sure. But before you rush into the fight, you must know that the British are attentive to your every move. When you feint left, they move right. When you charge forward, they find your open rear flank. Simply put, they are the best fighting force in Europe. To defeat them, we must be cunning, we must be daring, and we must be unexpected."

Smallwood took his place beside Cary with his arms behind his back. "I've invited Lieutenant Cary here today to act as our drillmaster," he declared. "Today, he will demonstrate the maneuvers and methods that must be mastered in order to break the British lines. And master them we will—even if we must practice one thousand times!"

With that, the commanders organized the recruits into practice squads, shuffling them like playing cards amongst each other until four groups were proportionately aligned.

Josh counted nineteen fellow recruits in his squad, mostly fresh-faced young men he didn't recognize. He was disappointed that neither Ben nor Paddy had been assigned alongside him, but he shrugged it off. If this training camp had taught him anything, it was that you learned to depend upon whichever compatriot happened to be next to you.

Cary once again addressed the men while gesturing toward Josh's group. "On my left-hand side are two battalions of twenty soldiers each. You are the patriot army and you must penetrate British lines. On my right-hand side are two other battalions. You are the British army and you must keep the patriots at bay."

He ordered the groups to stand opposite each other while he remained in the center between them. Josh gazed out over the ranks of his fellow soldiers, now play-acting as British troops. *So, this is what it feels like to face off against the enemy*, he thought—*exhilarating yet terrifying.*

Cary limped over toward the British side. "You soldiers will march in the tradition of the great European armies," he explained. "This means bayonets fixed against an army that is prepared to shoot you or stab you to death as you march toward them. You don't want to give them that satisfaction."

He pointed at a small gap between three soldiers on the British side. "Attack directly and the British have you where they want you," he said. "But at Lexington we learned the opposite: Look instead for their weak flanks, such as this one, and penetrate them. By doing this, you throw the enemy into disarray."

He shifted his attention toward the trees alongside the field. "Always remember that you live on this land. These British soldiers are foreigners. You know the forests, the waters, and the fields far better than they do. Always use that to your advantage."

Cary paused to take a deep breath. "Lastly—know that the British grossly underestimate you. They believe you are all untrained, undisciplined farmers. Show them the price of their vanity."

The militia commanders broke the group apart and sent the faux British contingent to one end of a long, grassy field down a small hill. The patriot side was gathered near a clump of trees a few hundred yards from the rise of the hill—out of sight of their opponents.

The objective was deceptively simple: A red flag fluttered deep behind British lines, while a blue flag waved behind patriot lines. Each side had to penetrate the enemy and steal their flag.

Each man was given a cloth-covered stick instead of a rifle. When struck by the stick, a recruit was considered dead.

Josh and the others toyed with their weapons. Many of the men assigned to the patriot side were young and quick, with a few grizzled western Marylanders thrown in the mix. They all waited for someone to speak up.

Josh finally did. "I have an idea."

The faces of his teammates brightened as they circled him.

"We need to split their ranks," he directed. "We're younger and faster than them by all marks. We need to lure them away from their defenses toward our lines, then swoop in when they've left their flag unguarded."

"It's like flushing birds," offered a gruff westerner. "We drive 'em into the sky and then pick 'em off one by one…. How 'bout you send your runners forward first as a decoy?"

"Yes, exactly," Josh agreed. "When they pursue the runners, we launch our second wave at the weakly defended flag."

"You easterners aren't as dumb as you look," the westerner remarked.

Josh chuckled, already accustomed to this type of interaction from Paddy. "Come on—let's map this out."

The group huddled. After a meeting of the minds, they stood up tall, raised their sticks in solidarity, and headed into the mock battle.

Josh didn't have any time to doubt his plan; everything had been set in motion on the spot. The first group of patriot soldiers roared over the hill toward the British lines. They held their position midway down the field, waiting to see how the British force would react. Josh nestled in the tree line a few yards away to observe the scene until it was time.

It didn't take long for the British side to launch their attack. Josh recognized Paddy and a band of westerners among those leading the charge—no surprise there.

The patriot forces hurried to form a defensive wall, but Paddy and his men were simply too quick. Their white sticks thwacked Josh's fellow soldiers roughly across the chest and shoulders. If he had to guess, at least ten of his fellow soldiers were "dead" and out of the game.

The surviving patriots fled back up the hillside with Paddy and his group in hot pursuit. Josh watched them shoot past him as he remained hidden in the trees. It would be only a few minutes before Paddy secured the patriot flag.

The reserve British forces that had remained behind did what Josh had hoped they would do: Sensing an opening against the retreating patriots, they plunged forward against the scurrying patriot ranks directly behind Paddy and his group.

Josh turned to the ten men waiting in the trees. "Time to find our opening."

They sprang out of the forest into enemy territory, where they encountered eight soldiers defending the flag.

Buzzed with adrenaline, the patriots surged past the British defenses with a flurry of stick strikes. Josh counted only two patriots down and a single British defender left. Josh dispatched him with a fierce blow from his stick. One of the youngest patriots swooped in and snagged the red flag, holding it aloft in victory.

Josh wasn't quite ready to celebrate. He gathered his eight remaining men and led them back down the field and up the hill. He caught Paddy and the bulk of the British force just as they reached the remaining patriot defenders. The enemy—including Ben, who was gleefully thwacking patriots left and right—swiveled and found themselves trapped between two charging patriot sides.

"It is done!" Smallwood's voice boomed from somewhere out over the field.

Men on both sides dropped to their knees, panting heavily. The fight had ended with the patriots in possession of the British flag and the surviving British soldiers helplessly surrounded.

Josh patted Paddy on the back. "That was fun." He winked.

"Sneaky bastard," Paddy said with a hint of admiration. "You took us down with a rotten hunting maneuver. Oldest trick in the book."

"And you fell for it," Josh countered.

Paddy's lowered head was all the concession he needed.

The men turned their attention to a soldier limping toward them. Cary paused in front of Josh and clapped. "Good work, soldier," he praised. "I was watching. You're a good listener."

"Thank you, sir," Josh replied.

Josh longed to ask him several questions. But before he had the chance, Cary had turned to speak to the wider group. "That goes for all of you patriots—excellent work. A command performance. As for the British side—hopefully your lesson has been learned."

Cary was interrupted by a flock of militia commanders, who circulated through the ranks. They formed the recruits back into a single line, collecting the cloth sticks and flags. Josh never had the chance to continue his conversation with Cary, as he was hustled into position.

A moment later, he became puzzled by the sight of a commander rushing toward him. His pulse quickened as he wondered if it had anything to do with his performance. Perhaps he had impressed them so much that he would be singled out for a special mission of some sort?

"Bolton—Joshua Bolton," he called him.

"Yes?"

"I have orders to bring you back to camp. You have an important message."

Josh followed the commander at a brisk pace. He hated the idea of leaving Cary and his fellow soldiers behind with his blood still thumping for more action, but clearly, something had happened—and he doubted it had anything to do with his heroics in the game. What could it be?

The commander stopped outside the tent flaps, inviting Josh to enter. Josh went inside and was surprised that the commander hadn't followed him.

A stoic militiaman stood alone in the tent with an open missive in his hand. "Joshua Bolton?"

"Yes. What's this about?"

"I'm sorry to inform you that a terrible tragedy has occurred—regarding your father..."

TWENTY-ONE

David Brown had been a young, ambitious soldier when his father was sent home. He still remembered the day. Brown had just returned from training camp, full of enthusiasm for the Crown and his chance to carry on a family legacy of military service. He was still wearing his cadet's red dress uniform as he stepped out of the carriage and hurried into his family's country home outside of Falmouth.

Usually, when he returned home from camp, his mother or sister had been there to greet him, offer him some food, and ask him to tell his stories "from the front". But that afternoon, the house was cold and silent, the window shades tightly drawn.

Brown didn't see much of his father in the years when Britain was at war with France and he was off raiding French colonies in America. But he had heard stories—legends, really—of Alistair Brown's prowess as a commander, how he had sent the enemy fleeing in places with evocative names, such as Niagara and Oswego. There was even talk that one day, Alistair Brown might lead the entire British army in the colonies.

But there was another side to his father—one that didn't make it into the legends. Brown knew that his father had been an unfaithful man, and that during his time away he indulged in loose pursuits in the colonies. He was a hard drinker and a heavy gambler with a wit that was sometimes cruel.

His son, by all accounts, could not have been more different. Serious almost to a fault, disciplined, and restrained, Brown made people feel incredulous that he was related to his famous father at all. Deep down, though, Brown was proud of his father's exploits—even though his excesses eventually got the better of him.

As he sat at the dinner table with a meat pie set before him, he imagined his father in the shadows sipping from a half-empty bottle. How would he handle the current situation—being berated by the people who had hired him to conduct his covert deeds? He would probably laugh it off, down his current bottle, start another, and then head off to a pub to cavort with a trollop. Alas, this wasn't Brown's style.

He was shaken from his reverie when Gibson, his dinner guest, reached over his plate to snatch a bottle of wine. "Not bad for a man in hiding," he said, admiring the label.

Brown forced a pained smile. He had been holed up in a Delaware inn for weeks, staying close to the shore, where he could more easily rendezvous with British visitors sneaking onto the mainland. In many ways, he was the perfect man for the job, having the ability to tamp down his posh British accent into a flat monotone and, in his dark plain clothes, pass mostly unnoticed among the colonials.

Since meeting with Howe weeks earlier, Brown had continued to spread his spy network throughout the colonies with the help of the Doans, who seemed to know everyone from Virginia to New Hampshire. Bit by bit, he had begun to amass critical information about the extent of the colonial rebellion. The British could not afford another Boston.

"Let's come to the point," Brown snapped. "May I ask why you're here?"

"My pleasure." Gibson grinned as he took a swig of wine before continuing, "Howe is disappointed—with you."

Brown feigned ignorance. "Oh?" he asked.

Gibson burst out laughing. "You didn't expect us to find out about the stunt you orchestrated in Annapolis?"

Brown had, of course, arranged for the gunman to attack the leaders of the Maryland resistance, in an effort to cut the head off the snake before this colony could join the rebellion. But the assassin had been anything but subtle, publicly shooting three of the men at a rally while shouting he was acting in the name of the Crown. Although it didn't go as planned, Brown regarded it as a worthwhile endeavor that likely frightened the Marylanders into silence.

"It was not a stunt," Brown retorted. "It was carefully planned based on good intelligence."

Gibson's guffaw nearly caused the wine to spill out of his glass. "Carefully planned! You killed a merchant who, as far as anyone knows, was no patriot mastermind. In doing so, you've shaken up the hornet's nest. You can scarcely walk a Baltimore street without hearing about the travesty—the innocent killing of unarmed civilians."

Sequestered all this time in Delaware, Brown had not heard about the fallout from the murder that occurred in broad daylight. He shrank in his seat. "That was not intended," he conceded. "Please—express my apologies to the general."

Gibson's chair screeched back from the table. "I must go," he said. "Thank you for dining with me."

Brown's eyes followed Gibson as he moved toward the door. That couldn't be all, he thought. There wasn't a chance Howe would have sent Gibson all this way for a meat pie, a couple of glasses of wine, and a verbal message that he was "annoyed".

"Oh." Gibson smirked, turning back. "There's one more thing."

He tossed a sealed letter onto the table beside Brown's plate.

Brown stared at it as he heard Gibson issue one final snide remark. "I see you've learned nothing from your father."

Several minutes after Gibson left, Brown gingerly broke the seal and unfolded the letter. It was a written order from the army command. He had been censured—a devastating blow to everything he had worked for.

On the other hand, he realized his good fortune at this serving as his only punishment. He could easily have been court-martialed and shipped home with nothing to his name, just like his father before him. It was likely only his spy network that had saved him. Without him, information about the rebels would dry up.

He took a long drink of wine and considered his next move. He must push his network even harder than before, gathering intelligence so crucial that Howe would have no choice but to decorate him.

He drew a candle closer and lit a corner of the parchment. "I will never be my father," he said, watching the flame consume the missive. "Even if it means burning every single colony down to the ground."

TWENTY-TWO

Sunday, June 23, 1776
Fell's Point, Baltimore, Maryland

When Mary Bolton received the news from a messenger that humid Wednesday night, she didn't scream or cry. Instead, she lay down in the darkness of their bedroom, resting on the bed where her husband would no longer sleep, staring upward into nothingness.

She had thought about crying, but the tears didn't come. She had thought about shouting out loud, but her voice couldn't ring out. She had thought about drowning her feelings in a glass of claret or a dram of whiskey, but she couldn't rise to fetch it. Mary was numb.

First she had lost her son...well, not literally. He was out on a field somewhere with hundreds of other young men, all waiting to have their hearts plunged by British soldiers. It was inevitable, like what had happened to that poor Smithson boy.

Now she had lost her husband...forever. Why? For what reason? What could he possibly have done to offend their masters from across the pond? Sam had been nothing but a harmless merchant—one who had for years tolerated their escalating taxes, tariffs, and all kinds of other

111

nonsense. As far as she had heard from Greenwood, Sam hadn't even had a chance to speak at this so-called protest. He'd been gunned down for no reason whatsoever, except that he'd been in the wrong place at the wrong time.

After the wake, she returned to her bedroom and shuttered the blinds. She lay back down and allowed the days to pass, not distinguishing morning from evening. She didn't eat—she had no appetite whatsoever—only she did have a blurred recollection of Lydia coming and going with tea, which she had cajoled her into sipping.

"*Why Sam…why?*"

"Mary?" Lydia asked.

Mary didn't realize she had uttered the words aloud and wasn't aware of Lydia's presence in her bedroom. She had no idea how long she had been hovering over her. "What do you want?" she snapped.

"It's time," Lydia answered, flinging open the blinds. The room instantly flooded with morning sunlight.

Mary, frozen on her bed, shielded her eyes with her arm.

Lydia had never seen her in such poor condition: She looked frayed and fragile, already shedding pounds from lack of sustenance. "Let me give you a hand…"

Lydia wasn't about to give her any say in the matter. She took Mary by both hands and coaxed her into sitting up and then onto her feet. Lydia hardened her grip to help Mary as she waivered. Mary's face flushed. "You all right?"

"A bit dizzy…but I'll be all right," Mary said, steadying herself on her own.

"We'd better get a move on; we're a bit late," Lydia said. "There's quite a fuss out there already."

Lydia helped Mary undress and hoist on an all-black dress with an embroidered matching shawl. She adjusted the silver brooch on Mary's chest and then reached for a brush on the nightstand. Mary plucked the brush out of her friend's hand. "No—I can brush my own hair, thank you very much."

"Ah, good," Lydia remarked, stepping back. "Returning to your wonderful old curmudgeon self, I see."

Mary brushed out her knotted hair, wrapped it into a bun, and pinned it all together. Her color and strength were somehow returning to her all on their own.

"What are you going to say?" Lydia asked, handing her an appropriate black hat and thickly netted veil.

"I suppose I'll know when I step out there," she replied.

After a bit more primping, Mary announced, "Ready."

They made their way through the house, opened the door, and paused together in the doorway, astonished at the sight in front of them: A stream of mourners dressed in black had gathered to pay their respects. Seeing Mary, they all began to remove their hats, out of respect. Further down the street, patriot supporters seethed with pent-up rage as they held protest signs and flags at their sides.

Mary felt her eyes become misty and gulped back tears. She was thankful to have the veil as a shield.

"Sam's death has changed everything," Lydia said, her voice quivering.

Mary smoothed the wrinkles in her dress with her hands and stepped forward into the mass of townspeople—whites and Negroes, men and women, merchants and dockworkers, city dwellers and local aristocrats in their finery—clapping in her honor. The reactions became deafening, engulfing her tiny frame.

When she reached the center of the crowd, she held up her pale hand and everyone fell silent. "Thank you all…for gathering here today," she sputtered. "Sam…would have been honored by your presence."

The crowd cheered. Mary could hardly believe that all of this fuss was for her husband, a reserved man who didn't particularly enjoy being the center of attention.

"I was informed that my husband was killed four days ago…a senseless act of cowardice," she said under her breath. "I have been trying to come to terms with it…to understand *why*. To know why the Lord would claim my husband…and why He did so in such a brutal manner.

Sam was a moderate, religious, and peaceful man. He never harmed a soul.... He deserved nothing but honor and respect."

Her surrounding audience responded with applause, but she would have none of it. She raised both hands and quieted them down with a voice that was unexpectedly strong and unbroken. "But that is not really the entire reason why you are all here, is it? It took me a long time—*far too long*—to realize that a terrible evil has infiltrated our land. They tax us with impunity. They force our businesses into debt. They march troops through our cities to the north. They treat us as if we are not worthy of their citizenship. Now they murder us in cold blood when we speak our minds. I say, '*No more!*' There comes a time when even the lambs must fight against the wolves. I believe with all of my heart and with all my soul that the Lord is on the side of the lambs. *We are the chosen ones who will be delivered!*"

The claps, whistles, and cries surrounded her with such force that she once again became unsteady. She could hardly believe such rebellious words had come from her lips. But she was not finished...not yet. When the crowd simmered down, she continued, "I know many people in our colonies remain loyal to the Crown. Until this week, I too had doubts about our cause. But I say to you now: Any sovereign who would tax, pillage, and murder his own subjects does not deserve our loyalty. We are *God's children*, not the king's!"

She gazed downward, exhausted. The crowd roared out of control, chanting and cheering. Lydia held her shoulders for support—and to assure her of how well she had spoken.

"That was the most inspiring speech I've ever heard in my life," a patriot said to her.

"Bless you, Mary, bless you," sobbed one of her female neighbors.

Greenwood, with his arm in a sling and his eyes wet with tears, somehow found his way to her for an embrace. "You do a great honor to Sam...and all of us."

She heard a familiar voice from behind. "Mother...I'm speechless."

Before this tragedy had occurred, Mary had ruminated over the lecture she would give her son the next time she saw him: a harsh combination of inducing guilt and scolding him for having treated his own mother and father with such disrespect. But now that Josh stood right there in front of her—his boyish face smeared with tears—she helplessly fell into his arms and wept.

* * * *

St. Peter's could handle a sizable crowd, but not the overwhelming crush of Baltimore's citizens and worshippers that flooded inside to attend the funeral of its martyr of British tyranny. The nave had quickly become standing room only, the crowd seeping out the door and spilling onto the street.

Father Fischer weaved through the congregation toward the pulpit, clutching his worn copy of the Bible against his heart. The eulogy was predictably on the traditional side; he commended Sam's soul to God's care and blessed the Bolton family. As he spoke, Josh couldn't help but contrast this version with the much more candid priest with whom he had spoken in private a few weeks earlier.

After completing his sermon, Father Fischer called Josh forth to speak on his family's behalf. An inexperienced orator, Josh walked uneasily toward the pulpit. The town was still buzzing from his mother's speech, and he felt a responsibility as the man of the house to speak.

Josh peered out at his audience. His mother's head was lowered in silent prayer. Lydia was there, of course, as distraught as if she had lost one of her own. Josh also spied Greenwood, who looked ready to strangle with his one good arm the next Englishman he saw.

He cleared his voice, but his throat cracked anyway. "My father had a favorite saying, which I never understood as a child. He said, 'I believe that all of us—every man, woman, and child—are simply heavenly spirits on a voyage through this world. We are merely visiting angels placed here to have an earthly experience.' I could never quite understand what he meant."

He swallowed dryly and continued, "It was not until I found out he was gone that I understood. He was a kind, generous man who believed in the power of good to vanquish evil. He lived his days as a visiting spirit among us—a better angel who remained true to his beliefs in this world and lived by example. And now, he has died supporting those beliefs.

"My father loved Baltimore. He also loved our colonies. He felt that we are uniquely blessed by God with an abundance of resources—but also with a special purpose to make this an exceptional place in this world."

Suddenly, Josh's mind went blank. His spine shuddered as he felt all eyes upon him. He stared down at his feet and wondered if he could go on. He hadn't had time to put quill to paper and felt impossibly speechless. If he went on too much longer, he knew his emotions would take over. "He taught me everything I know," he mustered.

He was about to step off the podium when something overtook him and he added, "I cannot let this stand. My father must be *avenged*. The Lord is on our side."

The congregation exploded with rallying cries, which echoed out into the street.

"Bolton! Bolton! Bolton!"

"The British shall pay!" Josh overlapped them.

As Josh stepped back toward his seat, he reddened from the outpouring of emotions from his fellow Baltimoreans. *Did I really say that in front of all of these people?* he wondered, filled with regret and despair. *What has come over me? What have I done? I've turned my father's memorial into a protest.*

As he passed by Father Fischer, he was unsure of what to expect. The reverend patted his back and whispered in his ear, "Do not worry, son. You said what they all wanted to hear…including myself. But I'm not so sure of what your mother thinks right now…"

Josh returned to his seat beside his mother, who still hadn't raised her head. Finally, she raised it and glared into her son's eyes. "You'd better keep to your promise. More importantly, you'd better come back *alive*."

* * * *

Josh had never been a pallbearer before. He certainly had never envisioned carrying his father's remains. He felt as if he had entered some other place, where nothing seemed the same and things didn't make sense anymore.

He wished Ben were alongside him—not necessarily as a pallbearer, but as someone who truly understood him and would empathize with his sorrow.

As the coffin was interred into the ground, Father Fischer said some final words over the grave, which seemed to Josh like an empty pit where his heart now resided.

One by one the townspeople extended their condolences and muttered how they too stood with the patriot cause. Merchants and their wives—whom Josh's father had scarcely spoken to in years—tearfully approached him, their rings and adornments glinting in the sun as they whispered their intentions to donate to Smallwood's forces in Sam's honor.

Even the assorted dockworkers who had snuck away from their duties and cleaned themselves up and dressed for the occasion promised they would throw an extra shilling toward the militia.

"It's for a noble cause," a large dockworker said.

"Your father was a good man," stated a bearded dockworker as he patted Josh's back.

A hunched old-timer, presumably retired, approached Josh and waved his cane. "The king can kiss my bloody arse!"

When the crowd thinned, Greenwood approached the family and wrapped Josh in an embrace while protecting his injured arm, which was now in a sling. "It's my fault," he admitted. "I never should have asked him to attend that rally…. He didn't even want to speak. I pressed him into doing it. I'm so sorry, my son."

"It's not your fault, sir," Josh pronounced. "My father made his own decisions. He always did what was just. He had *every right* to be there."

"You are indeed your father's son," Greenwood said. "We are lucky to have you fighting for us."

This nearly pushed him over the edge; such magnanimous praise was too much for him to bear. He intentionally redirected his thoughts to Tessa: He missed her now, more than ever. How he longed to be in her arms again…to feel her lips pressed against his. He hadn't seen her in the church or now at the gravesite and wondered if she had even been made aware of his loss. How was it possible for her *not* to have heard? The murder had to be the talk of the town. Why wouldn't she come even if someone else had informed her? *Of course* she would have been here if it had been possible, he decided. She simply didn't know.

He vowed that he would go straight to her as soon as he could escape this dreadful scene and he was comfortable knowing that his mother was safe and sound at home. He would tell Tessa *everything*. He would pledge himself to her and promise to marry her immediately upon his return from training.

It took nearly another hour for everyone to pay their respects and for the funeral to dissipate. Father Fischer said some final comforting words to Mary and bade farewell, insisting that he would stop by later that day.

On the verge of collapse, Mary, Lydia, and Josh climbed into the wagon and plopped onto their seats as they set off on their journey home. They remained silent for several minutes, which seemed like an eternity. Josh itched for two things: to apologize for his egregious error in judgment, and to conjure an excuse to skip off—at least for a while—to find Tessa.

"Mother," Josh began. "I did a terrible thing to you and Father. Something I deeply regret. I want you to know that I—"

"No," his mother interrupted him. "Please. Not now. Not after today."

He had to concede to her wishes. They were all too exhausted to deal with past emotions. He realized that quiet would be best for everyone for the duration of the ride.

At last they arrived home, and Josh helped each lady step out of the wagon. All three of them felt odd coming to a place where Sam Bolton would never again materialize, but they knew eventually they would somehow have to come to terms with it.

Suddenly, feeling hunger pangs, Mary finally came to the realization that she required some sustenance—perhaps she might be able to swallow a simple soup or porridge—and then a lengthy respite.

But their plans were again demolished: A cadet holding a dispatch stood at their front door, having waited patiently for someone to appear.

Lydia clutched her chest, as if preparing for the worst. Mary was emotionless.

Josh immediately stepped forward, as if to protect the women. "May I be of service?"

"You are cadet Joshua Bolton?"

Josh took a half step back, fearing the worst. He tried his best to stand upright like a soldier after everything that had occurred. "Yes, I am."

"I have a dispatch from Colonel Smallwood to retrieve you."

"But," he protested, trying hard not to sound like a whiny child. Under any other circumstances this wouldn't have been an issue. "I was told that I had a full day for bereavement. My mother needs me."

"Change of plan," explained the cadet. "The Continental Army needs you more. Your orders are to march to Annapolis—right now."

It dawned on him that no longer was he a cadet: From that moment on he was a *soldier*—a fighter, a warrior, a champion of the cause. And he was fully prepared to put his own life on the line to obey the orders of one man: General George Washington.

TWENTY-THREE

Monday, June 24, 1776
Patapsco Valley, Maryland

Josh barely had enough time to hug his mother and Lydia before gathering up his things and heading off with the cadet. The pair joined a contingent of a half-dozen cadets and marched from Baltimore to a designated clearing in the woods far from town, where they met up with a wagon train rolling south, advancing to meet up with the 1st Maryland Regiment.

Every moment winding their way through the back roads of central Maryland past the riverside mills and isolated small farms felt excruciating in the scorching summer sun. His hair beneath his tricorn hat was soaked with sweat. His feet and legs ached, and he could feel the stinging blisters on his heels open up as they scraped against the raw interior lining of his boots. No matter how much he adjusted his posture or the position of his weapon and rucksack, he couldn't find a way to keep up with the others without irritating something—his feet, his legs, his arms, his neck, his back…

All the while, he carried an even more grievous burden: the image of his poor lifeless father lying in his grave. He hadn't had a solitary moment to unload his pent-up sorrow and guilt. Before, during, and after the funeral he'd felt it necessary to conduct himself with the bearing of a soldier: standing tall, head high, stiff upper lip, dry eyes. Over the last twenty-four hours, he hadn't dared reveal even the slightest trace of emotion with everyone's gaze fixed upon him. He considered it somewhat ironic that he had gone home for his father's funeral before being obligated to march with his regiment toward the same city where he had been murdered.

At last, the sun receded behind some clouds and was replaced by a cool breeze. The soothing air on his face relaxed some tension as warm tears involuntarily slid down his cheeks. In a way, he felt relieved to be releasing some emotion. As the tears steadily fell, the rest of the journey from that point onward didn't seem quite as arduous.

The crack of a driver's whip and the shudder of wagons grinding to a halt snapped him out of his reverie. He brushed the wetness from his face with the top of his shoulder, coaxing the tears to stop flowing.

"Present arms!"

Josh and his fellow soldiers hoisted their rifles into position and stood at attention.

"At ease!" shouted a different voice—though Josh thought it sounded oddly familiar.

Gesturing broadly, Colonel Smallwood emerged from an opening in the woods with a smile. "Well done, men," his voice boomed above their heads. "You haven't forgotten your training. Come, meet up with the regiment."

He waved the group down the country road toward a clearing in the forest just beyond, where Josh could make out a cluster of wagons circled in a defensive position. He felt something sharp jab him in the back, followed by a phony British accent. "Surrender immediately, colonial dog!"

Josh didn't have to think twice: He spun around to embrace his attacker. "Ben!"

Ben, stiffly patted Josh on the back, as if embarrassed in front of the other soldiers.

"Ben?" Josh questioned, pushing back to look him in the eye. Immediately, Ben swung his arms tightly around Josh as they both tried to fight back their flowing tears. Tears of both sadness and of joy.

"I'm so sorry, Josh…I wish I had been there."

"I know…"

Josh was the first to release his friend. He shifted the weight of his musket to his other shoulder and looked out over the assembled wagons, swarming with soldiers loading and unloading gear. "You've been busy."

"They've worked us hard, that's for sure," he said. "The colonel thinks we're ready."

A commander hustled by them and grunted out orders, shoving them toward the wagon train. For Josh, this meant yet another continuous long day's march—first to southern Maryland and then, early in the morning, into Annapolis.

"I suppose we're about to find out if that's true," Josh said under his breath as the pair hurried to fall in beside a wagon that rumbled to life.

* * * *

The men of the 1st Maryland Regiment awoke hours before dawn and marched synchronously along the banks of Chesapeake Bay. As the sun rose, they kept their pace but marveled at the serene beauty of the glimmering water: the flies and water bugs dancing above; birds splashing down for a light breakfast; gentle ripples coasting and receding. The soldiers longed to plunge in fully clothed—anything to remove the harsh mud and stink from days in drills and marches—but knew they were a long way off from any kind of respite.

They weaved their way down a cobblestone avenue leading into the capital city. Blinking the sleep out of his eyes, Josh wondered if he had ever seen anything quite so impressive in his entire life: From all directions, groups of Maryland soldiers were marching and conjoining. There must have been hundreds of them. The drum corps pounded a rhythmic beat that kept the men's legs moving in tandem. Everywhere he looked he saw the glint of brass buttons, as if they had been shined in anticipation of their grand appearance through the city.

Curious about the early-morning noise and fuss, Annapolitans swung open their bedroom windows and front doors to poke their heads out and glimpse the fanfare. When they saw the troops parading down the streets in formation, a buzz erupted as the early risers urged their spouses and children to come forward and witness the spectacle themselves.

By the time the regiments reached the base of the statehouse—with its black-and-white dome that seemed to glow in the dawn sunlight—clusters of onlookers had gathered in the street, waving homemade flags and cheering the arrivals.

The patriots synchronously marched with the drumbeat down to the church spire of St. Ann's, which lay opposite the statehouse in its wide shadow. Then, all at once, the drums ceased and the boots tapping against the cobblestones stood still.

Annapolis fell silent as the soldiers awaited their next instructions.

Colonel Smallwood strode up and down the lines, his trademark sword dangling from his hip. He sized up from head to toe every soldier he passed; once he had completed his inspection, he stood front and center with his arms behind his back.

"General," the colonel called out, sweeping his arms outward for dramatic effect. "I present to you: the men of the 1st Maryland Regiment."

Josh's heart raced: Had he truly heard the word "general"? Is it possible *he* was here? Had *he* personally come all the way to Annapolis, just to greet him and his comrades?

An imposing figure stepped out from behind a statue, dwarfing Colonel Smallwood. His bearing, barrel chest, and muscular arms had clearly been sculpted from many years as a skilled horseman and farmer. Every soldier felt intense scrutiny raining down upon him from his steely blue eyes and unmistakable aquiline nose.

General George Washington, commander of the Continental Army.

His presence here had been kept secret, since officially General Washington was supposed to be in Philadelphia meeting with the Continental

Congress. Instead, he had chosen to make a special detour to review his troops up and down the middle colonies.

General Washington addressed the soldiers in the firm, methodical tone they expected. "Gentlemen of Maryland: This contingent will soon join citizen soldiers from all across our colonies. Alongside your fellow soldiers, we will face a British Crown determined to impose their will upon us and deprive us of our God-given liberties and freedoms. We cannot allow that to occur.

"In recent months, we have been able to inflict losses upon the British oppressors. We have sent them fleeing from Boston to Nova Scotia, from Charleston to Wilmington. Yet we have also paid for it dearly with our own blood in the streets of Norfolk and on the plains of Quebec.

"Our destination is New York. It is there that we believe the British and their mercenaries will be congregating their forces for the sole purpose of enslaving our people, of subjugating us, our wives, our children, to their tyrannical and corrupt rule.

"We assemble today as an army of free men—*patriots, warriors, and servants*—to prepare ourselves for that next battle, the battle to defend America, our way of life, and the ideal of liberty. There we will face British soldiers who have won the storied battles found in our history books; they will be fighting not only for their personal glory, but also for an unjust and immoral cause. They believe that we will cave under their military power and cower into submission. Let us therefore rely upon the goodness of the cause, and the aid of the Supreme Being—in whose hands victory will animate and encourage us to great and noble actions. The eyes of all countrymen are now upon us."

General Washington paused with deliberation. He raised his arm to make one final declaration. "In five days, we march."

TWENTY-FOUR

Tuesday, July 2, 1776
New York Harbor

David Brown stood at the prow of the frigate and inhaled the tangy salt air. In the distance he spotted the clustered brick counting houses and banks that formed the tip of Manhattan, from where the colonies' wealth was funneled halfway across the world. Beyond that, as the boat drew closer, he could make out Broadway, which seemingly stretched out forever into the horizon.

He snickered to himself as he visualized thousands of patriots, snug in their tiny homes, waking up to see the bulk of His Majesty's unrivaled navy sitting right at their doorstep—anchored in New York Harbor. He moved away from the prow past busy deckhands and marines in their pristine uniforms, arms at the ready.

So this *is what it feels like to have power*, he thought in admiration.

"A fine day, is it not?" a voice bellowed behind his shoulder.

Brown turned to face a man he presumed was the ship's captain and saluted.

"At ease, Mr. Brown." The officer grinned.

When Brown reacted to being recognized, the officer clarified, "I know quite well who you are...especially after what transpired in Baltimore."

Cringing at the reference, he brushed a tangle of dark hair out of his eyes and presented his callused hand to the commander. As they shook hands, Brown noticed the medals festooning the man's chest and realized he was in the presence of someone far more important than just a frigate captain.

"Admiral Howe." He genuflected.

The admiral was a legend among the British ranks: There were entire textbooks devoted to his acumen and strategic breakthroughs. His brother, William—coincidentally Brown's immediate boss—would be leading the British forces as they came ashore.

Brown knew he had to tread carefully and not appear intimidated. He had to presume the admiral was well aware of his demotion, given the Baltimore reference. "I did not expect to find you aboard," he added.

"I am quite fond of the first day our fleet arrives in a new port," the admiral spouted.

"Do you anticipate any difficulties from the rabble?"

"These rabble, as you refer to them, may be plain oystermen and crab catchers," he asserted, "but I have learned never to underestimate my foes—especially if they are defending land they are convinced is their own."

Brown was unprepared for this response and fell speechless: He considered the colonists inferior in every way. He trusted the admiral's skills, but couldn't he deduce the magnitude of the mismatch from just one glimpse of the ridiculous island that lay ahead?

Brown felt their conversation was interrupted just in time when a marine announced to the admiral, "Sir, they have arrived."

The pair headed for the stern, where a dinghy smacked up against the side of the broad ship, tethered by a flimsy rope. Two figures scaled a rickety boarding ladder tossed into the current, their grip slippery from the sea spray.

Brown was surprised to find that the visitors boarding the ship were none other than General William Howe—the admiral's brother and his own superior—and Henry Clinton, the general's right-hand man. He hadn't expected to see either of these dignitaries so soon, and wished he'd had more time to gather information for them. As it was, he had spent the last two weeks indiscriminately dispensing coins to his network to be on the lookout for morsels, but without much to show for it—yet.

"Welcome aboard," the admiral greeted them, with a tip of his hat. He gave no indication that he and the general had any kind of familial relationship.

Shaking the saltwater spray off their uniforms, the group traipsed along up the starboard deck and then down into the central cabin, where Howe invited them to seat themselves around an unsecured table that slid back and forth with the swells.

"It is not often that we welcome the leading commanders of the navy and the army together in a single conference," Admiral Howe said. "But we all know that this particular circumstance is, to put it mildly, unusual."

"Quite," General Howe agreed. "It strikes me that we are here as parents, preparing to spank our misbehaving little children."

The admiral chortled and Brown joined in. Clinton seemed less than amused. "Their offenses are *not* minor—nor are they to be counted among our 'children.' When Boston rebelled, these colonials ceased being British subjects. After we have decimated their forces, I shall enjoy seeing their leadership strung up by their necks for treason."

The statement lingered in the air for an uncomfortable few seconds until General Howe shifted his attention to Brown. "Speaking of their leadership…what can you tell us about them?"

"My findings are only preliminary," he began, hoping his voice didn't sound shaky. "Our contacts on the ground are, shall we say… developing."

Clinton slapped his hand down on the wobbly table. "Blast it, man, we are at war—stop this gibberish and tell us what you have found."

Brown knew he had to give them something substantive that they could chew on. His reputation had already been soiled, and he couldn't afford to disappoint these high-ranking soldiers at their first meeting. "I have one well-placed source within the elite society of New Jersey. He's a landowner—a farmer named Moody. He was recruited by the Doan brothers, whom, as you know, are helping to develop our spy ring here in the north."

"Yes, yes, get on with it," Clinton drawled.

"Moody informs me that there is much concern about the current state of the New York defenses under General Washington. They are grotesquely undermanned and underprotected in this area. It seems as though nearly every colony is desperately raising a militia. I have unconfirmed reports of troop movements up the coast, intended to bolster their defenses from a maritime attack."

"They must fear my brother more than me." General Howe chuckled, poking the admiral in the chest.

"They shall come to regret that," Clinton remarked, turning back to Brown. "Please, do you have anything more substantial to offer us? What you have told us is not worth what I hear you are being paid. We could have drawn these conclusions for ourselves."

Brown fidgeted. He didn't wish to divulge everything he knew all at once, especially since he didn't have that much more and needed something held back in reserve for later to demonstrate his continuous value. "Well…we have heard some interesting whispers about who Washington may be relying upon to lead these new recruits."

Now he had their full attention. They leaned forward in their seats, beckoning him as if they'd said, "Go on," all at once.

"We have only a few names thus far—no one very notable," he stated. "There is William Smallwood—a veteran of the wars against the French, but little more than a footnote—from Maryland. There is also Israel Putnam from Connecticut."

"A doddering old fool," Clinton dismissed. "Anyone else? Someone more worthy of our concern?"

"Perhaps you have heard of a man named William Alexander?"

"*Bill Alexander*? The so-called *Lord Stirling*?" Clinton yelped. "The drunk? The rich boy? The heir to the throne of some made-up Scottish nobility?"

"The one and the same," Brown replied.

"Ha!" Clinton cackled. "How pathetic. The 'lord' is the best they have? A man who gets drunk from his own homemade wine?"

"That will do, Brown," the general said while processing the information. "We look forward to receiving more information about the colonial troop movements and plans soon. *A great deal more information.*"

Sensing he had been dismissed and certain the gentlemen wished to conduct the remainder of their business in private, Brown excused himself and slinked out of the cabin.

He returned to his position on the prow and ruminated while guzzling some warm ale. It was imperative that the Doans come through for him. His future hung in the balance.

Damn colonials, he seethed to himself. *I hate each and every one of them.* He spat in the water, imagining a direct hit in General Washington's eye.

He heard an odd sound and turned to his left. A British soldier had lowered his trousers to urinate over the side. "D'ya suppose the colonials drink this water?"

Brown didn't hesitate to drop his own drawers and join the soldier to create a dual fountain. "I hope so…. I have a bucket of piss in me to flavor their soup."

TWENTY-FIVE

Wednesday, July 10, 1776
Podickory Point, Maryland

The colonists separated into several units as they ventured up the coast. Soon they would board converted barges and head to the northern reaches of the Chesapeake. A few days later, they would march through Wilmington and then enter Philadelphia. Ultimately, the hundreds of men from the 1st Maryland Regiment would coalesce in their final destination: New York.

Ben, having endured a two-hour march, plunked his pack down on the country road and leaned on his musket for a breather. Underneath his clothes straight down to his woolen socks, he felt his skin chafe and itch from pools of sweat.

Separated from Josh, Paddy, and his other mates, he felt emotionally and physically fatigued and homesick in unfamiliar territory. He didn't recall such isolation since his mother had brought him from the Carolinas to Maryland as a little boy. He couldn't understand how he could feel so alone when he was surrounded in front and back by dozens of his compatriots—all fighting for the same cause. *Freedom*, he questioned—*it's worth all this…isn't it?*

As he was taking a sip from his canteen, he heard muffled voices come from a thicket beside the road.

"I'd give anything to be down there," one man said.

He and a couple of nearby soldiers exchanged knowing glances, conveying to investigate. They stepped a few feet through the tall weeds and saw a muddy stream gurgling alongside the road, just down a sloping hill.

"Water!" someone screamed.

Several men—including Sullivan, Conway, and Morrison—scurried down the grassy slope toward the river. Hordes followed. Before long, some fifty Marylanders had dropped their muskets and rucksacks and plunged into the stream, splashing each other with muddy water and dunking their heads for relief.

Ben ached to join the others and cool off, but Conway was dead center among the men thrashing about in the water. He didn't have the patience to deal with him—not today, not ever.

When he heard the approach of horse hooves, he knew it was likely one of their commanding officers and was glad, at least, that he wouldn't get in trouble. No one had sanctioned their bathing in this stream.

"That's enough, gentlemen!" boomed a familiar commanding voice.

Ben peeled back a couple of feet to avoid detection as he stared up at the towering, proud figure atop his gray horse: General Washington.

The horse clomped a couple of feet into the stream as the general looked down upon the men, who froze in place. "Please, allow some room," he said, laughingly lightening the mood. "My steed is parched."

The men created a separation as Washington dismounted and permitted his horse to lean his head down and partake. Washington patted the animal and then hoisted himself back onto the saddle. "Carry on, men," he said with a tip of the hat. "We resume our march in a half hour."

As the horse strutted off, Ben impulsively pulled off his boots and socks, yanked off his shirt, and made a beeline headfirst into the stream.

The water was cool and murky, but refreshing beyond anything he had ever felt in his entire life.

This is what freedom feels like, he thought as he treated himself to another dunk underneath.

* * * *

Ben felt revitalized as he sat on the ground and tugged on his boots. Something unnerved him, and he turned to his left to see Conway eyeing him. Ben had seen that disgusting look before—and not just from this soldier.

Would he really start something *now*—after they had just marched all this way together and been in close proximity to General Washington himself? Ben wondered as he rose to his feet.

Conway mimicked his every move, his gaze fixed directly upon him.

A half-clothed soldier waving his musket weaved directly between them, sounding a frenzied alarm. "Hurry! Over there!"

The fifty-odd soldiers hastened their movements: Those still in the stream poured out, while the others threw on their clothes and gear. Conway, for his part, chose not to wait. He barreled through the weeds and took a glimpse. His expression flushed as he pointed. "The enemy! At least a dozen of 'em!"

Ben charged in Conway's direction, just as a musket ball tore through the man's neck, splattering blood and muscle in the air. His eyes bulged while he attempted to say something before he collapsed in a pool of blood.

Ben bent down to lay Conway on his back. His complexion was pale and his eyes had a faraway, glassy look. Ben went through the formality of taking his pulse only to conclude what he already knew.

Without hesitation, Ben snatched the dead man's musket and joined his fellow soldiers hiding in the weeds, their guns at the ready. Peering ahead, they made out the figures of at least twenty marching Tory militiamen—likely a gang of disgruntled loyalists from nearby New Jersey—who were led by four British officers.

Have we really come to this? Ben thought in disbelief. *Colonists firing on fellow colonists?*

The Tories wasted no time: They aimed their muskets and fired.

"Let's go, men!" someone yelled. "Form ranks!"

The fifty Marylanders fell into a tight formation, lining up in two rows as they had learned from their training. They packed their musket barrels with shot and gunpowder in rapid movements.

Since the commanders were not present, Ben knew he had to act as the firing line sergeant. Breathing heavily, he waited until he could make out the Tory lines more clearly through the smoke. With a wave of his arm, he ordered the first row of ten troops to squeeze off their shots.

As the haze cleared, Ben prayed that they had taken down a chunk of the loyalists, but this wasn't the case; only a couple had fallen.

Ben raised Conway's musket and fired, striking a Tory between the eyes. He tossed the empty musket to the ground, grabbing his own weapon for another shot.

Popping sounds cascaded all around him, and he threw himself to the ground. "Everybody down!" he shouted. Some followed his lead, but a few others were too late. Ben watched as two Marylanders were penetrated in their chests and shoulders and blood seeped through their uniforms.

"Next line—fire!" he yelled while scrambling to reload.

The men followed his command, but Ben could still make out the oncoming barrage of militia uniforms, moving inexorably toward them.

So this is it, Ben concluded. *This is the end—I won't even make it to New York.*

Just as hope had almost abandoned him, Ben heard the sound of hooves from behind. He wheeled around to see Commander Gist and three other higher-ranking officers on horseback charging toward the rear of the Maryland line.

The commander fired off a round from his musket and leapt down from his horse. He ordered the rear of the line to carry the wounded and move them out of harm's way.

"Make haste and reach the main lines!" he shouted.

He and the other officers distributed a few fresh muskets to the front line of Marylanders, who fired off a burst.

"There aren't many of them—we can rout them with a bayonet charge!"

Ben slid the rusty bayonet onto the front of his musket. The Tories were within twenty yards now; it would take quite a sprint to reach them without being hit. He awaited his orders with a few other soldiers nearby.

Commander Gist peered out over the advancing militia lines and grimaced; there were more of them than anticipated and his men were sitting ducks in an open area.

Suddenly, one by one, three British officers collapsed, their chests split open from rifle shots.

Commander Gist swiveled around to search for the source of the shots. He caught sight of Paddy and three of his fellow westerners crouching near the Maryland lines a few paces back, taking potshots with their long rifles.

Paddy lined up and fired another shot, catching a fourth redcoat officer in the temple. This was all the Tory militiamen could take; they broke their march and darted in the opposite direction back into the fields with gunfire at their heels.

After a final flurry of shots, all fell silent.

Commander Gist signaled for the patriot guns to cease. "Hold your fire, men!"

Paddy placed his massive, long rifle at his feet. "Bastards think they can catch us with our pants down." He grunted. "Let them go lick their wounds."

Once the wounded were properly attended, Commander Gist gathered the troops and ordered them to march back to the main lines. "Good work, soldiers! I imagine that was merely an expeditionary force, probing our defenses. But we will not take any chances. We shall rendezvous with the main forces at once. Mark my words: They have only witnessed a hint of what the men from Maryland can do!"

TWENTY-SIX

Friday, July 12, 1776
Philadelphia, Pennsylvania

As the son of a merchant, Josh felt he knew Philadelphia—at least by reputation, if not from firsthand experience. He recalled sitting in countless meetings in his father's study, listening to wealthy Philadelphian visitors boast about how much cleaner and more civilized their city was than all the others in the colonies. In their minds, while New York was a businessman's paradise and Baltimore a dependable port, Philadelphia represented something much grander—perhaps even freedom itself.

In spite of everything he had heard about this great city—including the patriotic rumblings of the revolution—Josh couldn't begin to anticipate the reception that awaited him and his fellow soldiers on arrival. Annapolis was nothing compared to this.

Colonel Smallwood marched at the head of the parade, followed by his closest commanders on horseback. Accompanied by drums and fifes, the fully reunited 1st Maryland Regiment marched in step through the heart of the city to the delight of frenzied Philadelphians, who mobbed the cobblestone streets for over a mile while flailing patriotic banners and signs. The cheers and chants were thunderous, especially as the soldiers made their way toward the Pennsylvania statehouse. Behind those windows, Josh knew, labored the men of the Continental Congress, who, at that very moment, were making fateful decisions that would impact the lives of everyone across these lands.

The soldiers drew to a halt and waited in position like statues, as the visitors from Congress—looking like portly sage men with white wigs from this distance—exited the statehouse and assembled. Colonel Smallwood joined them to address the men. "Soldiers: The Continental Congress welcomes you to the great city of Philadelphia. At the request of General Washington, I have been asked to read you a document that is most important to our cause. In fact, it is the very reason we are all gathered here. It was written and signed less than a fortnight ago by members of our own Congress, many of whom stand before you."

He raised a sheaf of parchment, cleared his throat, and recited, "*We hold these truths to be self-evident, that all men are created equal, that they are endowed by their creator with certain unalienable rights, that among these are life, liberty, and the pursuit of happiness…*"

As the colonel continued, Josh glanced over at his fellow soldiers—including Ben and Paddy, a long way down the line—to confirm what he had already felt: Like him, all were fighting back tears of pride. Josh found similar reactions among the crowd in front of him: Men, women, and children of all ages clutched handkerchiefs to their eyes and noses. He would remember this moment for as long as he lived.

As Josh tried to return his focus to Colonel Smallwood, he did a double take: A beautiful young woman was staring at him. She was some distance away and her hair was concealed by a blue bonnet, but what he could make out of her face and figure bore a striking resemblance to someone he knew and deeply cherished… *Tessa*.

The woman turned away with sudden disinterest, disappearing into a swirl of Philadelphians. *No, it couldn't have been her*, he thought. *It's impossible. What would she be doing in Philadelphia? And Tessa would never have looked away from me like that*.

136

The possibility flitted out of his head, at least for the moment. He attributed the mirage to being physically wiped out from traveling hundreds of miles on foot, not to mention being more than just a bit heartsick. *If only I'd had the time to find her when I returned to Baltimore,* he thought. *I only needed a few precious minutes with her...*

A soldier to his left nudged him out of his reverie. The speeches had all winded down and once again the men were on the move. Embarrassed at being a half step out of sync with the others, he adjusted his rifle and rushed to fall properly in line—fortunately without anyone's having taken notice of his lapse.

Yet the image of the woman in the crowd flashed in his mind: Remove the bonnet and she was the spitting image of his beloved...wasn't she?

TWENTY-SEVEN

Evening, Friday, July 12, 1776
Philadelphia, Pennsylvania

Mordecai Gist held court under the stars in the main barracks yard, surrounded by about forty of his men—including Josh, Ben, Paddy, and several other westerners. His eyes ventured from one soldier to the next as he addressed them in a low tone. "Gentlemen, I've asked you all to join me here tonight to offer you a special invitation. It is something of a confidential nature, so I trust that you will be discreet."

The men moved their heads up and down in unison as an emphatic "yes."

"As you know, I have been an agitator for colonial rights from the earliest days—first as a founding member of the Independent Cadets and now as a commander here in this regiment. With this in mind, I have made a request to Colonel Smallwood—a request that he has rather reluctantly accepted."

Gist swiveled the lamp around, which caused his face to appear as if it were cast in a shadow.

"I have been appointed commander of an elite squad of troops within the 1st Regiment—a contingent that I alone command. I have been granted the honor and responsibility of handpicking the exceptional soldiers who will fight alongside me in our upcoming campaigns.

"I have observed each of you closely and have admired your discipline and exceptional talents. That is why I asked you here—for you men to join with me. Together, we will achieve greatness on the battlefield."

He placed the lamp down on the grass and motioned for the group to scrunch closer. The men hung on his every word.

"As many of you know, we faced a small contingent of loyalist troops while en route to Philadelphia," he continued. "We fought by the book and sent the enemy on the run. But we cannot lose sight of the fact that we also lost five brave men as a result of that engagement. I assure you, they will not have perished in vain. Make no mistake. We have drawn an important lesson from this experience: We cannot fight the British by the book and win. We must fight a different kind of war. From this point forward, if you agree to join me, we will meet the enemy in new and unorthodox ways to confuse and disrupt their traditional warfare tactics. This is how we will win.

"Throughout history, you will find examples of legendary soldiers who were called upon to go up against insurmountable odds and accomplish the extraordinary. These elite, fierce soldiers were the best equipped and most feared individuals of their times. They were the bravest of the brave. In ancient Greece, they were the Spartan warriors of legend. In our colonial army, *you* are those elite soldiers. *You* are our Spartans."

He presented his hand facedown in the center of the group. "Let us swear our bond to each other. We are the Sons of Baltimore. *Sine pari*—without equal."

A soldier slapped his hand on top of Gist's. Josh, Ben, Paddy, and all of the others followed suit, one by one, while pledging a silent oath.

As the group solemnly dispersed, Gist blew out the lamp and headed back to his barracks. He knew he would sleep soundly that night.

* * * *

Josh paused outside the barracks door for a look up at the stars. He felt something tug at his arm. "You coming, mate?" Ben asked.

"I just need a few minutes," Josh said.

"Don't take too long," Ben warned him. "We need to rest up. You heard Gist. We have a lot riding on us."

"Got it," Josh said.

He wandered a few steps, contemplating everything Gist had said— especially words like "elite" and "brave." *Will I do justice to these words?* he wondered. *Not too long ago I was nothing but a merchant boy learning my trade. Now I'm a soldier—a Spartan, no less. What would my father have thought of all this?*

Either way, Ben's advice aside, he knew it was going to be difficult to fall asleep after the pledge to Gist—a man he had admired since he first met him in the Cat's Eye Pub. Now, only a few months later, he was taking up arms right alongside him.

He settled his thoughts and started to make his way back toward his barracks when he was spooked nearly out of his boots. A voice whispered to him, seemingly from out of nowhere. "Josh?"

He spun around. "Who is it? Who is there?'

A womanly figure stepped out into the moonlight: *Tessa.* He had to rub his eyes to be certain he wasn't hallucinating. "Tessa? How did you… what are you doing here?"

"I came to see you," she replied.

"You came all this way? I don't understand…. I mean, I've missed you terribly."

"I heard all about your father. I'm so sorry I wasn't there for you… so sorry."

Josh felt relieved: She was apologizing to him and not the other way around. She didn't seem to bear any kind of grudge for his having left without saying goodbye—and for not finding her when he returned to Baltimore. He knew both acts were explainable, but she didn't seem remotely interested in dredging up these matters.

"Thank you," he said, moving toward her to take her hands. His words raced out of his mouth. "I can't believe it's you—that you're *here*. I feel like I'm dreaming. Tell me, why did you come all this way to find me? Not that I mind. I'm so happy to see you and—"

She placed her finger on his lips. "*Sssssh*," she silenced him. "I don't have time to talk and this isn't the time or place. Meet me tomorrow morning at Arch and Race streets—*please, Josh*."

"Yes, of course…I will," he responded. "But I don't understand. What is happening? Are you in danger? Are you all right?" "I'm fine, Josh, trust me," she answered, looking around with concern. "Really, I must go. I'm sorry. We'll talk tomorrow, all right?"

Before he could reply, she planted a tender kiss on his lips.

Josh reached his arm around her for a full embrace, but she recoiled and shifted a few feet away. "*Tomorrow*," she repeated.

"Wait," Josh called after her. "Don't go…not yet."

She shook her head before turning around and picking up her pace. Josh pursued her a couple of steps and asked, "Tessa—I must know. Was that you earlier today…at the parade? Wearing a blue bonnet? I swear…I'm sure it was you…and now you're here."

Her head rotated sharply back to him, almost as if he were a complete stranger. "No. I wasn't anywhere near there. I don't own a blue bonnet. You must have mistaken someone else for me."

With that, she vanished in the moonlight.

TWENTY-EIGHT

Tuesday, July 16, 1776
Philadelphia, Pennsylvania

Josh didn't get much sleep that night. Not only was his head swirling from his pledge to Mordecai Gist, but now there was Tessa's surprise visit as well. He hadn't planned on seeing her for some time—and certainly not so unexpectedly in Philadelphia. And wasn't it an odd coincidence that the woman in the blue bonnet who resembled her so closely had been staring at him? Yes, it was possible for such a lookalike to exist… but what were the odds of such a thing occurring when Tessa had also happened to materialize right before him in this same city? If it had been her, why would she lie about it?

Josh was the last soldier to lie down on his cot and the first to arise. At sunrise, he dug out a clean outfit buried deep within his rucksack and did his best to tame the unruly mop of hair that flowed down to his shoulders. He made an attempt to run a razor over his stubble and splashed some whiskey onto his rough skin. He didn't have a mirror handy to review his hasty self-assemblage, but decided that his sludgy appearance would have to do. *The Spartan soldiers didn't care about how they looked, did they?* he thought.

Good fortune smiled upon him that sunny morning, as he somehow expected it would: His name was far down the daily on-duty list for later in the afternoon. He was *free*—if only for a few hours. No one questioned him as he hustled out of camp and hired a carriage to take him to the city center. The ride cost him nearly half of the coin he had stashed away, but he wasn't thinking about money. Only one thing consumed him: once again being in Tessa's arms.

He stepped out of the carriage and walked past the upscale neighborhood boutiques and other shops. The day had hardly begun, and the area was still sleepy with shopkeepers only now flipping the "Open" signs in their storefront windows. The empty streets and sidewalks gave him a chance to get a clear view of his surroundings, and it didn't take him long to spot his beloved seated on a bench shaded by a majestic cherry tree. He paused to absorb it: She looked as striking as ever in a trim rose-colored dress with her hair pinned up in braids.

He kissed her on the lips while plunking himself beside her. "I missed you so much," he said as he leaned into her. "You look as beautiful as ever."

"And you are as handsome as ever," she reciprocated, somewhat preoccupied.

He felt he had to fill in the void that followed. "This is such a wonderful surprise…seeing you here, I mean…"

Her silence made him slump back uneasily. "I know I left suddenly… but a lot happened. First my friend Christopher…then my father…"

"I know," she murmured, interrupting him. "That was so horrible for you. I'm sorry you had to go through all of that."

"But you could have written to me…. You knew I enlisted, didn't you?"

"I *did* write to you," she countered with a hint of defensiveness. "I mailed a letter they said would reach you when you arrived here in Philadelphia. You haven't received it?"

"N-no," he stammered, uncertain whether he should believe her. He wanted to and searched for a fitting excuse. "It must have been lost in transit…while we were on the march."

"How has it been? The march, I mean."

"I've never been on my feet so much in my life!" He chuckled in an effort to lighten the mood. "But it's worth every single step. First was the celebration in Annapolis—it was incredible. I actually heard General George Washington speak!"

Tessa placed her arm around Josh's neck. "So, what do you think of this General Washington?"

Josh didn't hesitate. "He's a masterful leader and an inspiration. I heard he was big, but seeing him in real life—it's so hard to describe. He has an air about him, a *presence*. It's an honor to serve under him."

"Is it?" Tessa snapped. "Back home we've heard nothing good about him. People are saying he's inexperienced, making bad decisions, and sending young men off to war terribly unprepared."

Josh folded his arms; it was if someone had tarnished the reputation of his own father. "That's not true. He's not anything like that."

"So, you're prepared to march under his command?"

"Of course! Our army will follow him *anywhere*. He is a man of the people, for the people. I trust him with my heart and soul," Josh announced. He moved in closer to her and smiled. "Listen, my darling Tessa, I didn't leave camp to meet you here to discuss military matters. I came to see *you*. And we haven't much time. We leave tomorrow for Morristown. Then we head on to New York, where we will make our final camp."

"Josh, I know this will be hard for you to hear"—she took both of his hands—"but I truly believe you are making a mistake…"

"Mistake…I…I don't understand," Josh stammered. "I thought you understood the cause…why I'm doing all this. Why we *all* are. I lost my father…"

"I know all that—and why you would want revenge."

"It's not just about revenge," Josh argued. "I mean, *it is*—I would like nothing more than to slice into the hearts of a few dozen redcoats—but it's far greater than that. We are fighting against *tyranny*, we are the chosen people—"

"Yes, yes, I've been hearing all of the patriotic, God-fearing blather." She shrugged.

Josh tried not to be further offended as she continued, "The more I learn about this war, the more I believe it's a death sentence. I…don't want to see you get killed because of a general's inexperience and bad decisions."

Josh stood up, his face flushed: This was more than he could bear. "How can you continue to repeat such things? You haven't even seen the great man—*I have*. I would follow his lead to the end of the earth. I would give my own life for him. He's *not* making bad decisions. We are well prepared to face the enemy."

Tessa shook her head. "That's not what I've heard. You barely have two hundred troops. Your weapons are old and don't shoot straight. You are just a boy with one month's training. Tell me: How does that prepare you to go up against one of the world's mightiest armies?"

The word "boy" cut him to the quick. *Is this how she sees me? As some stupid kid?* he thought. Not too long ago she had supported him and approved of his enlistment as a cadet. What had changed? For the first time, he felt his voice rising while conversing with her. "I will have you know I have been *personally selected* by Mordecai Gist to serve alongside him in battle—I would say that means something, wouldn't you? He thinks of Ben, me, and others as warriors—*Spartans*, in fact. We can take anything that gets thrown at us!"

Tessa raised her hand. "Stop. I'm sorry, that was wrong of me. I didn't mean to upset you," she said, patting the seat beside her. "Come here."

Josh calmed himself down enough to look past her biting words and resume his place next to her. He waited for her to speak. "I'm just frightened for you, Josh. I don't want you to be hurt. Please…come back home with me to Baltimore. We can live our lives together—just us— and forget we ever spoke of this."

She leaned her head against his shoulder and looked up at him, her tone softening. "You don't have to fight…"

Clearly, the disagreement was far from over. Josh felt the blood continuing to rush in his veins, and his head was throbbing. He struggled to sound stronger, older, and wiser than his years while maintaining a calm manner. "Tessa, you know I care for you deeply. But I'm fighting for something much bigger than myself—or even the two of us. Surely, you understand that."

She placed her hands on his neck; her touch felt warm and soothing. "I know you believe all that. But it's not you. That's just the rich colonial merchants, the manipulative politicians, and the chest-beating reverends talking. They won't be the ones doing any of the fighting. But you will be. And that's what scares me."

"You don't understand, Tessa. You don't know the people I've met these past few weeks with the regiment. You haven't seen their bravery and their commitment. You haven't witnessed the extraordinary leadership of our commanders. *I have.*"

"Well then." She sighed, rising to her feet. "Clearly your mind has been made up."

He stood up next to her. "Did you really think I could abandon my regiment? Betray my friends? Break my oaths?"

"No, I suppose I didn't," she answered. "But I had to try. I just… don't want to lose you."

"You won't, I promise," he assured her, clasping her hands and bringing his face closer to her. Her arguments and criticism suddenly made sense; she was worried about him. "Besides, my mother would die if anything were to happen to me."

Tessa forced a smile. "I care far too much to ever give up on you, Josh."

The two looked into each other's eyes as their lips met for a passionate kiss. He looked down while continuing to hold her. "I have to go back—I'll be expected on duty."

"Perhaps we can meet again in Morristown in—how many days did you say?" she asked.

"Three days' march, starting tomorrow."

Tessa placed her hands on her hips. "Expect to find me in Morristown—again begging you to come home with me."

"You are persistent."

"I won't give up until I know you are safe."

"And I won't give up until all of the redcoats are on their ships heading back across the Atlantic."

Their lips pressed together one last time. As they headed in opposite directions, they each felt baffled by the other's stubbornness—as well as disappointed that their final kiss had been so devoid of passion.

TWENTY-NINE

Evening, Saturday, July 20, 1776
Morristown, New Jersey

en rubbed his eyes as he paced back and forth across the dirt road, his musket at the ready for any sign of redcoats. It was his turn on watch, and he had to force himself to stay awake and ensure that all of his senses were on total alert. The skirmish with the Tory force back in Delaware and images of his fallen dead comrades filled him with trepidation.

Compared to the grandeur of Philadelphia, Morristown was nothing special to him. But the New Jersey town nestled in the woods did have one advantage the capital city did not: an easily defended, strategic location where an army could guard all sides of its encampment with ease.

Ben listened intently through the sounds of the outdoors—mosquitoes, crickets, frogs—for anything out of the ordinary. Everything seemed serene until he heard the rustling of something through the tall brush about ten yards off the road. He licked his lips and squatted behind a tree for cover and to get a good angle at whoever appeared. The noises drew closer; he could see something move. Ben cocked his musket in nervous anticipation.

He held his breath and nearly squeezed the trigger when a fawn skipped out into the clearing and pranced through some trees to the other side of the road. Ben exhaled and lowered the weapon with a grateful sigh.

His moment of relaxation was premature: He heard oncoming footsteps—this time, unquestionably from a human—and once again raised his musket. A shadowy figure appeared at the edge of the southern road to his left.

Hold on, Ben steadied himself. *What did they tell us? "Don't fire until you see the whites of their eyes."*

Crouching down low, he took several cautious steps toward the figure. Along the way, he convinced himself that it was probably a local drunk or a woman for hire whom he'd have to shoo back to town.

"Who goes there?" Ben demanded, cradling the weapon as he neared the figure silhouetted in the moonlight.

"At ease, soldier, I'm a patriot commander," the man barked. "Return to your duties. I...have a...rendezvous with someone."

"I'm sorry, sir, but I have orders that no one—absolutely no one—is to pass," Ben responded in a forceful tone. "Please raise your arms and show yourself."

"Yes, yes, of course," the man agreed. "But I am only able to raise one arm, as I am leading my horse."

The man did as instructed, moving forward into visual range and the moon's illumination. As he neared, Ben could make out the etched features of Colonel Sharpe—the leathery, lean commander of another contingent with a reputation for being short-tempered. He held the reins of an oversized gray horse.

Ben lowered his rifle; the last thing he needed was an argument with a superior, especially one as irascible as Sharpe.

"Thank you, Colonel, you may lower your arm," Ben said, his hands still on his weapon.

"Ah, good. You know who I am. May I get along now? You have done your duty."

"With all due respect, Colonel, my orders are to stop anyone from loitering past sundown while the regiment is encamped. I regret that you will need to return to your quarters."

The colonel stood nose to nose with Ben. "You are a darkie, boy—and of an inferior rank. You are not in any position to order me to do a blessed thing."

Ben had a feeling it might come to this: He was damned no matter what he chose to do. "Again, sir, Colonel Smallwood directly ordered me to enforce this rule. I must request that you return to your quarters."

"Damn your mouth, boy!" he growled. "What is your name? I'll have your head for this."

Ben was about to respond when another figure emerged into the moonlight. A woman in a blue bonnet approached and embraced Sharpe with a giggle.

Colonel Sharpe assisted her onto the horse. As her legs were hoisted on the saddle, her bonnet fell off. Ben watched as her strawberry blond hair tumbled down her shoulders. Tessa and Ben locked bewildered expressions, neither having expected to see the other.

Sharpe drilled holes through Ben with his stare as he tucked Tessa's feet into the stirrups. He thumped the horse's rear, and the animal clopped away. "I would advise you to keep your mouth shut about this," the Colonel threatened. "We don't need any diversions interfering with our effort, now do we?"

Ben held his ground, uncertain of his next move.

"We also don't need to see another nigger's corpse hanging from a tree."

The two scowled at each other before the colonel turned on his boot heel and headed off through the trees in the direction of his camp.

In Ben's mind, there was only one thing he could do—even if he hated doing it. He scrambled up the sloping hill back toward camp.

He ran with such determination that he startled Johnson, his fellow patrolman. "Wright—what are you doing away from your post?" he called.

"No time to explain," he said.

"Is everything all right? Anything I need to do?"

"Take over my post," Ben instructed him. "*Please*. I'll be right back. There is something urgent…I'll explain later…"

THIRTY

Evening, Saturday, July 20, 1776
Morristown, New Jersey

Josh was in a deep, fitful sleep when Ben came bursting into his tent, rousing him to hurry with him toward the center of the camp.

"Wake up!" he hollered, giving him a shove.

Josh could barely get one eye open as he grumbled, "I don't hear any trumpets.... Are we under attack?"

Ben was stymied. *What did I really see?* he pondered, feeling a shudder of doubt. *And how do I explain whatever it was to my best friend?* "Not exactly...but it's an emergency."

Josh rolled over to the other side of his cot. "I just got off duty. If it's not redcoats, there's no emergency."

Ben couldn't afford to waste another second. He kicked the cot with such force, it nearly tipped over. It was enough to jostle Josh and convince him to sit upright and shout, "Hey, what the...was that necessary?"

"Yes, it was," Ben shot back. "And if you don't get up right now, I'll kick you somewhere much worse!"

"Fine, give me a moment," Josh said, still battling grogginess. As he stretched and yawned, Ben drew closer while pumping his fists. "All right, all right."

Josh quickened his pace, pulling on his shirt and trousers while seated on the cot. He tugged on his boots, tied his laces, and rose. "Ready," he announced, grabbing his hat. "Now, do you want to tell me what this is all about?"

"No time to explain," Ben said, hastening out of the tent.

Josh, charging behind, grabbed Ben by the back of the shoulder. "You wake me up in the middle of the night and tell me there's an emergency. Goddammit, tell what it is."

Ben took a deep breath and looked down. The words spilled out. "I saw Tessa…with another man."

* * * *

Josh became increasingly flustered as he fired questions at his friend along the way to Commander Lawton's, only to be ignored. Josh's thoughts turned dark and pained: *Tessa with another man? Impossible! What does Ben think he saw? He must be mistaken…. And why are we heading toward Commander Lawton's tent? What's going on?*

A corporal ushered the young men into Commander Lawton's tent. It didn't appear as if the white bearded man had been asleep; he was sitting on his cot by candlelight in his overalls and suspenders holding some papers, most likely war briefings. Standing erect, he placed the papers down and turned to the young soldiers. "Yes? You boys have something to report?"

"I beg your pardon, sir," Ben said with a slight bow while clasping his hat with both hands. "I'm terribly sorry to disturb you, but it is urgent."

The commander's expression turned impatient. "All right, soldier. What is it, man? Get it out. Did you see a threat?"

Josh, who also had his hat in his hands, looked at his friend as if to say, "Go on. This is your show." Josh had seen his friend in a lot of scrapes over the years, but never agitated to this extent—not even when he had to stand up to people like Conway. And how did all of this relate to Tessa?

"No, sir, not exactly," he answered, struggling to get the words out. If it came down to Colonel Sharpe's word or his, who would his commander believe? He fretted, fearing he knew the answer—but had to take a chance anyway. "I was on duty this evening, outside the camp."

The commander's eyebrows lifted. "Ah—someone broke the curfew order?"

Ben's pained look provided the answer.

"Come on, out with it," the Commander barked. "Who was in violation of a direct order?"

"Colonel Sharpe, sir," Ben replied, looking at Josh out of the corner of his eye. "He was…helping a woman onto a horse. She rode off as I left, and then he headed back into camp."

Commander Lawton rubbed his temples. "This woman was leaving camp, eh? Had you ever seen her before?"

Josh and Ben exchanged tense glances. "Yes, sir, we both had. She is a barmaid from Baltimore. Her name is Tessa."

Josh was unprepared for hearing her name aloud, even though he had known it was coming. What on earth was Tessa doing in the middle of the night with Colonel Sharpe? And then she rode off on a horse? He couldn't possibly have been more confused; there had to be an explanation. Maybe he was mistaken? After all, it was pitch black….

"How do you know for sure it was her?" Josh challenged him.

Ben gave his friend a look that said, "I'm not a blind idiot."

"You know this woman? You recognized her?" the commander spat at both men.

Ben raised his chest as he answered, "Yes, I do. Like I said, her name is Tessa and she is a barmaid I—*we*—know from back home in Baltimore. She wore a blue bonnet to disguise her hair, but it fell off…and I knew for sure it was her when her strawberry blond hair was revealed."

Josh's heart fractured with this newest detail: The woman who had looked at him from the parade sidelines wore a blue bonnet, a fact he hadn't mentioned to anyone. Yet Tessa had denied even being at the parade. What if she had lied to him? What was she up to? Her appearances and behavior had been strange...

Commander Lawton paced in front of the two soldiers. He knew something was amiss when he caught Josh's reactions. He pressed his face up close to Josh. "I am under the impression you know this woman far more than you have admitted thus far."

Before Josh could speak, Ben rallied to his defense. "Sir, it's true that my friend has been courting Tessa—but I assure you he did not have anything whatsoever to do with the events of this evening."

Commander Lawton squinted at him. "When did you last see this barmaid?"

"L-last Tuesday...in...in Philadelphia," Josh stammered.

"What has she been up to here, in Morristown?"

"Honestly...I have no idea," Josh spluttered.

The commander's jaws tightened as he continued the inquisition. "And you have no reason to believe she arrived at camp to see you?"

Josh shrugged. "She had mentioned coming to camp...but I've received no letters; I had no idea—"

Lawton thrust his finger in Josh's face to silence him. "You understand that information about our soldiers or our movements could make someone quite rich in these parts. Did you communicate any piece of information to her at all? Something she might be able to sell?"

Josh steeled himself. "No. Of course not. But please...there must be an explanation. Tessa isn't a traitor...this must be some sort of misunderstanding."

Commander Lawton gestured toward a spot on the opposite side of the fire. "Wait there until Colonel Sharpe arrives."

Josh obeyed the commander and stared into the firelight.

Ben shuffled toward him. "Josh, I'm sorry all of this is happening and for you to have heard it this way—but the watch commander had to know as soon as possible."

"You saw her?" Josh snapped, trying to process all of this. He longed to give Tessa—the only woman he had ever loved—the benefit of the doubt. Perhaps there was a lookalike out there—someone who wore a blue bonnet. If he could mistake a total stranger for Tessa, it was entirely possible Ben had done the same thing—especially since it was dark and he was probably overtired. He had sensed from the beginning that Ben disliked Tessa. "You're telling me that out of all the soldiers here, you happened to be the one on duty who saw the one woman you've never liked—who has come all the way here from Baltimore and then Philadelphia not to see me but another man instead? That sounds like quite a coincidence."

Ben tipped backward in disbelief. "Are you saying I'm lying? Why would I do that? We've been friends since—well, forever."

Josh threw up his hands in frustration. "I don't know. All I can say is that you've never liked her, you've never trusted her, and you've always been jealous that we were together."

Ben's laugh came out as a snort. "You truly believe that I would risk my place in this army just to get your girl in trouble? Even if I *were* jealous, which I'm not, I would never do such a thing to you. Have I ever lied to you or made anything like this up?"

Josh struggled to produce an answer and then stated, "Answer me this, Ben: What was she doing here with some colonel she's never met?"

"I'm sorry, but you already know there are only two possible answers to that one."

Josh turned away from his friend as he responded, "Don't say them."

"I think you need to hear them said aloud and face the facts," Ben concluded. "Either she's a traitor and selling secrets—or she was here selling something else."

With that Josh snarled and flung himself at Ben, seizing him by the uniform lapels and shoving him to the ground. Ben thrust his friend to the side, struggling back to his feet and crouching into a defensive position. Josh lunged on top of Ben one more time, but hearing the scuffle, a group of soldiers ran into the tent and separated them.

Once Josh and Ben were both on their feet, Commander Lawton paced between them. "If anything like this happens again, I'll have you both sent to the stocks."

Still breathing heavily, Josh and Ben shared blank looks. Neither thought a day would ever come when they would find themselves at odds, much less exchanging blows.

Commander Lawton addressed Ben, "Soldier, which way did this woman ride when she left town?" he asked.

"West, sir, on the main road," Ben responded.

"Damn, she could be miles away by now," the commander grimaced as he turned to a staff soldier. "Ride west and retrieve that woman!"

The rest of the soldiers, followed by Commander Lawton, turned to exit the tent. Josh and Ben started to follow them, but the commander spun around to halt them. "Neither one of you moves," he directed. "And no more fighting between you—or else!"

THIRTY-ONE

Friday, July 19, 1776
Knowlton Township, New Jersey

Tessa felt the night breeze rushing across her face as she brushed her hair out of her eyes. She wasn't much of a rider, but the horse was familiar with the route and took the lead galloping through the dark, meandering New Jersey back roads.

The crisp air invigorated her, yet she could not sweep away these past few days. She felt no shame in what she was doing—she had to survive, didn't she? What had the revolutionaries ever done for her? She was a woman getting on in years who had been raised in a cesspool of an orphanage, bereft of family or friends. She escaped and traveled from town to town where men frequently had their way with her whenever and however they liked. When they didn't beat and abuse her, they stole her money and abandoned her after having led her on for months with false hopes and empty promises.

Then she met Josh—the poor young fool. He was not like the others: He was gentle and delightfully naïve. He truly loved her, she knew that for certain. But, as she had discovered, he was on the wrong side of this skirmish; the colonials didn't have a prayer of winning this conflict. They were too stupid to even recognize the myriad traitors right under their very noses. She was convinced that his fate was to be shot or stabbed to death or, at best, maimed and crippled. What good would he be to her in any of these circumstances?

Her treatment of Josh was her sole regret. She had used her relationship with him as her means to visit the army on the march and gather useful information—a job that had already paid her handsomely, more than she'd made in her entire life. Along the way, she had no choice but to be unfaithful in order to loosen officers' lips and extract much-needed information on colonial activities.

As soon as she surmised the hopelessness of the cause and the insurmountable odds the Continental Army was up against, she tried to get Josh to relinquish the cause and return to Baltimore with her. Once the British rolled over the colonial forces and all the independence foolishness was over, they could at last lead a normal life together with her recent ill-gotten gains to help them along.

But that was now just a pipe dream. She would never see Josh again. How could she look him in the eye after his friend had caught her with Colonel Sharpe back in Morristown? Of all the people on duty that night, how could it have been him? *That infernal black man never did like me*, she thought. *He most certainly told Josh about what he saw.* The two were inseparably close—friends since childhood, she recalled—and there was a good chance Josh would believe the tale he told. At the very least, Josh would ask her too many questions. No matter how clever her answers might be, he would always retain some doubt about her. She couldn't face him again knowing that mistrust would always come between them.

So here she was, alone yet again, riding some stranger's horse in the middle of the night. Josh, unable to listen to reason, had cast her aside to fight for glory. Tonight she would turn over her information, claim the rest of what she was owed, and head straight for British-occupied territory, where she would change her name and start anew. Who knows?

Perhaps at some point she would meet up with a royal dignitary and set sail with him for England. Wouldn't it be grand to become nobility?

The horse finally slowed down, enabling her to loosen her grip on the reins. She had been in the saddle for over an hour and felt relief at the prospect of being close to her destination. She could make out the King's Lancer tavern in the distance—a tiny square box of an edifice emanating light and laughter in the darkness. As the horse came to a halt in front of the tavern, she leapt from the saddle and tied it to a hitching post. She wrapped her hair in a black scarf, since she had lost her blue bonnet in her hasty retreat following her rendezvous with Colonel Sharpe.

Straightening her clothes, she extracted a pistol from her saddlebag and tucked the barrel into her skirt. It would do her no good to walk into a way-stop tavern without being prepared—especially this late at night.

She squinted through the tavern window, trying to see past the grime and cracks. Not much there—just a bunch of drunks and an older gentleman in the back. Perhaps that was him? She moved toward the door; it creaked open and she hesitantly stepped inside. She was met with the rank odor of stale beer and low-grade cassia cinnamon, which was used to add much-needed flavor to cheap tavern food.

She surveyed the room, her hand close to her pistol. The corpulent barkeep kept his head down as he poured a drink. A couple of half-drunk patrons sleepily hunkered at the wooden bar. Three or four other scattered bar guests were spread out unconscious across their tables.

Only one man—the older gentleman in a western hat—appeared to be awake and not inebriated; his back was turned to her as he swallowed down ale. Tessa slinked toward his table and stood before him.

"Moody?" she asked under her breath.

The middle-aged, dark-haired man in a plain white shirt and faded gray jacket tipped his hat to her. Tessa didn't know much about her interlocutor, except that he was a loyalist and that she had been instructed to deliver the information in her possession into his hands.

"What did you bring me?" he demanded.

She placed her hands on her hips, all business. "Payment first."

"Of course," he responded, reaching into his jacket pocket and tossing a pouch onto the table. Tessa weighed it in her palm and judged it to be light; she tugged it open to review the quantity of coins within.

Her arms slumped to their sides. "Where's the rest?"

"You'll get the other half once I've heard what you have to offer," Moody insisted.

Tessa glanced over her shoulder. Most of the drunks were oblivious, if not comatose. The barkeep had moved on to polishing silver. Sitting opposite Moody, she leaned her elbows on the table and whispered, "Their forces number about seven hundred—mostly from Baltimore, all newly trained. They are encamped in Morristown before marching to join Washington in New York. They will take up defensive positions within three days' time, but clearly don't have enough men or supplies by themselves to guard the full extent of New York. There is a possibility that regiments from Pennsylvania and Delaware may join them."

Impressed, Moody completed his ale and asked, "What about their armaments?"

"I counted twenty mortars and twelve cannons, carried on fully stocked wagons. Each man is equipped with a musket and knife. And there is a contingent of riflemen from somewhere in the Maryland mountains. These men may be trouble. Their shooting accuracy is already causing a stir."

Moody closed his eyes, committing these details to memory. When his lids snapped open, he tossed a second pouch onto the table that was equal in size and weight to the first. He took a final swill of ale, tipped his hat, and slid off his chair with a closing, "Good evening, madam." Instead of heading through the front door, he stepped behind the bar between swinging wooden doors that presumably led to the kitchen.

Tessa leaned back in her seat, a heavy burden lifted. Before squirreling away the second pouch, she extracted a couple of coins and slapped them on the table. "Barkeep! If you have any ale left, bring me a double!"

* * * *

Standing in a private back room behind a locked door, Moody lit a candle and spread out a writing parchment on a table as best as he could, given the confined surroundings. The King's Lancer was an ideal out-of-the-way haunt to conduct his business, especially since the owner shared his loyalist sympathies and the barkeep had no issue with minding his own business until his services were needed.

The woman's information is good, he considered—*very good, in fact.* His benefactors would be most pleased. He smoothed out the parchment with one hand and dipped the quill into a vial of black ink. Sliding a second piece of parchment over the top—this one with a series of shapes cut into it—he scratched out words into the empty spaces, copying down Tessa's information in vague terms, using plain language to make it read like an everyday correspondence.

He then lifted the second sheet away and finished the letter, filling in the gaps in the sentences to make them legible. As he stepped back to inspect his handiwork, the incriminating troop information was buried within the body of the letter, decipherable only by someone with the same template as his own. Fanning the parchment, he watched the ink dry and seep in. Once satisfied the process was complete, he folded the paper and slid it into an envelope, scribbling the address on the front and sealing it unmarked.

He unlatched the door, blew out the candle, and made his way through the kitchen to the swinging wooden doors leading to the bar. As he snuck past the barkeep, he stuffed the envelope into the back of the man's trousers. The barkeep was unblinking as he wiped a mug with a dishrag.

Moody didn't pause to look at the barkeep or any of the drunks, but out of the corner of his eye he spotted the woman in the same spot guzzling down some ale. He wished she hadn't remained there; she was putting them both at great risk of detection.

He tilted his hat down over his eyes and made his way through the front door. The next day his missive would be handed to a reliable courier, who would deliver it to the Hudson Inn—the final roadhouse along this route. Within another day, it would arrive in the hands of the Doan brothers, the men who had solicited his services for this mission. From there, the Doans would pass the information to the British camp in New York and, finally, into the hands of General Howe.

Moody whistled a ditty as he strutted toward his horse. His thoughts filled with reverie of British medals pinned on his coat and British trollops in long gowns cowering at his feet—that would be the life, indeed.

THIRTY-TWO

Dawn, Saturday, July 20, 1776
Morristown, New Jersey

Whispers of Colonel Sharpe's "being seen" with "some woman" against direct orders filtered throughout the camp that night. By dawn, his bedraggled figure was hauled out of bed and into the center of camp by two armed soldiers.

"Lawton! Lawton!" he squawked. "What's the meaning of this?!"

Ben and Josh—who were allowed to return their tent—remained wide awake but refused to say a word to each other. Upon hearing the ruckus, they charged out together as if in a competitive race. They came to a skidding stop when they saw Colonel Sharpe being thrust forward by the scruff of his neck toward Commander Lawton, who was now fully dressed for the day.

Commander Lawton wagged his finger in Ben's direction. "This soldier reported seeing you with a woman who was leaving town tonight on horseback. Can you explain it?"

Colonel Sharpe cackled. "*That* woman? Please, Commander. She was a loose wench who entertained me for a couple of hours. I was merely sending her back from whence she came."

Lawton circled around him. "Before midnight? Why such an early departure?"

"I had no more use for her after I was satisfied. To be honest, she was a bit of a disappointment, if you know what I mean..."

Josh's fists curled at his side. He ached to thrash the colonel. *This can't be true*, he convinced himself. *It can't. Tessa would never be unfaithful to me...would she? What do I really know about her or her past? Has she played me for a fool?*

"What was her name, sir?" Commander Lawton asked, continuing the investigation while oblivious to the crowd of soldiers witnessing.

"I've no idea. Why would it even matter? She is of no consequence; she was just a plaything."

"What did the two of you discuss?"

"Are you certain you wish to hear me recite all of the sordid details in such company? I mean, there are young soldiers here to consider." The colonel smirked.

Commander Lawton *humphed* while continuing to admonish the colonel with a penetrating glare. "Indecency and breaking curfew are crimes in the Continental Army—assuming those are your only misdeeds," he berated.

The commander paused, perhaps considering his options. Josh knew that there was a lack of evidence in any one direction. After all, Ben had only seen him help Tessa climb upon a horse. There was nothing solid whatsoever to contradict Colonel Sharpe's story.

A soldier lounging by the fire interrupted before the commander could say anything, "Sir, over there—two riders are approaching camp."

"Ah—perhaps we shall at last have some answers," he declared. "Bring them here at once."

The soldier jumped to his feet, sprinting toward the pair on horseback. He led them toward the campfire. As they drew closer, it became clear that a second rider sat behind one of them.

Josh coaxed himself forward to get a better look. He nearly keeled over when he saw an unmistakable figure bound by a series of ropes pinned to the saddle and gagged: *Tessa.*

165

"So now we are at war with harlots, eh?" Colonel Sharpe sneered.

Enraged, Josh made his move toward Colonel Sharpe, but Ben grabbed him and held him back. "Stay out of this—*please*. If you get in the middle of this, you'll get blamed. Don't do it for me. The cause needs you, Josh…*please*."

The soldiers unraveled the ropes connecting Tessa to the saddle and helped her dismount. Once on the ground, a soldier removed her gag but kept her hands tied behind her back. The words screeched out of her mouth, "How dare you! What is the meaning of this?"

Commander Lawton approached her. "I apologize for your rough treatment, Miss. We are investigating what may be a serious matter." He turned toward the two riders and asked, "Where did you men find her?"

"No more than thirty minutes' ride north of the King's Lancer—on the main road," one replied.

"Soldier," the commander addressed Ben. "Is this the woman you saw last night with Colonel Sharpe?"

"Yes, sir," he answered.

Josh couldn't stand seeing Tessa this way, so wild-eyed and distressed. She seemed to have aged a decade. Her beautiful hair was scraggly and strewn about her face and neck. Her clothes were splattered with mud. Her eyes were glazed, as if she had been drinking.

Something compelled him to stand forward. "Sir," he began, "I know this woman. She's innocent. I would bet my life on it."

Tessa faced Josh. Her expression softened—if only for a moment. Then it twisted in disgust as she wrestled with her ropes like an animal. "Let go of me at once! You have no authority to hold me here!"

"I would advise you to remain silent until spoken to, Miss," the commander warned her, swirling around to reprimand Josh. "That goes for you as well, soldier."

Commander Lawton moved closer to Tessa. "Tell me, what were you doing at the King's Lancer last evening?"

Tessa struggled to maintain eye contact as she replied, "I stopped for a meal. I was on my way to Pennsylvania to visit my family."

Josh contained his stupefaction: Tessa had relatives in Pennsylvania?

"You were seen leaving Morristown last evening in the company of Colonel Sharpe," he said. "Why were you in Morristown, and what is your relationship to the colonel?"

"I told you," Colonel Sharpe snarled, "she's nothing but a tart I hired for the evening."

"No, it's not true!" Josh exclaimed. "Tessa, tell them!"

The commander allowed Josh to step closer to Tessa so the drama would play out; perhaps this would finally reveal the truth.

Tessa stared at the ground. "Please, Josh," she said as tears fell down her cheeks. "I know you would defend my honor—even if I have none left. The truth must come out."

"What…what do you mean? Tessa?"

"I swear to you—all of you—that what I am about to say is true. Colonel Sharpe provided me with confidential information about your soldiers—including the number of men you have in camp, your weapons, and supplies," she admitted. "By now, that information is already in loyalist hands."

Tessa was not nearly finished. She referenced Josh and Ben with a tilt of her head. "These two soldiers are innocent. They had no part in this. In fact, they should be commended for their honesty and bravery."

Her shoulders slumped down in defeat.

The commander's stern gaze returned to Colonel Sharpe. "What do you have to say on the matter, sir?"

"The woman speaks nonsense!" He scowled. "She would rather be hung as a traitor than labeled a whore!"

"Around my waist you'll find a satchel within my dress containing three pouches filled with coins. In the smallest, you will find coins that match three in the colonel's possession."

"Nonsense!" Colonel Sharpe protested.

The commander directed a soldier to carefully remove the three coin pouches from Tessa's satchel. He sorted through them, easily figuring out which was the lightest, and then opened it up.

"How on earth can you match coins in there to any others? It's absurd!"

"Each of them has a notch in the same spot," Tessa said. "Look, you'll see."

The soldier extracted the remaining coins in the satchel: All of them bore the same markings. "All notched, sir," he said.

"Search that man top to bottom!" the commander bellowed. "Search his quarters! Find me any coins in his possession!"

Soldiers scattered toward Colonel Sharpe's quarters, while a couple of others forcibly searched his body.

"Commander Lawton, this is preposterous!" He struggled. "You are going to trust this whore's word over mine?!"

"Quite possibly," answered the commander.

"Commander," called one of the soldiers who were rummaging through the colonel's pockets. "I think I have something."

"Leave me alone! How dare you disrespect me like this? I shall have you all court-martialed and hung!"

The soldier extracted three coins and gasped as he held them upright for all to see. "All notched!"

"Arrest that man," the commander ordered.

Colonel Sharpe cried out as two of Lawton's guardsmen seized his arms and forced them behind his back, looping a rope tightly around his wrists. His screams echoed through the camp as they dragged him toward the brig.

"As for you, Miss," the commander said, shifting to Tessa. "I'm afraid you must follow him."

"I accept my fate," she relented.

As the guard began to escort Tessa away, Josh intervened. "Please, Commander, I beg you—"

"No, Josh," Tessa interjected. "I knew the risks."

Tears flooded her bloodshot eyes as the guards carried her off. "I did love you, Josh…"

Josh mouthed the word "goodbye" but could not produce the sound. At that moment he felt no concerns about death on the battlefield. A bayonet had already pierced his heart.

THIRTY-THREE

Tuesday, July 30, 1776
New York Harbor

Brown's head pounded as he tugged a thin blanket over his head to protect his eyes from the morning glare. The swaying he felt from his hangover, coupled with the vibrations of the morning tide slapping against the ship's hull, was making him nauseous. His cabin teetered and bounced, causing the prior evening's empty bottle of gin to roll back and forth across the length of the cabin.

He felt lousy but could no longer hide from the day: Too much was afoot. Staggering to his feet, he stumbled to a basin and splashed some lukewarm water on his stubble-coated face.

It had been nearly two weeks since the armada had sailed within sight of New York Harbor, as the British invasion forces coalesced. They had taken Staten Island with ease, sweeping into the island's sleepy little towns and commandeering fields to provide training grounds, campsites, and foodstuffs for the hordes of arriving soldiers.

He had spent these dreary days aboard the smelly, cramped frigate to bide his time until his spy network came alive once again with information about the patriot advance. As the fortnight passed, he became increasingly alone and desperate and washed his sorrows down with gin. He could barely stand another minute. *Today is going to be the day*, he vowed to himself. *I know it.*

He was startled by an abrupt knock on the door. Hardly anyone visited him or paid him any mind, which made any intrusion seem urgent. He lunged across the room to the door, sliding it open.

A clean-cut soldier in uniform stood at attention. "You have a visitor, sir," he announced.

At this point, Brown would have welcomed anyone—but he had to demonstrate some semblance of importance to the soldier. "Who is it?"

"See for yourself, sir," he answered. "He's right here."

The soldier stepped aside to reveal a rumpled Moses Doan waiting outside his cabin. "That will do, soldier. Dismissed."

Brown's morning gloom turned into a wolfish smile as he gestured for his guest to come inside. "Mr. Doan, to what do I owe this pleasure at this fine hour?"

"I have news for you," he replied, maneuvering inside the cabin room. "News I believe you shall greatly appreciate…"

* * * *

Generals William Howe and Henry Clinton begrudgingly agreed to sit down with Brown and Doan. They welcomed information of any kind about the rebels, but scoffed at the idea of accepting battle advice from such dreck—a two-bit horse thief and criminal ringleader from the uncouth backwoods of Pennsylvania and a discredited British officer. It was almost too much for them to bear.

They suffered for hours listening to Brown and Doan babble on and would have tossed them out on their asses except for one thing: Their intel was exceptional. In fact, this Doan creature put on quite a show, unwrapping a leather-bound folio stuffed with information from his network of low-level informants scattered throughout the northern colonies—everything from expected patriot troop levels to the number, type, and condition of weapons stored in camp.

By the end of the briefing, the generals pondered what they'd heard while Doan smugly sat back in his chair with his hands behind his neck. Brown stood in the corner, soaking it all in; his hangover faded with every revelation.

At last, Howe spoke. "Mr. Doan, leave your papers with us. The commandant is waiting for you outside with your final payment."

Doan rose, bowed, and proclaimed, "God save the king!" before walking out.

When the door closed, Howe gestured for Brown to take a seat among them. "If this information is accurate, it demonstrates several fatal flaws in the patriot defense," he said.

"*If* it's accurate?" Brown sniggered. "Mr. Doan does not make mistakes. I can vouch for his reliability. He's the best spy in the colonies."

The generals exchanged knowing glances, yielding to their good fortune. There was no reason to doubt a single triangulated detail of what Doan had provided.

"Give us four days of good weather and we'll have them all in chains," General Howe declared.

"I concur," General Clinton added, spreading a crumpled map of the coast across the table. He tapped his finger at several points on the map. "Look at these positions—all of them will be virtually exposed. Washington has made several costly decisions that are to our benefit."

"Let us exploit them, shall we?" General Howe proclaimed.

"Agreed."

"You are dismissed, Brown," General Howe concluded.

"Yes, sir," Brown said, rising with a salute.

When Brown reached the door, General Howe turned his head back forty-five degrees to the right—not enough to actually see the man—and called, "And Brown…?"

Brown spun back around, half expecting the other shoe to drop. "Yes, sir?"

"Good work," the general complimented him. "Jolly good work."

THIRTY-FOUR

Friday, August 23, 1776
Brooklyn, New York

Over one month had elapsed since Colonel Sharpe's and Tessa's capture. Josh didn't know what had become of Tessa and didn't care to ask. He presumed she would face trial, be judged guilty, and be imprisoned or sentenced to death by hanging or firing squad. Whatever the case, she was dead to him.

Colonel Sharpe's fate was a different story entirely. Josh learned all of the sordid details from Ben, who gave advance testimony against Sharpe for the upcoming court-martial at the end of the month. Ben was awarded a commendation for his integrity. Josh congratulated him but otherwise treated him frostily, leaving them both to wonder if their friendship would ever be the same again.

Meanwhile, it was a rough entry into New York for Smallwood's troops. A summer thunderstorm washing over the city turned their campsite into a mud field. As the rains continued over the next few days, sickness began to spread.

Josh huddled under his tent with a blanket pulled around his face and head as he listened to the rain pelting the canvas. The sounds were soothing and in a way helped him think through and come to terms with certain realities—the deaths of Christopher, his father, and most likely Tessa. That is, until his tent mate gagged and threw up three days' worth of gruel in a corner behind him.

Josh had largely avoided the trenches of mud and human waste on the edge of the camp, but the germs were everywhere—in his own tent, in fact—and he wondered how long his system was going to hold out. He couldn't tell if his own nauseous sensations were symptoms of illness or reactions to the fetid odors surrounding him.

His roommate continued to wretch, causing Josh to tighten the blanket against his nose and mouth. He was almost thankful when he was summoned to help some soldiers push a wagon of provisions through a mud-filled crater posing as a road.

Josh flung the tent flaps open and scurried into the downpour toward the group of men shoving the back of the wagon. He noticed that Ben had also emerged two tents away from him to do the same. Josh ignored him and quickened his pace when suddenly his boots gave way underneath him and he flew in the air; he landed splashing on his rump in a thick puddle of mud.

He heard scattered snickers from his fellow soldiers and struggled to his feet. The ground was so slippery that he had nearly plunked down a second time when a familiar hand grabbed him. "Three possibilities, mate," Ben said, grinning ear to ear as he held Josh in position. "You've been drinking too much, you have the stomach ick, or you're just a bumbling idiot."

"What do you think?" Josh asked as Ben hoisted him to his feet.

"Most likely an idiot," Ben snapped.

Standing up tall, Josh tried in vain to wipe the mud off his uniform. The more he tried to clean himself, the worse the smears became. Ben couldn't resist laughing.

"What...are you laughing at me?" Josh asked.

"I suppose I am," Ben said, trying to control himself.

After a few more hapless attempts at brushing himself that resulted in a splotch of mud's spraying across his cheek, he surrendered in defeat and started chuckling at how ridiculous he must have appeared.

"I'd say you never looked better," Ben remarked, slapping his friend's shoulder.

Their smiles diminished as they studied each other through the onslaught of rain. "Ben, I…I never had a chance to say I'm sorry."

"Sorry? For what?"

"For not believing you…about Tessa. You were right all along. I was just too dumb to—"

"Stop beating on yourself," Ben comforted him. "The British are going to try to do enough of that to us—no reason to help them along."

After another thought Ben added, "Listen, if a barmaid that beautiful cast me in her spell, I may have been just as helpless…. On second thought, no I wouldn't have. You're the bumbling idiot, not me!" Josh couldn't resist a smile.

The soldiers managed to guide the wagon out of the trench without their assistance. The two men stared at each other, unsure of what they should do next. All at once, someone made the decision for them; a soggy figure shoved them both into Josh's tent. The bulky man showered the cots and rucksacks as he took off his coat.

"Whew—I am pruned from top to bottom!" Paddy exclaimed. He swung out a bottle of a pale, cloudy liquid toward Josh and Ben. "Howdy, boys. This camp is swimming in shit. Imagine: I left the beautiful mountains of western Maryland for this cesspool! Well, now that the two of you gents have finally kissed and made up, how about we celebrate and warm ourselves at the same time?"

As soon as Josh took a swig from the bottle, the intense liquid seared the back of his throat, causing some food to charge up his esophagus. He somehow swallowed it all back down. "What is this vile concoction, Paddy?!"

Paddy belly-laughed as he yanked the bottle back from Josh's hands and downed half of it with one gulp. He smacked his lips and cackled, "This is my private reserve, boy! Finest product of the Monocacy waters!"

Josh, feeling paralyzed, wiped tears from his eyes.

"Too strong for you, eh?" Paddy asked, preparing for another swig. "It's the only cure for the pestilence that's all over this goddamned place. Washes the sickness right out of you."

He thrust the bottle toward Ben, who pinched his nose and gurgled it down. Paddy seemed impressed.

"It's not so strong. The moonshine my pop made back in the Carolinas was stronger," he said. He then added a belch for good measure.

Paddy and Ben laughed uproariously and slapped each other's backs. Feeling left out, Josh snatched back the bottle and downed another swig.

With friends like these and enough liquid courage, Josh thought, *the British had better watch out.*

THIRTY-FIVE

Evening, Friday, August 23, 1776
Wall Street Tavern, New York

The mood was somber at the Wall Street Tavern, where the colonial military leaders were meeting to assess their situation and determine next steps. The charges of lightning and thunderclaps shook the establishment and strobed light on their drawn faces: gaunt and pale Mordecai Gist; weather-worn and craggy Lord Stirling; sullen Lieutenant Colonel Samuel Smith; reserved General George Washington; several anxious lower-ranking officers; and Colonel Smallwood, who kept a stiff upper lip as he addressed the group. "Gentlemen, as you know, in three days' time we will convene court-martial proceedings against Colonel Sharpe for passing vital information to the enemy. As his commanding officer, I am obliged to preside over those proceedings. This means—and it is with a heavy heart—that I must temporarily relinquish my command, in spite of the imminent British assault."

His audience reluctantly murmured in agreement. They could hardly afford to lose a single leader at such a critical time—especially one as capable as Smallwood—but Washington insisted on maintaining decorum.

"I place my full confidence and trust in the regiment's commander—my close friend and fellow patriot General Stirling. Gentlemen, I wish you all success on the battlefield. I will rejoin you as soon as my duty has been completed."

He raised and tipped his wine glass in a silent toast to his fellow leaders. After drinking it down, he took his seat with a regretful sigh.

The room remained silent as the rain and wind whipped against the windows. General Stirling tugged his coat down to remove any creases as he rose to his feet. The taciturn general with squinty eyes and an elongated forehead downed his whiskey in a single swallow and made his way to the front of the room. He moved back and forth several times before his gravelly voice erupted. "Thank you, Colonel Smallwood. It is a true honor to be given command of your forces. It is due in no small part to your monumental efforts that they are well trained, well disciplined, and eager to bring the battle to the enemy."

After his abrupt start, he was momentarily at a loss for words. He stared at the chipped plaster wall across from him before reclaiming his voice. "It…is no secret to most of you that my family and I have been disrespected and ridiculed by the elite of England for some time…. Thus our fight for freedom has even greater significance for me than you can imagine. It would give me extreme personal pleasure to see those bastards sent running from our land as soon as possible…*extreme pleasure*."

The commanders thumped their fists on the tables in approval.

"Gentlemen, know that I am thoroughly dedicated to our cause…. I will fight for as long as will be required…and will do whatever is required to achieve victory," he stated, once again fumbling for words. Before his audience lost patience, he addressed one person directly. "Colonel Smallwood: I would like you to know that I intend to take your position at the lead when the battle ensues."

The leaders in the room were taken by surprise at the announcement. This was a serious departure from the traditional rear-observation role of a general. The commanders whispered amongst themselves and then stood to raise their glasses in honor of Stirling's bold demonstration of service.

General Stirling looked away from the group as they completed their silent toast. He plunked himself down, relieving his nerves with another dose of whiskey.

General Washington rose with a wave of his arm. "Thank you, Colonel Smallwood and General Stirling. I do not have much to add to what has been expressed here tonight. I will say only this: We have exorcised the British from Boston and we will without a doubt prevail here, even with the full might of the British armada arriving upon our doorstep. But mark my words: New York will *not* be the final battleground of this war. We must keep our wits about us and ensure that our troops are resolute for a drawn-out conflict. We must outfox the enemy, not engage them on their terms. I believe that the Lord will see to it that the true engagement we must win is the *final battle*—the fight for our freedom from oppression."

Washington raised his glass up high. "Gentlemen, to victory!"

The men clinked their glasses together with Washington's final crescendo. The cocktail chatter resumed as Washington and Stirling slipped out of the room.

Sipping wine from his refilled glass, Mordecai Gist turned to Samuel Smith. "What is your honest impression of him? Stirling, that is."

Smith shrugged. "I would be lying if I didn't say he has a certain— shall we say, reputation."

"So he does," Gist concurred. "Then again, I believe he is whip smart."

"In business matters perhaps," Smith considered. "But on the battlefield?"

"He did capture a British squad vessel with his own assembled troops…"

"So I heard," Smith admitted. "I am more concerned about how the soldiers will respond to him. I heard he threw lavish parties at his New Jersey estate but would mysteriously disappear halfway, bewildering his guests."

"My impression is that the men like him quite a bit."

"What if they don't trust him to stay sober?"

"General Washington gave Stirling's daughter away at her wedding," Gist said. "If Washington trusts him and believes he is the right man for the job, then so do I."

Smith drained his glass and smacked his lips. "I hope you are right, my friend. If not, New York will indeed be our final battleground."

THIRTY-SIX

Midday, Monday, August 26, 1776
Fort Half Moon, Brooklyn Heights, New York

Thanks to the work of hundreds of local farmers—chopping down a large chunk of forest—a fortress had been built within the past week to fortify the Brooklyn perimeter. Piles of raw, chewed-up dirt around the vicinity were evidence of the farmers' hours of backbreaking labor, which they performed without a single complaint—even as they toiled during the torrential rainstorms.

Crouched down within the fortress, Josh tried to look past the massive trench works that spread across Brooklyn Heights and nearly blotted out the view of New York and its famous harbor. Even with the crisscrossed fortifications towering into the sky, he could still make out the ominous masts and shadowy hulks of the British armada looming in the distance.

The thought struck Josh head-on: *I can't believe I'm really here—and the British are out there. It's all come down to this, as I somehow felt it would—even when I was unloading cargo back at Fell's Point.*

He hoisted a log barricade into place near the side of the trench and gestured to the three soldiers who stood guard. When it was adjusted to their satisfaction, Josh retreated into the dim, cavernous trenches within the fortress.

He joined a group of his fellow soldiers, including Ben and Paddy, who were huddled together in the hazy glow of a lamp. Major Gist bent down to address the troops. "Men, as you are well aware, we are here to defend this island from British incursion. General Washington has ordered us to stave off any landing parties identified here in Brooklyn. His troops in Manhattan will do the same on that island."

The soldiers ruminated on this for a moment as it sank in that they were defending a series of islands—not just a massive city.

"I can tell by some of your reactions that this comes as a surprise. I admit this geography is not our ally," Gist conceded. "But it's not theirs, either. This is *our* land—the swamps, forests, and these hills on which we stand. And we will use it to our great advantage."

Gist stood up with a brush of his uniform. He studied the group, locking eyes with one soldier after another. Once he acknowledged everyone, he trumpeted the words they longed to hear: "We march in an hour."

Josh and Ben lingered as the men began to disperse. Their expressions hardened as they would during a staring contest, each waiting to see who would speak first. Paddy's sudden rush startled them, as he pushed between them, wrapping his bear-like paws around their shoulders. "Ah, I've seen that look before—your balls have finally swollen up and you're ready to hunt some Englishmen!"

* * * *

Gist turned a corner into the narrow, constricted trench leading to the makeshift officers' quarters, where he found Stirling leaning against the log wall with a silver flask in his trembling hand.

"You are a fine speechmaker," Stirling croaked, pressing the flask to his pursed lips. He dropped it down and continued, "The men—they like you and they respect you. That is a valuable asset."

"I trust them with my life, and they do the same," Gist said.

Stirling leaned on his arm to balance himself against the wall as he groggily reflected,

"I don't have your gift for oratory, as you can no doubt tell. But I am persistent."

Stirling took another nip from the flask and swallowed with contentment. He offered it to Gist, who declined it with a half wave of his hand. Stirling didn't seem bothered by the reaction as he stated, "When someone tells me that something cannot be done, I immediately want to prove them wrong. They said I did not have royal lineage, yet here I am—a lord. They said I could not grow grapes in the colonies, yet here I am a vintner. And they said I could not lead men, yet here I am— a general."

Gist was about to speak when Stirling held up his hand, not wishing to lose his fragile train of thought. "Today, my friend, there may come a time when you feel that you must drop back. Retreat to fight another day and so on and so forth. When that time comes, look to me. I shall serve as your guidepost. Whatever flaws I may have—and, to be sure, there are many—I more than compensate with relentlessness. I will fight tooth and nail with my last breath before General Washington falls back, surrenders, or gets crushed. I do not retreat—*ever.*"

Visibly stirred by Stirling's words, Gist changed his mind and extended his hand to request the flask. Pleased he would no longer be imbibing alone, Stirling handed it over and relished watching Gist guzzle it down. Gist smacked his lips and returned the flask with the pronouncement, "I don't retreat, either."

For the first time ever, Gist saw Stirling crack a smile.

"Then we shall get along quite nicely," Stirling toasted, before sucking down the remains of the flask's contents. He wrapped his arm around Gist's shoulder as they headed to the officers' corridor, where his aides were busily plotting their advance on a vast parchment chart, which was stained and weathered by the recent weeks of rain and travel.

Gist leaned over to get a closer look at the dark outline of Long Island and the markings that indicated their position. He shook his head in dismay. The patriot camp was wedged inside a corner of the

Brooklyn peninsula that overlooked Manhattan Island; their position was juxtaposed against a harbor full of British ships watching their every move. Beyond their fortress, swaths of farmland dotted with small towns and way stations were vulnerable behind an undefended coastline. Patriot forces were hemmed in by the Guan Heights, an imposing range of hills that split down the center of Brooklyn and overlooked the swampland below.

Somehow, the patriots—with their ragtag forces and diminished numbers—had to protect the entire scope of Brooklyn, battling difficult terrain and occasionally severe weather just to confront the enemy. As if that weren't all, they needed to block the British from reaching Manhattan, where General Washington and the bulk of his forces had set up a series of defensive forts.

Gist rubbed his face. "Not exactly what we would consider optimal."

Stirling tucked the empty flask into his coat pocket. He leaned over the map to study the intricately drawn lines. "What do the scouts tell us from the front?" he asked an aide standing around the map.

"Early reports indicate a primary force from General Grant—moving northward," the aide said, adjusting the lenses at the bridge of his nose.

"Grant's a pompous fool," Stirling said, turning sharply to Gist. "He seeks to create a spectacle. We can head him off"—he paused to tap his pointer finger upon a strip of open land between the Heights and the coastline—"right here."

Gist didn't think twice. "Agreed."

"Ready your men and prepare to meet Grant's troops head-on," Stirling growled. "He shall pay a steep price for underestimating us."

THIRTY-SEVEN

Evening, Monday, August 26, 1776
Near the Red Lion Inn, Brooklyn, New York

Pop. Pop. Pop.

The unmistakable sound of musket fire echoed into the night as the first shots of the Battle of Brooklyn reverberated up the coastline.

Josh's eyes fluttered open as he heard the sounds ricocheting across the colonial camp, which spread along the rolling hills overlooking Gowanus swamp—a mess of soggy ground and drowned marsh reeds.

He and his fellow soldiers were guarding the Gowanus—a one-lane road that ran up the hill toward Brooklyn Heights, where the bulk of the colonial troops were hunkered down behind the thick fortress walls that had sheltered Josh and Ben a day earlier. If they were to lose control of the Gowanus, the British would have a straight shot to the heart of the colonial forces in Brooklyn.

Josh sat up to take a look around through the slit in the tent. All around the camp—which had been silent and still only two minutes earlier—men were staggering to their feet, trying to make sense of what was happening.

Ben, with his musket slung over his shoulder, slipped inside Josh's tent. "Those shots were close, don't you think?"

"I don't think so," Josh said. "They would have sounded our alarms if they were that close. I think they just carried in the night. It may even have been from colonial watchmen taking practice shots at some birds. We can probably go back to sleep—for now."

"Sleep after that? Ha—you must be crazy," Ben said, rubbing the back of his neck.

Josh lay back down and turned on his side, dragging the blanket over his back. "This crazy soldier is getting more shut-eye."

Ben wanted to chat some more—at least to help calm his nerves. But Josh's eyes were shut, and the camp was already quieting down. He shrugged and left.

Josh stirred uncomfortably and rolled over several times before he lay on his back with his eyes wide open. Ben was right; there was no way he was going to fall back asleep after that, and he wished his friend hadn't left.

He hadn't given much thought to what the sounds of war might be like until these last few minutes. But those *pop, pop, pop* sounds magnified in his head: What would it sound like with hundreds—perhaps even thousands—of muskets firing? And cannons?

The reality of what lay in store made both his heart and mind pound.

THIRTY-EIGHT

Late evening, Monday, August 26, 1776
Near the Red Lion Inn, Brooklyn, New York

"General Stirling, wake up!" the aide yelled, shaking him awake. "It's General Putnam. Hurry!"

Stirling managed to raise his head—which felt like it contained a ton of bricks—three inches from his pillow and snap open one crusted eyelid. "What the hell...? Why is Put here?" he snarled.

The aide's blank expression was useless; he knew he had to go out and find out for himself what his commanding officer could possibly want at this ungodly hour. Not bothering to put on his pants, he stumbled out of his quarters on the northern perimeter of the Gowanus encampment.

He spotted Israel "Old Put" Putnam—Washington's favorite commander—leaning against his horse, wheezing and struggling to catch his breath. He must have raced all the way from the Brooklyn Heights fortress to their hillside camp in the darkness, which wasn't a good sign. The man was a devout pipe smoker, which didn't help his lungs any.

"General Stirling," Putnam managed to say, "The British have overrun our southern flank…about three miles south of here…down Gowanus Road…"

Stirling cursed under his breath as Putnam informed him that the shots heard earlier in the evening had been part of a calculated British ruse. The British had sent a few soldiers rummaging through a watermelon patch near the Red Lion Inn—a tavern to the south of the Gowanus camp. Since watermelon was unheard of in England, it made sense that the fruit might lure a few British stragglers out of position to score a prized treat.

The colonial guards fell for it. They fired off a few shots at the redcoats, who scurried off into the night.

As the British anticipated, the colonial forces had developed a false sense of security. The experienced night watchmen handed their duties off to a handful of junior militiamen. The inexperienced young guards joked and clowned in the moonlight, passing around a flask until they all passed out.

Two hours later, the British struck: General James Grant and three hundred British regulars descended on the Red Lion. It took only two flurries of musket balls for the colonial defenders to retreat. A few managed to escape and pass the news on to the colonial lines, where it reached Putnam's desk an hour later.

"We can't afford these amateur losses," Stirling grumbled. "How long do we have?"

Putnam gestured toward the south, deep into the marsh. "Mobilize your regiment, general. I believe we shall see the British main force hit us from the south within the hour."

Stirling started off to obey his orders when he heard Putnam interject, "Lord Stirling—you might wish to put your pants on first."

* * * *

Mordecai Gist tended to be a light sleeper. It was an annoyance when he was at his home in Baltimore and awoken by every drunken sailor or screeching cat that happened by. But what was an everyday nuisance under normal circumstances was an asset on the battlefield, as he found himself wide awake and alert long before the exchange of musket shots became an all-out gun battle. He tugged on his uniform and fastened his saber to his waist, tucking a pistol into his wide leather belt before charging toward Stirling's quarters.

On arrival, he found the cantankerous general frantically issuing orders to his aides, who were dashing around him in a whirlwind of activity. He waved Gist over and demanded, "Where's Haslet?"

"Sir, Colonel Haslet is away on court-martial duty alongside Colonel Smallwood," he answered. "Major McDonough is now in charge of the 1st Delaware."

Stirling threw up his hands in frustration. "Goddammit, we have a war to fight and we're worrying about court proceedings…. Gist—find me Major McDonough!"

It didn't take long for Gist to track down Major McDonough, who joined him on his return to Stirling's quarters. Gist was surprised to find that Stirling had transformed from a harried and aggravated tyrant into an intense, energized, and supremely focused leader.

"Gentlemen," he welcomed them. "This is the hour we've waited for."

Gist ushered them toward a table draped with tactical maps. "The British have engaged us *here*," he said, pointing to the location of the Red Lion. "We believe that this is the main force of their army, driving up Gowanus Road to our position." He traced his finger up the map toward their current position atop the Guan Heights. "If the British advance in this direction, I propose that we confront them with the kettle."

Stirling spread his index and middle finger to form a "V," inverted them, and placed his hand on the map to demonstrate his point, in case his subordinates didn't follow him. He scissored his fingers together to illustrate how they would wrap around the enemy upon attack.

Gist and the others signaled that they concurred with the plan. Bolstered by their approval, Stirling continued, "Gist, you take up position on this small hill, which the locals call Blokje Berg—or some such Dutch nonsense. McDonough, you stand guard with your men here to the left."

He paused to study the map, then stabbed at it with his index finger. "I will move Atlee to this apple orchard, up and just to the right of the road. We will absorb their attack here and funnel them through the low-lying ground into the apex of the 'V' to create a crossfire. The more they move forward, the more they will become flanked."

Gist stepped back to catch his breath, which had been taken away by Stirling's instant grasp of the topography and the tactics he planned to employ. It was a bold but risky strategy, given that all units from Delaware, Pennsylvania, and Maryland amounted to only sixteen hundred soldiers against the British onslaught. The remainder of the colonial troops in Brooklyn were either stationed to the east under their fellow commander Sullivan or ensconced in the fortresses at Brooklyn Heights. General Washington, meanwhile, was guarding against an imminent British assault in Manhattan.

"Gentlemen," Stirling concluded. "You have your orders."

"Yes, sir," Gist and McDonough simultaneously said, exiting the tent.

Gist slapped McDonough on the back and said, "We will meet again on the other side." When they separated, he made a beeline toward the Maryland ranks at the edge of camp and to Sergeant Gassaway Watkins—a hulking mountain of a man who had been at his side from the earliest days of the regiment.

"What is the news, sir?" Watkins asked, polishing his rifle near a fire.

He steeled himself for his response, "It's time. Ready the Maryland Regiment for battle."

"With pleasure, sir," the sergeant said, raising his bugle to his pursed lips.

THIRTY-NINE

After midnight, Monday, August 26, 1776
Howard's Half-Way House, New Lots, New York

Old man Howard was about to depart his son's inn for the evening when heavy rain pelted the windows like a roll on a snare drum. He was still fit as a fiddle, if a tad overweight, as he neared his eighty-seventh birthday—but why take a chance on getting a chill? He decided to stick around for another beer until the storm subsided.

Howard had spent his entire life on this sliver of Long Island farmland between the forest to the north and the waters of Gravesend Bay to the south—almost within sight of the colony of New Jersey. It was a bountiful place for a farmer like him to live and work, where the soil was rich and the climate tolerable.

Now everything was on the edge of ruin. Never in all his years of peaceful farming life could he ever have imagined he would see an entire fleet of ships anchored right in his own backyard. Whatever the result of the imminent battle, he envisioned his crops and years of toil laid to waste.

"Quite a storm out there, hmm?" mused his son, William, who happened to be both owner of and barkeep at the tavern. He plunked a beer in front of his father and wiped the counter with a rag.

"Maybe it will sink a few of those damn boats," Howard grumbled.

"Those are British vessels," William said. "If they made it all the way across the ocean, I would think they can take a little rain."

"Maybe the soldiers will catch a cough and drop dead."

"One can only hope." William grinned.

The door swung open and a man in a long black rain cape stomped inside, splattering rain across the floor. Behind him were two other men: one dark and scowling, the other thin and pale.

Howard sized them up. He knew almost everyone on this part of the island, yet these were strange, unfamiliar faces. He couldn't imagine what had brought them into his son's inn during a rainstorm past midnight.

The man in the black cape strode inside with the stature of someone accustomed to being obeyed. "Pardon me, sir," he addressed William with the hint of a British lilt. "My companions and I have traveled from afar away and would like your best whiskey."

"Certainly," William acknowledged, pouring three vials of his finest whiskey and sliding them in the direction of the three strangers. The men brooded with dark stares around the room as they swallowed their liquor.

Howard didn't like the look of these men, not at all. If he were a much younger man, he would already have been out the door and summoned the town constable. His advanced age, coupled with the continuing onslaught of rain, made him think twice. Just as he mustered enough fortitude from a final swill of beer to rise to his feet, the three men spread out and blocked him as if participating in a well-rehearsed ballet.

The man in the black cape whisked the garment off his shoulders, revealing his pristine red dress uniform. The other two men followed suit, although they wore more understated military outfits. All three men clutched muskets with one hand while holding their swords close at their hips with the other.

"By the order of the king, I place you under arrest," the leader declared to Howard.

The old man raised his hands high in the air. He glanced over at William, who he knew was going for his rifle.

"Don't do it, Son," he warned. "For some reason, they seem to want me as their prisoner—not you."

The leader directed his musket at William. "That is right, Son. Be a good lad and do what the old man tells you. Politely hand me the rifle hidden under the bar. If you do otherwise, I assure you that the interior of this fine establishment will be splashed with a fresh coat of red paint— your blood."

* * * *

David Brown had to admit that he relished watching the fat old colonial turn pale as Henry Clinton unveiled his British army uniform in all its glory. *This is going to be a fun evening, indeed,* he thought—*so much better than the "wait and see" grind of spying.*

Clinton flicked Howard's nose with the tip of his musket. "What is your name, old man?"

"Howard," he answered while holding his breath. "William Howard the senior."

"Very well, then, William Howard the senior. You shall have the honor of being my very first prisoner of the evening," Clinton spouted, taking clear pleasure in every word. "How well do you know these parts?"

"Born and raised here…"

"Excellent," he said, tossing Howard a rain slicker. "You shall serve as our guide—for as long as you are of use to us."

Howard pulled on the rain slicker with guarded movements, his eyes never veering from the tip of Clinton's musket. He followed Brown, Clinton, and Clayton, his taciturn bodyguard, outside into the rain. William remained a fixed statue behind the counter, alarmed at how anyone could be so cold-hearted as to take an old man prisoner amidst such nasty late-night conditions.

Outside, the pub was surrounded by a dozen British cavalrymen on horseback—weapons at the ready.

"At ease," Clinton ordered the soldiers as he headed toward them. "We have what we came for."

The bodyguard and another soldier hoisted Howard onto a waiting horse, while Brown and Clinton settled into their own respective saddles.

"Well, get on with it," Clinton barked at Howard, whipping the back of the old man's horse. "Point us toward Jamaica Pass."

As they rode, the soggy plains gave way to rolling hills and then a thick forest. Winding through the undergrowth, Howard pointed out the local trails and ancient routes once used by the natives. An hour into the ride, as the forest once again receded into grassland, Howard gestured toward a clearing and Clinton signaled for the group to halt. The cavalrymen shifted anxiously in their saddles while awaiting instructions.

"This is the moment, Brown," Clinton hissed. "If you are right, we sail through. If you are wrong, you go the route of your father."

Brown bit his tongue; he had several replies in mind but decided that silence was the best option under the circumstances.

Clinton interpreted the nonresponse as his answer. "Very well then," he said, unsheathing his sword. He turned toward the cavalrymen and flicked his fingers at the opening in the tree line.

The soldiers charged through the trees in a thundering crash of mud, hooves, and horse spit. Clinton took up the rear, while Brown kept a watchful eye on Howard, who trotted closely behind.

Brown detected some dim lights glinting in the rain ahead as the cavalrymen tore into the clearing. He heard desperate shouts, the whinny of horses—and then nothing.

Brown and Howard cautiously moved ahead to find out what had happened: How could the skirmish have ended so abruptly? As the trees opened up, Brown saw five colonial soldiers on their knees with raised hands, their weapons tossed aside.

Clinton, who had dismounted, circled the captured men with his sword extended.

"See this, Brown? Is this the best the colonial army has to offer? If so, we shall see London even sooner than expected!"

A colonial soldier on his knees beside Clinton spat on the general's riding boot. "You'll see hell sooner than London, you English dog!"

Clinton wheeled around and, in one motion, slashed the soldier across the width of his throat. The man slumped over as blood spurted from his artery; his body shook and convulsed in the mud. "How undignified," Clinton critiqued, driving his blade through the man's back.

Brown couldn't help but notice that both of Clinton's boots were now soaked with the soldier's blood—a stain far worse than the man's spit.

The battle for New York had begun.

FORTY

David Brown watched in awe as thousands of British troops passed him, marching in unison down Jamaica Road. *This is all my doing,* he thought. *All of my hard work is coming down to this moment.*

He was startled by a hard slap on his back from another man on horseback. "Well done, Brown, well done," Clinton said, revealing himself. "Not a single colonial in sight—just like you said."

"The Doans do not disappoint," he said, his head raised with pride.

If the surprise attack were to prove successful, it would mark a new day for Brown's career and for his family. He would be hailed as a decisive military leader, a master spy, and a hero of Britain's campaign to reclaim the colonies. Mostly, though, success would mean the stains would be removed from his family's reputation. All of the death and destruction would be worth it in the end.

He tightened his grip on the reins as his horse lurched forward. It would be more than two hours before they reached their ultimate destination: the rear flank of the unsuspecting colonial forces tucked along Gowanus Road. Moving this many soldiers without alerting the sleeping townspeople along the route would be a victory unto itself. There were so many things that could go wrong, so many ways to tip off the enemy and spoil the element of surprise. But they had come this far, and Clinton had more than proven himself up to the task. Unlike the British commander's golden boy, Charles Cornwallis—who sometimes dithered over decisions and worried over whether he was obeying the laws of war—Clinton made rapid-fire judgments, leaving little room for doubt and second thoughts. Brown recognized that this was precisely the type of attitude that was necessary to beat back the colonial incursion. After all, it was how the colonials themselves made all their decisions—by the seat of their pants. While Clinton was a trained military leader—educated in the best British military academies and experienced in battle—he could think like the colonials and act accordingly.

Knowing that the colonial forces would keep a close eye on the British encampments to the south in anticipation of an attack along Gowanus Road, Clinton had left General Grant and his men there while directing his troops to flank the unsuspecting colonial forces from the eastern side. As if that weren't enough, General Cornwallis and his Hessian allies were not far behind with another regiment to mop up any leftover resistance.

Brown amused himself with thoughts of the sleepy colonial watchmen pondering when the British attack would come, readying their toy hand-me-down guns for an attack coming from the south.

As the British forces crested a steep hill, Clinton held up his gloved hand into the night air. He dismounted and Brown followed suit. While the advance guard of horsemen stood watch, Clinton and Brown walked a few paces down the road to a farm field that stretched into the distance. Brown extracted a tallow candle from inside his jacket, struck a flint, and lit it. The sputtering flame was the only light for miles around.

It barely took an instant for the farm field to crackle with activity: One, two, three…and, finally, four men in black stepped into the road. Half of them were clean-shaven while the other pair sported thick black ponytails; they were all equally intimidating, with black grease rubbed along their cheeks to camouflage themselves in the night. All four were armed with sizable blades at their waists and pistols strapped to their hips tucked into thick leather holsters.

So—these are Hessians, Brown considered. As a young military man, he had heard legends about the tough Germanic warriors. The one that stuck most in his head was that the Hessians were said to leave their young boys to fend for themselves in the wilderness to determine who would survive; those who did were placed in military academies as soon as they could walk.

Fact or fiction, Brown knew that they were among the most respected fighters in the world. And, luckily for the British, their services were for sale. A rumor had made its way around camp that Clinton was paying them by the head count.

"General Clinton," rumbled one of the ponytailed men in a thick Germanic accent.

"You'll forgive me, but we haven't been formally introduced," Clinton said. Even he seemed to be paying nervous respect to these four mercenaries.

"It doesn't matter; we have been sent by General von Heister," he said in broken English. "My men are sheltered at the mouth of Battle Pass. We await further orders."

"Excellent," Clinton stated. "You will await two cannon blasts from my lines. When we reach the colonial forces guarding Gowanus Road, we will signal you to intercept the remaining colonials."

"*Verstanden*," the Hessian replied, thumping his fist toward his compatriots, indicating for them to cut back through the field.

As they turned to leave, Clinton delivered one final message. "Make sure to tell your men that not a single injured colonial shall be left alive on the field of battle. If they see survivors, bayonet them. Healthy prisoners may be taken—we'll ransom them later. Understood?"

"*Vereinbart*."

Clinton didn't follow a word of German, but he could tell from his ally's bloodthirsty smirk that his instructions had gotten across. He was duly impressed by these four men and glad to have them on his side. Barbarians or not, they seemed capable of claiming the island entirely on their own.

FORTY-ONE

Dawn, Tuesday, August 27, 1776
Gowanus Road, Brooklyn, New York

The rain ceased and all fell silent along the Gowanus. At long last, Josh managed to drift back to sleep hours after the gunshots had disturbed the camp. The skies opened up as dawn approached. But before the first rooster crowed, horn blasts echoed in succession throughout the Maryland ranks.

All of the soldiers knew the instructions of these warning sounds and did not hesitate. In fluid movements they slid off their cots, assembled their weapons, buttoned up their uniforms, and tugged on their heavy boots.

In the center of the camp, figures scurried in all directions to perform their duties in preparation for battle. Josh, who hadn't the time to fall into a deep sleep, was among the first to rise and fall in formation by the fire. He was pleased when Ben materialized a couple of seconds later and was able to position himself by his side. Come what may, the brothers were determined to fight side by side.

Soaking it all in, they exchanged frenzied glances while sharing the same thoughts: *This is it? Where is everyone?* There weren't nearly as many soldiers as they had seen in training camp. Perhaps some had drifted away out of boredom, fear, or plain disgust at the conditions. The rest, like Josh's tent mate, had likely fallen ill from the stomach sickness that had swept through the camp.

Josh felt queasy and dizzy himself. Nerves, he presumed. Ben had already been involved in a skirmish in Delaware, but Josh had never fired his musket at another human being. Today would be the first true test—not just for him but for the entire regiment who had made it this far.

Sergeant Gassaway Watkins took charge, bellowing at the troops until his voice turned hoarse. "Soldiers, prepare for battle! It's time to kick some Limey arse!"

The men cheered and whooped, their guns waving high in the air. Josh kept his musket close to his chest, where he felt the emotions and camaraderie deep inside. *We are the true believers,* he thought, *the ones brave enough—or crazy enough—to risk our lives for our God-given colonies and the ideals of liberty.*

"Maryland, attention!" Watkins shouted. His voice was met with instantaneous silence. Josh steeled himself in readiness to receive his first battle command. Watkins' finger extended south in the direction of a lumpy hillock. "On my order, we march to that hill. Two lines, double time!"

The regiment's drummers took up their positions at the head of the line, tapping out a tempo for the men to follow. The Maryland lines followed, marching in sync double-time. Josh watched the campfires recede, eventually becoming glowing specks behind them.

The soldiers trudged down the back side of a slope and then climbed up the small hill to where the sergeant had directed them: Blokje Berg, their home for the next few days.

When they reached the crest, Watkins reappeared up front. He raised his arms up and down while issuing commands, "Front line kneeling, second line standing!"

Josh and Ben, as part of the front line, clambered onto their knees, which sank into the soggy ground. Josh placed his cartridge box of pre-fashioned ammunition beside his right elbow, from where he could easily reach over to it and reload his musket. Ben, meanwhile, squinted into the sight of his musket, trying to focus on shapes below in the swamp. Both men could feel the presence of the standing second line of Maryland troops, leaning forward and taking aim. If either of them stood up suddenly from kneeling, he was liable to lose an ear.

Dawn's first light appeared over Brooklyn, and the haze gradually lifted. From his position on this unimpressive little hill, Josh could make out a good swath of the Gowanus swamp. In the far distance, he saw the glimmering lower reaches of the New York Harbor, where the outlines of the daunting British ships were starting to come into view.

Josh closed his eyes in mock surprise when he heard a familiar growl from above. "Don't you worry none; I've got your back, boy."

Josh peered up and saw Paddy, the giant mountain man, stooping over him with his long-barreled hunting rifle jutting outward.

"Say what you will about the 'Earl' in charge, but the man knows a good battle formation," Paddy chortled, referring to Lord Stirling by his nickname among the troops. "At this angle, we'll be picking off redcoats faster than squirrels in the fall."

Josh figured he was right. The British would be advancing up the hill, which made them easy prey. Not to mention the six short-range cannons that were being wheeled into position behind the forward lines, which would discourage any frontal attacks.

Josh was caught off guard by the sound of retching to his side. Ben wiped his mouth and averted his eyes, coughing up chunks of the prior evening's meal.

"You okay?"

"Must have been the salt pork," Ben joked, swallowing back another lump. "I'll be fine, don't worry about me."

"All right," Josh said, his eyes returning to his musket barrel. "But I'm here if you need me."

The sound of indiscernible shouting voices drifted from the back of the line. Watkins' voice drowned them all out. "Do you see 'em, boys?! They're coming! Take aim—but hold fire!"

Josh leaned his cheek against the cold metal and well-worn wood of the musket stock. He could barely see a faint glimmer of lanterns in the swamps below. Then, as if a hill of ants had been released, the redcoats swarmed into view. The procession of identical soldiers swelled, overtaking the field, swamp, and road below.

Josh inhaled and readjusted his aim. *There are so many of them*, he thought; *they must outnumber us by at least three to one.*

"Look down, boys!" Watkins yelled. "You are in for a treat today! Each of you has the privilege of killing ten redcoats apiece!"

Watkins' continued shouts of encouragement were drowned out by a sudden explosion of muck and soil five hundred yards to the left of the regiment's hilltop position. Another explosion followed, rocking the muddy ground close to the first—but still a safe distance away from the readied colonial soldiers.

There was no telltale smoke drifting from the valley below—whoever was firing upon them was doing so from some long distance away.

"Hold positions!" Watkins screamed. "Those Limey sailors are just testing their cannon range!"

Josh squinted toward the harbor; he could barely make out the sudden bright flashes from the shadowy ships.

Another thunderous explosion sprayed mud and grass all over Gowanus Road, but still fell short of the Maryland lines.

"Heads down!" Watkins roared. "You don't want to miss the fun straight ahead!"

Watkins waved a lantern above his head. The Delaware and Pennsylvania regiments, stationed on the hills to the right, raised their own lanterns—tiny pinpricks of light.

The sergeant blew out his lantern, directing his attention back to the men. "Hold fire until you see the battle flags! Then let 'em have it!"

In the distance, behind the advancing first line, Josh glimpsed the first British regimental flags as a second line of British soldiers began their march. When they crossed a midpoint in the fields, they began to form into two even stacks of men.

"Happy hunting, boy," Paddy said in jovial tone.

The first rows of British soldiers were almost within firing range, but visibility remained an issue. It was going to be difficult striking them at this distance in the half light of dawn, Josh thought.

Another explosion ruptured, sending a shower of soil over the edge of the Maryland ranks. A moment later, a cannonball hit its mark, crashing into the wooden fortifications at the edge of the hill with a terrifying roll of thunder. Warm sawdust, wooden splinters, and dirt crashed down upon the Maryland soldiers.

Josh barely had enough time to catch his breath and wipe the muck off his face before he saw the British soldiers charge up the embankment toward their position. They reached within a few hundred yards before they hunkered down to take aim. The cannon fire from the British ships had served its purpose, staving off the colonial soldiers long enough to allow the British forces to get within striking distance. But the patriots still had the advantage of their hillside position.

"Front lines, fire!" Watkins barked.

Josh squeezed the trigger at the same time as hundreds of other soldiers. Instantly the area was enveloped by a cloud of bitter smoke; it was so thick, it became impossible to determine if anyone had struck a single soldier.

The colonials held their collective breath until the air lifted enough to see that at least a few of their shots had been effective. The British line drifted back a few yards, leaving behind a trail of corpses in the mud halfway up the hillside.

"Not bad for shooting blind," Ben said as he reloaded along with the others.

A round of musket pops from Paddy and his men standing above prevented Josh from responding. Their gunfire was accompanied by blasts from the patriots' short-range cannons.

Once again surveying the field, Josh was astounded by the body count of redcoats amassing in the mud one on top of the other. Still, more continued to press forward toward them.

"Now, we won't have any of that," Paddy mused. He and his fellow westerners let loose another round, sending three British flag bearers to the ground.

"That's it, boys!" Watkins shouted. "Knock them off their toes!"

The redcoats' assault didn't seem to be causing much damage, since they were firing uphill into a hazy, smoky dawn with low visibility. Their musket fire whizzed above the patriot lines or thudded into the hillside. Even their cannon blasts were falling short of the tiny hills, which were difficult targets for ships at sea.

Still, the advance continued in droves. Eventually, the sheer number of British soldiers would overwhelm even the most determined patriot defenses. Something needed to happen to turn the tide in the patriots' favor.

"Forward line—take aim and fire!" Watkins ordered.

The patriots fired at the next wave of British soldiers marching up the hillside. Paddy and the westerners took potshots at the advancing redcoats, picking off individual soldiers with remarkable precision.

"No time for napping, boys!" Watkins exclaimed. "They're coming again!"

After reloading, Josh raised his musket to his eye and took aim. The patriot volley burst out into the British forces below.

"I'm running low on shot!" Ben yelled over the crash of musket fire.

Josh flipped his box of rounds toward Ben, who snatched a handful.

"We can't hold them back like this forever," Ben said, squeezing off a shot into the sea of redcoats.

"Just keep firing!" Josh responded, firing off a shot of his own. He refused to admit it, but now he felt sick to his stomach; the acrid smoke in his nostrils wasn't helping any. But he refused to allow himself to throw up; imagining himself getting pelted to death while helplessly regurgitating gave him the extra incentive he needed to force it back down. He had to continue the fight, no matter what. Their independence—their entire country—depended on him. He had to do it for his father's memory… to return home alive to his mother…

Reload, take aim, fire…

He had no idea how much longer his troops could last against the unrelenting British ranks. Still, they refused to give in.

Reload, take aim, fire!

FORTY-TWO

Morning, Tuesday, August 27, 1776
Gowanus Road, Brooklyn, New York

Mordecai Gist peered out over the swamp to assess the situation. Since the break of dawn, his men had been fighting back the unending wave of redcoats. He was impressed with his troops' grit, considering this was the first battle for many of them, but could see the toll the stress was taking on the front lines. Not only were they showing signs of physical and emotional exhaustion, but their heated-up weapons were jamming and they were running low on gunpowder and shot. Did they have the stamina to sustain this? Who knows how long they might need to defend this hilltop.

Luckily, the casualties remained low. Thus far he had seen only a few Marylanders picked off by the British troops.

Gist knew it was going to take more than a strategic stalemate to drive the British off Long Island. He spotted Lord Stirling making his rounds behind the line of small cannons; he was busily inspecting their aim and ordering adjustments.

Wondering what Stirling next had in mind, Gist called out, "My compliments securing the ground, General."

Stirling stared out over the troop lines firing into the swamp below. He wagged his finger in the direction of the scruffy western Marylanders taking down British soldiers with unrestrained glee.

"In all my years, I've never seen men shoot like that," he said. "And I guarantee you that the British haven't, either."

"Yes, we have quite the regiment, sir," Gist concurred.

Stirling's gaze remained transfixed on the sharpshooters for another moment and then turned sharply to Gist. "Come with me."

The pair set off at a rapid clip back toward his temporary quarters on the far side of the hill. Once inside, Stirling tossed a tattered map on the field table. "How many British soldiers do you believe are still marching toward us?"

Gist did some quick calculations in his head before relating the information. "I'd hazard at least three thousand—possibly more. And Grant would always hold a sizable force in reserve."

"The men must not find out the extent of the forces we face," Stirling said. "If they keep this up, the British will be penned down in the swamp—stalled from reaching any further on the island. For now, with the number of men in our ranks, a stalemate is the best we can hope for."

"What would you propose I tell the troops, sir?"

Stirling removed his silver flask from inside his vest for a quick drink before he returned it to its hiding place. "Leave that to me."

The colonial leaders returned to the battlefield and marched up to Sergeant Watkins, whose voice was so shredded he could barely squeak the word "sir."

"Sergeant, please gather the men on rest," Stirling ordered.

"Yes...sir," the sergeant managed to spit out.

Through hand gestures, the sergeant collected a hundred or so men who at that moment were not engaged in the battle.

"Patriots!" Stirling's voice uncharacteristically thundered. "You have been as brave as lions this morning!"

The soldiers raised their fists and cheered.

Stirling was pleasantly surprised by their gung-ho reaction as he continued, "Not long ago our adversary, General Grant, stood up in front of the House of Commons and boasted that he could march across America with only five thousand men!"

The troops yelled back in mockery.

"I say to that dandy—*not today!*"

The soldiers could hardly contain themselves; they screamed as loud as their voices would carry. Savoring the attention, Stirling continued, "I promise you he'll march no farther through our continent than those mill ponds below us!"

The regiment let loose with unbridled jubilation. Even the men on the front lines who overheard the commotion cheered while continuing to fire upon the enemy.

No one had ever heard Stirling address a crowd like that before, and it produced the desired effect. Gist was duly impressed, especially when Stirling interacted with the men by slapping their backs and pumping their hands while issuing statements like, "Keep up the superb work, soldier!"

Gist prayed that the celebration wasn't premature and offering them false hopes. How could they possibly hope to ward off five thousand British soldiers in one day?

FORTY-THREE

Midmorning, Tuesday, August 27, 1776
Blokje Berg, Brooklyn, New York

The deafening musket roars continued throughout the morning.
Taking their turn for a much-needed break, Josh and Ben slumped near the back of the battle lines to rest their throbbing shoulders before reloading and returning to the front. The battle had been so fierce that both soldiers had already jammed and busted a musket apiece.

The British ranks, by contrast, didn't seem to be suffering any such hardships. No matter how many redcoats the colonials gunned down, the enemy was persistent and kept moving up the hill. Everything the patriots had heard about British training and discipline was true; they marched in tight formations that never faltered. Their weapons were new and reliable, and their pristine red uniforms gleamed with braggadocio. When one soldier fell, another replaced him with machine-like precision. Somehow, against all odds, the ragtag patriot army clung to the low hillocks circling the swampland, and the British were pinned down in the valley below—unable to reach the top of the hillsides.

Josh noticed that his friend was uncharacteristically tight-lipped. "You all right?"

Ben continued to clean his weapon as he droned, "I feel like we're going be stuck here forever—shooting at redcoats until we die."

Josh struggled to come up with a response that would deflate his friend's gloom—and privately offset some of his own. "At least we'll take some of them with us."

Ben continued his work with fervor. Josh wondered if this was how it would end: on some no-name hill, facedown in the mud.

Explosions pounded all around them, but neither soldier flinched. The sounds and vibrations had already become part of the environment and just background noise to them.

"Boys—over here!" Paddy called to them.

Josh and Ben leapt to their feet to join the mountain man, who was cradling his rifle in his arms before taking occasional potshots at the redcoats below.

"Look—down there," Paddy said to them. "They're veering off. It doesn't make any darn sense."

Josh could see that the British advance was dwindling, despite the fact that the enemy had plenty of soldiers to spare. Paddy seemed disappointed that there were fewer redcoats to target.

"Do you think they're retreating?" Josh asked.

"I doubt it. They're up to something…"

Mordecai Gist appeared at the end of their line, his face blackened and weary. "They are on the move. This battle is far from over, boys."

He motioned for Paddy and Josh to join him toward camp. Ben resumed his position on the firing line, oblivious to their imminent separation.

About thirty yards behind the front, Gist gathered twenty men, including Paddy and Josh. The mountain man extracted a clay pipe from his buckskin coat, lit it, and inhaled as Gist pointed toward a massive hill in the distance, lit by the rising sun, and addressed them. "That hill is the highest on the island—it will be their next target," Gist proclaimed. "If they gain the higher ground, they will have the advantage they need to drive us off our hillside…"

Josh licked his blistering lips. He tried to swallow, but his throat felt like a desert tomb encrusted with sand. He had no choice except to tap into his precious water reserve. He tipped his head back and sipped. He felt his passageway clearing enough to concentrate on Gist.

"…General Stirling and I will remain here with the regiment to force the British into a stalemate. You men will head toward that hill to join Colonel Atlee and the Pennsylvania regiment—they are marching up there now."

"Does that yonder hill have a name?" Paddy asked between puffs.

"For today, it will be known as Battle Hill," Gist answered.

"Battle Hill, eh?" Paddy considered. "It'll do."

* * * *

The mud of the Gowanus swamp soaked into Josh's boots as he and the other soldiers followed Paddy's meandering trail through the underbrush. They had trekked a roundabout route off Blokje Berg, parallel to the advancing British lines but hidden behind a thick curtain of scrub trees.

Josh wiped the sweat from his forehead and peaked through the foliage. If even a toe was exposed past the line of small trees, the British would instantly pinpoint him.

The soldiers placed their complete trust in Paddy. He was, after all, a skilled hunter, and this was perhaps the first time he'd truly felt at home since he left the mountains. To him, this was as commonplace as stalking deer.

"A few more yards and we'll be at the hill." He winked at the group. "Follow my lead and don't make a goddamned sound."

The soldiers did as they were told. Once they had safely reached the base of the hill, Paddy signaled for them to crouch low in the underbrush. He began to climb the outer edge, zigzagging through the tall grass so he would be harder to detect. Once he determined it was safe, he gestured for the men to follow him in the same manner.

About midway up the hillside, Josh caught a glimpse of the swamp below. They had managed to cross the entire field between Blokje Berg and Battle Hill undetected, despite the mass of British troops laying siege to the hills in the north. In the faraway distance, the massive British flotilla bobbed up and down in the East River. To the far left, plumes of chimney smoke ascended from the heart of Manhattan, as if it were any other normal day.

They were nearly at the crest of the hill when Paddy paused behind a clump of trees. He held up his palm to freeze the soldiers in place. The mountain man perched on his heels behind a scrubby tree in order to eavesdrop on some men only a few feet away. As he listened to the muffled voices, he withdrew a long hunting blade from his leather satchel.

Paddy broke through the branches and leaves, descending upon the British soldiers with the rage of a bloodthirsty animal. Josh emerged from the clearing to find that Paddy's knife was pressed tightly against the throat of a man in a worn blue outfit who had been pummeled down to his knees. Meanwhile, four other men in outfits similar to those of the Maryland Regiment were fumbling for their muskets.

"Toss the weapons to the ground—now!" Paddy threatened.

Muskets and knives were dropped by Paddy's feet as Josh and the other colonial soldiers surrounded them.

"Who the hell are you? Speak now or this fella loses his head!" Paddy snarled.

The newcomers exchanged glances before one stammered, "We... we're with Atlee's men, the P—Pennsylvania regiment."

Paddy dug the knife tighter into the soldier's Adam's apple. "Prove it!"

The same man who had spoken before gestured with his hands to his jacket interior. "May I?"

Josh aimed his musket at the soldier's throat with a warning: "Slowly."

The man agreed and then fished in his jacket for a thin scrap of parchment. "These are our assembly orders," he said, extending them in Paddy's direction. "Come on, read them."

Josh snatched the paper and examined it. The order was signed by Atlee and stamped with the Pennsylvanian colonial seal.

"It seems legitimate," Josh proclaimed.

Paddy lowered his blade and slid it back into the satchel. He clasped the soldier's hand, raising him to his feet. "No hard feelings, soldier— never can be too careful behind enemy lines."

"I understand," the soldier said, massaging his throat where the blade had brushed his skin. "Glad you're on our side. The name is Maham; I'm commander of this Pennsylvania contingent."

"Name's Paddy," he introduced himself. "We're from the Maryland Regiment. We've been sent from that shit pile up north to make sure this shit pile doesn't fall into British hands."

"Seems like we are in this shit together." Maham grinned. "There are about thirty more of my men on the other side of this tree line. We expect to rendezvous with a contingent of Atlee's troops before making a charge to take the hilltop. We'll be supported by the men from Connecticut, under General Parsons, who are en route."

"How many men do you think we'll have in total?" Josh asked.

"Not enough, I can tell you that." Maham shrugged. "But my men like to fight."

"Sounds like we'll all get along well," Paddy said, wrapping his arm around Maham's shoulder.

"Yep," Maham concurred, turning to his four comrades. "Men— grab your weapons back and let's continue where we left off."

* * * *

The climb upward was much steeper than they had anticipated. All of the soldiers—Paddy included—had to dig the butts of their weapons into the soil to push themselves forward. They paused for a breather when they reached a cluster of scrub trees and bushes a short distance from the top of the hill.

Peering down, Josh could see why the British would want this place: It had a commanding view over all of Brooklyn and Manhattan. Any

British bombardiers lucky enough to make it to this hilltop would have their pick of targets laid out in front of them.

"All right, break over," Paddy announced before the others even had a chance to rub their aching hamstrings.

Withholding their groans, the men resumed their climb. It didn't take long before they heard the sounds of musket fire and smelled tell-tale gunpowder smoke in the wind. In anticipation, Paddy sheathed and unsheathed his knife. *Soon*, he thought, *soon…*

Josh tried to see what lay just ahead, but the hilltop remained just beyond his view. All at once he heard a jumble of shouts, gunshots, and the thundering of feet on the muddy peak. He had hoped Atlee's troops were already there, decisively claiming the hilltop. It would be only a matter of time before they would hear an all-clear trumpet signal.

They waited—but no trumpet came, just more gunfire, errant screams, and puffs of smoke.

Paddy couldn't take it any longer. "We aren't doing any good biting our tongues down in this mud pit! Let's scalp some redcoats today!"

He leapt to his feet with his knife extended outward. The soldiers fixed bayonets to their muskets and charged up the hill with a whooping war cry.

The instant they climbed over the top of the hill, they found themselves engaged in chaotic hand-to-hand combat. Knives, bayonets, and fists were hurled against flesh; bodies wrestled on uneven mud, sending soldiers on both sides tumbling down the hill.

Atlee's men had been putting up a good fight, but there were many more British soldiers there than they had expected—and they were excellent street fighters. Determined to even the odds, Paddy launched himself toward the center of the skirmish, knocking down every soldier in his way with ferocious blows to their skulls. When he encountered a redcoat entangled with a patriot, he drove his knife deep into his back, yanked it out, pivoted, and struck it into the jugular of an attacking soldier.

"Get in here, boy!" Paddy exclaimed to Josh as he unsheathed a second hunting knife and simultaneously barreled two redcoats in their chests.

Josh recoiled at the grisly sight in front of him, preferring to focus his energy on where he thought his skills could be put to best use. Crouching down, he targeted his musket on a British soldier who was about to attack Maham from behind. Josh squeezed the trigger; the redcoat collapsed as the musket fire struck him in the chest.

"Much obliged!" Maham said, flipping his cap to Josh. He drew his sword and yelled for his fellow Pennsylvanians to follow him as he plunged deeper into the melee.

Josh didn't have time to respond. Musket shot whizzed near his head and he ducked down, desperately reloading and lining up another shot. He took aim at a redcoat captain on the edge of the field and lifted his finger to the trigger.

Before he could fire off the shot, his musket buckled underneath him and sailed into the mud. A British soldier struck him across the chest and he thudded into the ground. The redcoat buried his body on top of him while pulling a knife from his waistband.

Josh's hands instinctively pressed against the soldier's face in a furious attempt to shove him away. The soldier plunged his knife downward, but Josh was able to divert it into the ground by his shoulder. Josh drove his knee into the attacker's stomach, and he rolled off into the mud, momentarily winded. Josh kicked the knife out of his hand, grabbed his musket, and blasted him in the face.

It was clear to him that his musket—which worked well at a distance—would be useless for this close-quarters fight. He bent down to the dead British soldier's waistband and tore his sword free. The well-balanced British blade felt comfortable in his hand as he swirled it in the air.

Josh spotted a squad of British soldiers snaking their way up a deer trail to reach the summit of the hilltop. Figuring it was ideal to confront them while they were still winded from the climb, he gestured for a few Marylanders to join him at the edge of the slope. Josh managed to get there just as the first soldier was climbing over the top. He slashed the first soldier in the stomach before he could gain his footing. Stunned by the attack, the redcoat tumbled backward on top of three other soldiers, sending them all spiraling downhill. The oncoming British soldiers stepped over them, as they hastened their charge upward with extended bayonets.

Josh swung his sword at a charging redcoat, ripping through the soldier's arm, spurting blood in all directions. As the soldier reacted in horror, Josh finished him off by plunging his sword into his heart. The other Marylanders, meanwhile, picked off the approaching redcoats with small pistols. Josh barely dodged an oncoming bayonet from another redcoat, instinctively raking his sword hilt across the man's face and forcing him to stagger back down the trail with blood cascading from his nose. The Marylanders chased the straggling British soldiers back down the path, driving them to lower reaches away from the main battle.

Smeared with blood, Josh wheeled around to survey the battle-field. So many bodies lay facedown in the muddy grass that the soldiers involved in hand-to-hand combat were stumbling over their limbs, barely able to keep themselves steady.

As he watched British soldiers fall at the brutal hands of Paddy, the Marylanders, and the Pennsylvanians, Josh realized that their numbers now exceeded those of the British. The British reinforcements heading up the hill had slowed, and the patriots were holding their own—a miracle in and of itself.

With a blast of trumpets accompanied by thunderous footfalls, a wave of fresh patriot forces rushed through the opposite bank of trees. Josh recognized them as reinforcements from Parsons' Connecticut regiment; they could not have been a timelier, more welcome sight.

The exhausted redcoats saw the onslaught coming their way and retreated to the opposite hillside, eager to escape rather than be hacked apart by fresh colonials.

Within minutes, the patriots stood at the top of the hill having accomplished the near impossible: They had seized Battle Hill.

* * * *

Lacking enough energy to celebrate the victory, the surviving colonials collapsed on the ground to recover their senses and replenish themselves with water. Josh did the same at first, but then collected himself—and his newly prized sword—to find Paddy.

He discovered the mountain man hunched over a listless body, murmuring a few words. As Josh drew closer, he could see it was Maham's—the Pennsylvania commander. His chest was riddled with bullet wounds.

"Damn shame," Paddy said, puffing on his clay pipe. "Didn't know 'im long, but I liked 'im."

"Yeah," Josh mustered.

Paddy hoisted Maham's body over his shoulder and carried him to a few men from the Pennsylvania regiment, who said they would make sure he received a proper burial nearby.

"You did well, boy," Paddy complimented Josh, tracing his finger over the edge of Josh's British sword. "Oh, I like this…"

"Uh-uh, you can't have this one," Josh said, retracting it. "I earned it."

"Fine," Paddy growled, exhaling a wreath of smoke into the warm air. "What next?"

"The Maryland camp. If we move now we can arrive before noon."

Josh stashed the sword at his side, adjusted his musket, and trailed behind Paddy. He hoped and prayed that Ben had found similar success and was safe. Ben didn't share his fortune of having a friend—a hulking mountain man, no less—fighting by his side. He could hardly wait to see him again…assuming they could get down this hill and across several farms to the Maryland camp without being discovered and butchered by British soldiers.

FORTY-FOUR

Midmorning, Tuesday, August 27, 1776
Blokje Berg, Brooklyn, New York

Despite being barely able to see through his watering eyes, which stung from burning gunpowder, Ben managed to spot a redcoat ducking behind a thick tree stump. He lined up his musket and inhaled. When the redcoat peeked out from behind the trunk, Ben exhaled and fired; the weapon's recoil against his shoulder and surrounding cloud of smoke were now intuitive to him, and all he had to do was wait.

When a breeze drove away the smoke, Ben could see the redcoat slumped over the tree stump: a direct hit.

"Excellent shot, Wright," said a familiar voice behind him.

Ben turned to face Gist. "Thank you, sir," he said.

"I wonder how many redcoats you've shot down today."

"I haven't been counting, sir," Ben replied.

Gist leaned over to inspect Ben's shoddy musket. "I'm sure the number would have been significantly higher if you had a decent weapon," Gist observed. "Listen. We've just taken a delivery of supplies from Brooklyn Heights, courtesy of General Putnam. Head to the rear of the encampment and help yourself to a musket in better condition. If anyone objects, please tell him it's under my order."

"Thank you, sir," Ben said, brushing dirt off himself before leaving.

"Make it quick, soldier," Gist followed up with. "We need you back."

"Yes, sir."

Ben sprinted to the rear of the encampment, where he saw a group of four men in baggy work clothes struggling to push an overloaded wagon past the officers' tents. He rushed to assist them, throwing his shoulder into the side of the wagon as a sergeant shouted, "All together now, on the count of three—one, two, three!"

The five men shoved at the wagon in unison, and it lurched forward several feet to its designated stop. "That'll do!" the sergeant said as the wagon stopped with a jolt.

"Thank you," the sergeant said to Ben as the three other men began unloading the wooden crates of muskets onto the ground. They opened each container and stacked the weapons in a neat row.

"Sir, if I might," Ben said to the sergeant, gesturing to his musket. "May I replace this piece of junk with one of those?"

The sergeant eyed him with suspicion.

As if required to provide further explanation, Ben added, "I promise, I'll put it to good use."

The Sergeant continued to hesitate. Ben had a feeling he knew why. "Something wrong, sergeant?" he asked, pointing to the weapons right at his feet. "Is there a reason I can't just take one of these—you know, to help fight off our common enemy?"

"I was told to hold off dispensing these weapons until I was given specific orders by Colonel Gist," he explained.

"Well then," Ben said. "Perhaps you should know that the colonel did specifically order me to come here to replace my musket with one of those."

"Did he give you a written order?"

"No, he didn't give me a written order," Ben said, his voice rising. "I don't think he happened to have quill and paper handy in the middle of a battle."

"I'm sorry, but I can't—"

Suddenly, another party intervened. "Is there a problem, Sergeant?"

Both Ben and the sergeant turned to see Colonel Gist standing outside his tent.

Ben folded his arms, tempting the sergeant to make a false move. The sergeant sensed a connection between this darkie soldier and the colonel and blurted, "No, sir" before bending down, selecting a musket, and presenting it to Ben. "Here you go. The finest of the lot."

Ben examined it closely: Not a mark was upon it. The surface was so clean and smooth, he wondered if it had ever even fired a shot. "Sold." He grinned. "A pleasure doing business with you, Sergeant."

The sergeant groaned and stepped away to handle other matters. Ben headed toward the colonel to show him his new weapon, but Gist had already entered his tent. Ben shrugged and was about to move away when a woman appeared within the tent flaps—not just any woman, but an attractive *black woman* who was around his age. *What could she possibly be doing in the middle of a battlefield?* he wondered.

She and Ben exchanged curious glances. She seemed just as surprised to see a black man in a colonial uniform bearing a shiny new musket.

"Sarah!" Gist's voice barked from within the tent. "Get back in here! *Now!*"

The woman panicked, disappearing within the tent.

All at once it struck Ben to the core—how could he not have surmised right away that the young woman was Gist's slave? He had been free his entire life and enjoyed his freedoms to the fullest. But what of that young woman inside the tent? He felt pangs of guilt. Was he so spoiled and removed from the plight of his people that he couldn't even recognize the suffering of another?

And what of Colonel Gist? He was a brave man and a superb leader. The colonel had treated him like any other soldier—perhaps even better. Ben liked and respected him—at least until that moment. How could he justify serving under a man who had enslaved another? *Under a different set of circumstances*, he realized, *Gist could have owned me, too.*

Survival, Ben concluded. *I need him for survival. We are in the middle of a war. If any of us are to make it through the day, we need unity. He needs me to fight, and I need to fight for our freedom—for all of our freedom.*

Ben returned to the front lines—but not before he spat on the ground outside Gist's tent.

FORTY-FIVE

Midmorning, Tuesday, August 27, 1776
Blokje Berg, Brooklyn, New York

Josh, Paddy, and the rest of the Maryland squad made it safely back to the edge of the Maryland lines without incident. They cautiously passed through the swampy no-man's-land between Battle Hill and Blokje Berg, their muskets held close to their chests and their eyes on the lookout for any redcoat soldiers or snipers.

After the grueling, nonstop activity since daybreak, the sudden quiet and absence of the enemy felt ominous. Surely, they had slain and wounded only a fraction of the British army. There seemed to have been so many of them, they all thought, *torrents*; where did they all go?

The westerner stopped short and looked to the south. "Something's wrong." He sighed.

"We crossed with no trouble," Josh said. "Isn't that a good thing?"

"That's the problem, city boy," Paddy shot back. "It's often what you *don't see* that's more important than what you do."

"I don't follow you."

"Just think about it," Paddy stated. "The redcoats spend every second from daybreak fighting us tooth and nail over two shitty mud hills. Then, after a few hours, they pull back into their camp, leaving just a few soldiers behind. Doesn't that seem a bit odd to you?"

"We fought them to a standstill all morning," Josh reasoned. "They're licking their wounds and regrouping."

Paddy unleashed a belly laugh so powerful, Josh had to take a half step back. Was the man going crazy?

"Licking their wounds? Ha! This isn't some junior militia from Piss Junction," Paddy snapped. "This is the *goddamn king's own British army*. They don't lick their wounds—*ever*. And definitely not from a bunch of civilians fighting them with shitty old weapons that don't shoot straight."

Paddy took a second to collect his thoughts and scan around—as if the answer lay somewhere right in front of him and he just couldn't see it. "No, they're out there. Somewhere. Waiting for us. Waiting for the right moment when we are sitting ducks."

He paused to take a long sip from his canteen. When he sealed it up he concluded, "And then they'll devour us."

FORTY-SIX

Midmorning, Tuesday, August 27, 1776
Guan Heights, Brooklyn, New York

The British troops under General Clinton had marched toward the patriot lines all night and now nestled along the edge of the Guan Heights, on the back side of the patriot ranks. They kept a low profile as they awaited the signal—two cannon blasts—to attack the colonials' unprotected flank. Clinton would direct his forces into the back of the patriot lines from the northeast, while the Hessians would rush at them from the southeast. Grant would continue his bombardment of the regiments guarding Gowanus Road. If all went according to plan, the force of the three armies triangulating against the puny patriot lines would crack their resolve and send them scurrying like rats back to their paltry farms. In the meantime, they had to bide their time.

David Brown kicked at the sputtering remnants of the morning fire with the heel of his boot. He rubbed his bloodshot eyes. An all-night march was not his favorite way to prepare for battle.

General Clinton, standing beside him, disliked the silence. "Honestly, Brown, I wonder why we've even bothered to sail halfway around the world to this muddy, insignificant island."

"You never know what the future holds in store, General," Brown mused. "Someday this muddy, insignificant island may actually hold some value."

The two men chuckled at the ludicrous thought, but then stopped abruptly when an unknown figure approached from the hillside. One of Clinton's bodyguards raised his weapon and took aim. Clinton waved him down when he realized the interloper was a British scout who had traipsed through the thick underbrush of the Heights to take measure of the patriot army.

"What have you found, soldier?" Clinton demanded.

"As you expected, sir, the patriots have not moved their position since this morning, except to defend the hills to the south," the soldier reported. "There's no indication that they expect an attack from our direction. They are solely focused on General Grant's men."

"Perfect," Clinton said, turning to Brown. "Are the cannons prepared?"

"Yes, sir," Brown replied. "They are positioned atop the Heights. Everyone between here and Manhattan will hear them."

"In that case," Clinton sneered, "today will be a bloody day that the patriot forces are unlikely to forget. I'd wager we shall capture Washington himself before it is over."

Brown enjoyed hearing Clinton's ruminations. When he spoke, anything seemed possible.

"Douse this fire and break down our quarters," Clinton ordered. "Be ready—our march to the hillside is imminent."

Brown kicked dirt onto the fire and felt a stiff breeze pick up through the trees. He looked up and saw black clouds coalescing over the city. How ominous. How fitting.

After all these months of careful planning and weathering the controversy of his intricate spy rings, the true test was happening this afternoon—probably during a deluge.

It's about bloody time, he thought.

FORTY-SEVEN

Midmorning, Tuesday, August 27, 1776
Washington's Headquarters, Brooklyn, New York

The colonials' break from the bad weather was short-lived. A late-morning rainstorm burst over the island, drenching the little Maryland camp, the trampled Gowanus swamp, and the forested hillsides all around them. Any soldier not manning the front lines scuttled into a tent for cover.

In order to mask the size and locations of his regiments, General Stirling had restricted the lighting of campfires. The British camp, meanwhile, was aglow with fires, as they kept their own soldiers warm and dry, taunting the water-soaked colonials.

Stirling stood at the entrance of his tent as he tried to determine the impact the weather would have on the ensuing battle. He shivered, despite the thick, humid air.

"General, I beg your pardon," an aide interrupted his thoughts. The aide pointed out two waving torches in the distance high over Brooklyn Heights and added, "We have a signal...*two* torches."

Stirling knew right away that two torch signals meant he was being called to immediately assemble at the Brooklyn Heights headquarters with the other generals.

"Fetch our horses at once and accompany me north," Stirling ordered. He took off his uniform jacket and tied a nondescript gray cape around himself to help prevent any unwanted attention on the ride.

"What is it, sir? Who summoned us?" the aide asked as they mounted their respected horses.

"General Washington," he murmured as he kicked his horse forward.

* * * *

The rain-swept ride was miserable for both men. In spite of their turned-up collars and extra layer of clothing, they were soaked to the bone. They could hardly see where they were headed—much less detect any enemy soldiers—through the storm, which spewed at a horizontal angle directly upon them.

Regardless of the brutal conditions, they found their way to Washington's headquarters in reasonable time. The entranceway was cast in a pool of rain that was clearly deeper than the height of the general's boots. The aide diligently hopped off his horse first, landing with a splash into the water. He moved a wooden plank on the ground beside the general's horse to prevent his superior from suffering the same experience.

As the general dismounted and angled his foot down toward the plank, he barked, "Tie the horses to that hitching post on the left and then join me."

"Yes, sir," the aide obliged, sloshing through the water with both horses.

The plank supplied by his aide had afforded only a few feet of protection and, after just a few steps, his legs were nearly a foot high in water.

A few candles flickered in the front windows of the imposing gray brick mansion. *Cornell House—better known as Four Chimneys*, Stirling thought with a deep breath. An instinct directed his hand to search within his garments for his flask, but then he thought otherwise and withdrew it. He steeled himself: *I must face General Washington with a clear head.*

The aide rejoined him, and they hopped across the cobblestone pathway toward the front porch. Stirling pounded his closed fist against the massive door three times.

"Who is calling?" a muffled voice on the other side asked.

"General Stirling and his aide. Open this door immediately. We've ridden all the way from Gowanus…"

The door creaked open and one of Washington's immaculately dressed aides ushered them inside. The aide cordially removed their drenched outer garments and led the pair of doused soldiers into a warm, well-lit dining area. The room contained only one piece of furniture: a massive elongated table on which several maps had been spread.

Washington's private war room.

The man himself appeared from a side room with his hands behind his back. Stirling had an instant reminder of his commander's noble stature: Unlike the fatigued, muck-covered officers and soldiers battling back at the front lines, Washington stood before him impeccably clean, erect, and bulky from his chest; he radiated a fearless and irrepressible presence.

"Come this way, General," Washington invited him. "Your aide may accompany you."

The two stepped forward. General Stirling felt somewhat embarrassed as their wet boots squeaked on the polished wooden floor. He was glad, at least, that he had resisted the temptation of his flask.

Washington extended his hand to the general. "Thank you for joining us so quickly."

General Stirling became tongue-tied for a response as he clasped his gigantic hand. Washington didn't mind filling the conversational gap. "How is the battle going?"

Stirling cleared his throat before responding, "Quite well—under the circumstances. Our Maryland men have performed admirably. We now control both hills. The redcoats have pulled back."

Washington listened intently and took this in as he paced around the table. "You realize that was merely the prelude," he said.

"Of course," Stirling agreed. "I'm sure they are readying for another assault—like nothing we have ever seen."

Washington's head tilted in agreement.

"If I may ask—where are the others?" Stirling inquired.

"They are in the back, conferring," Washington answered. "They will join us momentarily."

True to Washington's word, the leaders assembled in the war room a split second later. First was a grumpy Putnam, who was wreathed in smoke from his pipe. Behind him were Generals Charles Lee, Nathanael Greene, and John Sullivan, as well as their aides. All had severe expressions on their faces, recognizing the stakes involved.

"Shall we begin?" Washington asked, as the men gathered around the table.

With that, an aide summarized the British and patriot positions and their estimated strengths. Stirling became restless—this was old news and a waste of his time to trek all this way in a rainstorm when he should be with his men in the field—when the aide said something he hadn't expected to hear.

"Our scouts report that the British have been moving troops into this area," the aide reported, highlighting a ridge near the left flank of Stirling's current position. "They are also heading here," he continued, indicating the right flank, where Sullivan's regiment was based.Stirling gasped; he stopped himself—barely—from letting loose a raft of expletives. This was an unexpected—and ominous—turn of events.

"Has all of this been confirmed?" Putnam asked, sucking on his pipe.

"The left flank has been confirmed—but not yet to our right," the aide responded.

"What of their ships?" Washington asked.

"No movement yet…but we speculate they are mobilizing to move up the East River—behind us," the aide answered.

Stirling absorbed the new information as he surveyed the map. If all this was correct—which he had no reason to doubt—the British had successfully managed to maneuver two sections of their armies within striking distance of the rear flank of his Marylanders and the other troops guarding Gowanus Road without a solitary colonial soldier's knowing. If the redcoats struck without warning—which was entirely likely— there was no way his seven-hundred-odd Marylanders, who were already exhausted from the day's fighting, could hold off such an onslaught. In fact, the impact would be immediate and devastating.

After a moment, Putnam set down his pipe and spoke. "General, it's clear that this leaves us no choice. We must immediately pull our positions from the south back into our fortifications in Brooklyn Heights. We will be far stronger standing our ground—consider the fortress walls we have there!"

As Putnam tossed his hands in the air for impact, there was a general murmuring of consensus from the other leaders—minus Stirling.

"I agree with Putnam's plan," one of the generals interjected. "It's our safest option, sir."

"It is our *only* option, sir!" Putnam corrected, exhaling pipe smoke.

The room fell silent as Washington considered the recommendations. "And if they surround us here in our fortress positions?" he probed.

"Then we fight," Putnam said, his teeth clenched around his pipe.

"Suppose they lay siege to our positions here?" Washington pressed, testing the general's self-assuredness.

"Then we fight," Putnam quipped once again.

Washington looked over to Stirling, who had kept his thoughts to himself throughout the exchange. "General Stirling, what say you?"

Stirling broke his concentration on the map to peer up. "I have only one question: What if we *lose*? The British will have us surrounded and will wait us out. What then?"

He allowed the question to settle among the group.

Stirling recognized that if they were to follow Putnam's advice and concentrate the bulk of Washington's remaining fighting forces in the Brooklyn Heights fortifications—including some of his most talented commanders and bravest lieutenants—and those fortresses fell to the enemy, there would be few left to lead the fight. It would be a devastating blow to Washington's army. Even the general himself could fall into enemy hands.

"Again, I ask: *What if we lose?*" Stirling belted in a more forceful tone. "What happens to our army? What happens to our fight for our freedom? Our revolution?"

"I invite you to propose another alternative, Lord Stirling," Putnam snapped back, pointing with the tip of his pipe.

Stirling did not hesitate to respond. "I propose we evacuate all colonial soldiers from Long Island back to Manhattan immediately. We regroup there and live to fight another day."

What Stirling was proposing was both risky and unorthodox: abandoning the field of battle altogether and retreating to join the main camp. But, if the British had in fact outflanked the colonial forces, no amount of defense could stop their overwhelming numbers from claiming the Brooklyn Heights fortresses.

"Pardon me," Putnam said with more than a hint of sarcasm as he cupped his hand to his ear. "Did you say '*evacuate*'?"

"I most certainly did."

Putnam walked toward the window, upon which rain was pelting the glass. "Do you see what is happening outside? The volume of this storm is no doubt already causing the East River to swell. I would estimate it is at least a mile wide by now."

Putnam spread his arms wide to emphasize his point. "Evacuate into *this*? With British ships out there? I think you've taken leave of your sanity, General!"

"No, I am not mad," Stirling began. "Though my troops may say otherwise at times."

There were a few nervous chuckles—but Stirling was not in a joking mood. "General Putnam," he continued. "You are exactly right. The storm has swollen the East River, and it will continue to do so as the surrounding creeks and rivers overflow into it. That is precisely my point: We must take full advantage of this."

Stirling could tell the others—including Washington—were confused by his reasoning. "You see, the added volume of water and the already strong current and tidal swirls of the river are actually pushing the British ships backward. That will continue to occur until the inflow subsides and the river returns to normal."

Though Putnam remained indignant, the other leaders seemed to be following his train of thought.

Stirling continued, "Gentlemen, as a youth growing up along these shores, I have seen similar atmospheric effects. The storm has brought winds from the north, rather than the south, as is customary this time of year. The wind direction—in combination with the force of the flooded river—will make it virtually impossible for the British to reach the stretch of river between here and Manhattan in time to stop our movement—*if we move with haste.*"

The men digested Stirling's analysis and recommendation as he scanned the room. One of the commanders raised his hand to ask the obvious question, "But, sir, if it is unpassable for the British ships, how will *we* be able to cross the river in small boats and barges?"

Stirling answered without hesitation. "As the weather cools down this afternoon and evening, the winds will shift from north back to south and calm the river. What's more, the East River is very unusual in that it reverses direction approximately every six hours—even longer when it's swollen like this. This means that, even if the British wanted to sail toward our position, they would be traveling against the strong current. I expect we will have up to nine hours to execute an evacuation."

Stirling eyed his compatriots, especially Washington, to gauge their reactions. He recognized this was all a gamble. But at least it preserved Washington's army and was a far better alternative than bottling them all up inside an untested fortress against a vastly superior force. In his scenario, at least they had a chance of living to fight another day.

"I've never heard such irresponsible blather," Putnam assailed Stirling, his face reddening. "You actually think we should head to sea in the heart of a rainstorm rather than hunker down and fight off the—"

Washington held up his hand. "I've heard enough."

Putnam clamped his mouth firmly around his pipe, his eyebrows knitting in frustration. He had to demonstrate self-control and respect to his superior.

"Gentlemen, as commander of our Continental Army, I am entrusted with a responsibility," he declared. "That responsibility is not to fight until the last man is standing or to humiliate the British. It is to make the most prudent decisions for the men under my command and our burgeoning nation."

There were chirps of agreement, withheld only by Putnam, who nearly gnarled off the end of his pipe.

"We have thousands of soldiers here on Long Island—and thousands more on Manhattan. We cannot—and *will not*—lose this army. Though I respect General Putnam's bravery and willingness to stand and fight, we must take stock of our enemy's numbers—which are far greater than ours—as well as their ground and naval positioning."

He placed both palms down evenly on the table to prepare the group for his decision. "We will evacuate to Manhattan, as General Stirling suggests."

The room buzzed with activity as Washington blasted out a series of orders to respective officers and aides while Putnam seethed at Stirling.

"Round up the mariners from Marblehead to captain the boats…. Send word to General Heath to send every flat-bottomed boat from Kings Bridge that he can commandeer…. Round up all the other small craft that can be found…. Muffle the oars with cloth—we must evacuate safely and silently."

Putnam couldn't take any more and slammed his pipe onto the table, unwilling to accept defeat. Everyone hushed as he spoke. "General Washington—with all due respect, sir, this won't work. We only have ten boats—there's simply no way we can withdraw everyone to Manhattan safely within this window of time."

Washington turned to the general who had steered them in this direction. "Stirling?"

"General Putnam is correct," Stirling admitted, his voice not faltering. "Ten boats will not be nearly enough, even under the best of circumstances. We would be lucky to transport one third of the men out before the British realize what is happening. We will need to commandeer more boats and find ourselves more time."

Washington was on the verge of making another statement—likely reversing his own decision—when Stirling volunteered, "I have a proposition…"

Stirling paused abruptly for dramatic effect before dropping a bomb of his own in the middle of the room. "My Marylanders will create a diversion."

All eyes swiveled toward him. Washington seemed unconvinced but was willing to give him a chance to explain. "General, what do you propose?"

Stirling straightened his jacket and stood erect, well aware of the significance of this moment. "My men are in the best possible position to strike back against the British forces and hold them at bay long enough for the men elsewhere on the island to escape."

Putnam's craggy expression softened as he relit his pipe. "A noble thought, General Stirling. But surely you recognize that it is a fool's errand. Your dedicated Maryland troops would be sacrificing themselves; it's nothing short of suicide. The British outnumber your men by thousands of soldiers."

"I admit the option is far from ideal," Stirling conceded. "But it is the *only option*. If my men throw their lines into disarray—for even a few hours—the majority of the Continental Army will have enough time to reach Manhattan."

Washington's face turned ashen; his pale blue eyes, rimmed with red, narrowed. "You have come to terms with what this maneuver will cost you?"

Stirling didn't blink. "Yes, I have, sir. My men…are the cost of our country's freedom."

Washington held out his hand for a firm handshake with the general. "Very well, then. Begin preparations for your bold maneuver. May the Lord be with you—and all of us."

FORTY-EIGHT

Late morning, Tuesday, August 27, 1776
Blokje Berg. Brooklyn, New York

Stirling arched his back in the saddle and drove his heels into the side of his horse, prodding him to continue the ferocious pace. As the rain pelted his shoulders and soaked-through cape, he took in a deep, concentrated breath. The air felt clear and crisp, the storm having washed away much of the summer humidity. For a moment, he felt different—perhaps like the hero his men—at least a portion—believed him to be.

While he exhaled, a familiar darkness once again clouded his thoughts. He was aware there also were those within his camp who whispered behind his back, wondering if he was worthy of his rank and title or had just bought them. His drinking habits were long-established, and there were some officers and soldiers who were skeptical about his fitness for command.

It had been like this all his life. Each time he had managed to prove the naysayers wrong to have underestimated him. Now he had to announce the inconceivable news to his men about the colonial strategy—the plan he had devised himself and emphatically proposed to Washington—and wondered if he had the fortitude to see it all through. He was going to set in motion a plan that would put his own men in harm's way, and he had sudden doubts about whether it would work at all.

Crash my men into the oncoming British lines to buy the rest of the patriot forces enough time to retreat back to Manhattan? What was I thinking? What if it is a complete failure, and Washington and all the troops get slaughtered? The Maryland men would have perished for nothing.

He forced himself into retreading his own arguments. There truly was no other option. If the British were to rout the Continental Army on Long Island—let alone capture Washington and his senior commanders—the war would be over. There may be pockets of resistance, of course, but those, too, would easily be snuffed out by the British iron fist. Without Washington, there was no leadership; without him at the army's helm, the revolution would be squashed forever.

Upon reaching his tent, he slid free of his saddle and ordered his aide—who remained on his horse—to summon all of his commanders and assemble them within. Stirling's boots suctioned into the mud as he tromped toward the tent, shrugging off his gray riding cape and tossing it into a heap.

Within minutes, his aide was inside the tent with his intensely curious commanders in tow, including Mordecai Gist.

"Gentlemen, please, gather in." Stirling motioned to them to huddle closer in to make room for everyone inside the crowded tent. Once they were settled, he prefaced with, "I have just returned from Four Chimneys. We have our orders from General Washington."

He stared at the eager faces gathered around him and felt a momentary pang of regret. Many—if not all—of these men would not survive the day because of his recommendation.

"I shall endeavor to keep this brief," he began, unrolling a map onto a wobbly table. "Our scouts report that British forces are executing flanking maneuvers to the left and right of our position."

He used both hands to trace a rough outline of the troop movements to illustrate. "This means that, in all likelihood, the British forces we have been fighting up until this point have been a diversion—a tactic designed to keep our attention fixed to the south while the bulk of their army secretly moved into flanking positions to strike from a different direction."

The commanders traded bewildered expressions. Only one aide had the courage to ask the burning question on everyone's mind. "Are we surrounded, sir?"

"Not yet, no," Stirling fielded. "But there is a chance we will be—if we hesitate. We have no more than nine hours to shift from our current position to Brooklyn Heights, where we will await an evacuation to Manhattan."

The group digested the information until a commander volunteered, "We are *evacuating*, sir?"

"Our mission is beyond critical. We have a single avenue of escape and a narrow window in which to accomplish it," Stirling replied. Then, sensing his words lacked transparency, added, "Yes, it can be interpreted as an evacuation—for some of us.... The Maryland Regiment will remain behind, under the command of Colonel Gist.... Are you here, Colonel?"

"Yes, sir," Gist said, as he made his way through the staff with his hand raised for visibility.

"Did you understand the command?"

"I do, sir," Gist asserted.

"Very good," Stirling said. "General Washington has instructed the Marylanders, under Gist's command, to form an extreme rear guard to provide protection for the evacuating troops and, if necessary, push the British back to provide our comrades time to escape."

He raised both hands to address the entire crowd. "If you are a commander responsible for a regiment that is *not* under Colonel Gist's command, ready your men for immediate evacuation. Time is both our enemy and our friend—you must reach Brooklyn Heights and be at sea before the storm passes and the tides shift.... As you can all imagine, it is imperative that our escape be completely silent. The men must wrap their wagon wheels in cloth and abandon the cannons and tents. Carry only weapons and powder. Is this clear, gentlemen?"

The leaders in the room unleashed a wholehearted "Yes, sir!" before Stirling dismissed them with the words, "Go now, and Godspeed."

The commanders hurried out of the tent and into the rain. Stirling listened to the muffled orders being passed along the chain of command. He turned around to face the one man who had stayed behind. "Colonel Gist," he began, holding his shoulders. "Mordecai…I think you should know that it was not General Washington who suggested that we form a rear guard—*I* did. I know it is a great sacrifice that you and your men will be making—but it is the only way to ensure the rest of our troops survive. Without the Marylanders' efforts, *everyone* may perish and the cause we have all fought so valiantly for may be lost."

Gist did not flinch. "I know. If given the chance, I would have volunteered."

Stirling patted Gist's shoulders as if to say, "Good man" without the necessity of verbalizing it. "Godspeed to you as well, General," Gist said with reverence as he headed out of the tent.

"Oh—Mordecai, one more thing…"

Gist turned to await a further command.

"I intend to remain with you and the Maryland Regiment."

Gist, at a loss, stared at Stirling for a prolonged moment while trying to absorb the statement. *Apparently, my superior is full of surprises*, he thought.

"Very good, sir," Gist acknowledged as he shook his head and made his way out.

Stirling, alone in his tent, felt the full weight of everything that was about to happen. He reached inside his coat pocket for his flask and whispered upward, "May God save us all…"

FORTY-NINE

Late morning, Tuesday, August 27, 1776
Blokje Berg, Brooklyn, New York

Josh and Paddy returned from Battle Hill unscathed. Whereas Paddy had no qualms about heading straight to the front lines, Josh was so weary and weathered that on reuniting with Ben he could muster only one word: "Nap."

Now that the fighting had subsided—at least for the moment—Ben agreed this was a fine idea. The two sprawled inside a cramped tent, trying to stay warm and calm their frayed nerves enough to sleep as the rain thundered around them.

Within ten minutes Gassaway Watkins beat his thick fists against the fabric of the tent and shouted, "Assemble at once, Marylanders!"

Josh roused himself and shook Ben, who flailed his arms in horror. "Are you having a bad dream?"

"Are we still on a mountain of mud in New York fighting thousands of redcoats?"

"Yes," Josh answered.

"Then I'm still dreaming," Ben said.

Josh chuckled to himself, though he could hardly tell whether Ben was joking or not. In silence, the pair pulled on their muddy boots and readied their rucksacks and muskets.

They staggered from the tent, whereupon they saw Watkins gesturing wildly to the Marylanders to get into company formation. Both men sensed something grave was happening.

As he joined the others in formation, Josh glanced out over the Gowanus swamp ahead of them—only about half the number of British troops were holding their positions. It was as though the rain had temporarily paused the battle. The British encampments twinkled with bonfires; Josh wished he, too, were drying up inside a warm tent.

Josh whispered to a western Marylander, "What's all this about?"

"Hell if I know," he grumbled.

As the last of the Marylanders fell in line, Watkins pumped his arms and called them to attention. He hoisted a freshly lit torch and addressed the group, "Men, as you may know, the Pennsylvania and Delaware regiments have already begun marching north. They are abandoning this post and heading to our embankments in Brooklyn Heights…. There have been reports that the British are massing forces on our left flank. This position is no longer safe."

He paused before continuing, "Men, we have been ordered by General Washington to secure the army's extreme rear guard and stave off the British while our other regiments can evacuate. I cannot overstate the importance of the immense responsibility we have been given. I believe our revolution depends on our efforts. As does General Washington. That is why the Maryland Regiment has been asked to secure the army's safe escape. It is my privilege and honor to be part of this regiment. We will do our job. We will not give in. We will fight back the British until it is our time to retreat north—we will prevail!"

The Marylanders cheered Watkins' rousing speech: All of them were willing to do whatever it would take to help the cause. Josh was right there with all of them, but he couldn't help recalling Paddy's concern during their trek back from Battle Hill. It seemed like only hours ago that they had beaten the British back to a standstill. How he and Paddy had managed to traverse the mountains without hardly seeing a redcoat along the way. Was everything the British had done up until that point a mere decoy?

The Marylanders saluted their officer. As Josh lowered his hand, he noticed Gist and Stirling standing by the edge of the troops. "I hope they know what they're doing," Josh murmured to Ben.

"It sounds like we're surrounded, either way," Ben countered in a morose tone. "Even if we lose…maybe some good will come of it."

"On my mark, fall into firing formation," Watkins ordered, waving the torch for emphasis. "I will take the front; General Stirling and Colonel Gist will bring up the rear."

As Josh sunk his feet in the mud and readied his musket, he tried to comprehend what he'd just heard. It was unusual—*unheard of*, in fact— for commanders to accompany their men so closely on the field of battle. He would have expected Stirling to ride ahead and rejoin the other companies, rather than test his luck in the mud with the soldiers.

Watkins doused the torch in the mud and skirted past the empty tents toward the hillside, where a skeleton crew of Marylanders sat in wide puddles, aiming at the battlefield.

The line surged forward through the muck. Josh shoved the heels of his boots into the spongy ground and plodded behind the others. He felt he was losing every trace of security: the tents, the half-lit lanterns swaying on their poles, the excess crates of food, and his temporary home—which at least had the advantage of being atop the hill.

"Watch yourselves, boys!" Watkins shouted. "It may be quiet now, but it won't be for much longer!"

Josh braced himself for the worst. Although the storm clouds were lifting and a ray of light was breaking through the sky, everything somehow seemed off. He shivered with uncontrollable terror. Was death imminent? Had all of this fighting been for naught?

And then he saw them—a line of gleaming redcoats marching inexorably toward them from the south. Paddy was right: They hadn't been licking their wounds from a patriot victory at all. They were reserving their strength for the real battle to come.

In that moment he closed his eyes and prayed: for his colonial brethren…for Ben…for the troops…for his poor father's soul in heaven…for his mother…for Washington…for himself…and even for Tessa, though he couldn't understand why.

As he pictured her beautiful face, his earnest pleas suddenly turned to rage. There was nothing worse than being a traitor, was there? He *despised* her for what she had done. Maybe her shameful actions had even played some kind of role in this British trickery. *She* lied *to me*, he thought; *she* betrayed *us all. How could she have done such things after she knew what happened to my father?*

When his eyes snapped open, he became overtaken by a venomous fury. He would make her pay. He would make *every last English soldier and officer pay*. It was long past due for these invaders to get the hell out of his country.

FIFTY

Late morning, Tuesday, August 27, 1776
Guan Heights, Brooklyn, New York

David Brown squinted into his spyglass with his left eye. When he had seen enough, he lowered it with smug delight.

The patriot commanders had done exactly as he had predicted: They had funneled their troops down Gowanus Road back toward Brooklyn Heights, leaving a remnant behind to guard their rear flank.

"They are spooked," he sneered to Clinton, who was crouched beside him. "Running like pigs back to the barn."

Clinton peered down through the trees on the hillside where his men had been hovering since daybreak. The patriot forces seemed like tiny specks in the distance, scurrying north along the rolling grasslands away from their Gowanus encampment. A cluster of a few hundred men—a sparse cluster of lost birds—lingered, as Grant's soldiers began their assault.

Smoke wafted over the battlefield with the sounds of scattered musket pops. *Finally, the real battle is beginning*, he thought.

243

"Is it really so easy to make them run? I thought this was going to be a fair fight." Clinton snickered.

Brown found this irresistible. "They know we've flanked them, but they don't know where or when to expect our full attack. I doubt they will be able to resist our next maneuvers."

The plan was deceptively simple: fool Stirling into thinking that Grant's men were just a diversion, then strike them down the center with a punch from Grant. As the colonials were sent reeling, the Hessians would charge down from the left and crash into the retreating forces. The best, most delicious part was saved for the end: Clinton's men would swoop in, followed by Cornwallis. As the second-in-command general, it seemed fitting that he would have the honor of forcing the surrender.

Just like that, the British would claim Long Island. It was only a matter of time after that, that Manhattan would fall and the colonial war effort would grind to a halt. The cherry on top would be for General George Washington to be wounded and captured—not killed, not yet at least—and paraded in chains through the occupied colonial streets by week's end.

The pair studied the patriots' movements and found them to be sluggish and feeble. Their pitiable defenses were already fraying, and Grant's men were only the tip of the poisoned spear.

"They won't last long at this rate." Brown yawned with mock boredom.

"I'm going to enjoy watching the Hessians tear into these bastards," Clinton savored. "But they'd best leave some for me. This campaign has shown the colonials to be a most disappointing adversary."

"Yes." Brown chortled. "Perhaps if they had greater support from their own natives, they would be more formidable."

The smoke became thicker in the swamp below. Clearly, Grant was accelerating his attack. Freshly outfitted with thousands of new soldiers from a midmorning rendezvous, Grant seemed eager to crush the patriots before any of his colleagues could have the chance to steal the limelight.

"We'd best act soon," Brown advised, "or else Grant will wipe them all out before we have any fun."

This was all Clinton had to hear. He gestured toward the soldiers who were guarding their two prized cannons.

"Gentlemen—on my mark, fire your shots," he commanded.

The bombardiers busily prepared their cannons and signaled they were ready.

"Fire!" Clinton hollered.

In unison, the cannons blasted out into the morning air.

Brown removed his pistol from his waist holster. *Thank heaven*, he thought, *I can finally get my hands dirty.*

FIFTY-ONE

Late morning, Tuesday, August 27, 1776
Gowanus Road, Brooklyn, New York

The British cannon blasts thundered across the hills, enveloping the colonial positions with gray smoke. With each devastating impact, bodies were gruesomely torn apart and flung in the air; they became indiscernible from the chunks of rocks, mud, and twigs scattering in all directions.

The patriots tried to collect themselves and duck for cover as the British let loose another roaring volley of musket fire on their rutted hillside position.

Josh and Ben, both covered in grit and flecks of blood, fired their weapons into the blurred morass, hoping they were hitting something. "Remember what I said earlier, about being trapped here forever fighting the British?" Ben shouted over the gunfire and cannons. "This is a hell of a lot worse!"

It was evident to Josh based on the multidirectional assault of the British fire that they had overtaken much of the Gowanus valley. If the

British were to charge now, there was no way his regiment could hold them back.

"Maryland, fall back!" Watkins shouted in desperation. "Abandon this position and fall back to the northern side of the hill!"

The Marylanders marched double-time toward the back side of the hill. Josh felt a chill of hopelessness; it was as if they had abandoned all discipline and were simply running for their lives.

They reached the sloping, trampled edge of the hill and headed straight down, mud caking their uniforms. Watkins' hands became full trying to keep the men together and sane.

A few soldiers tumbled over their own feet as they tried to evade the oncoming redcoats, and Watkins was quick to berate them. "If you break your goddamned legs, we aren't waiting for you! March like we taught you, like soldiers!"

A couple of soldiers sank down to their knees in the mud and began to cry. Watkins raised each of them back up on their feet and back in line. One soldier, though, continued to sob and shudder. Watkins smacked him back to his senses while yelling, "It's all smoke and no fire! They can't hit you from there!"

The hundreds of remaining Maryland soldiers, decimated by the British bombardment, regrouped and huddled at the base of Blokje Berg. Many were dizzy and disoriented, with blood smeared across their foreheads; others stared vacantly, oblivious to their injuries and pains.

Watkins circled the soldiers, ensuring no one fled to surrender to the British. He desperately needed each and every one of them; they had to hold tight together if they had any chance of surviving. Not to mention that they needed to buy a lot more time if the other colonial regiments were to have any chance of escaping.

Struck by a flash of inspiration, he pinpointed a direction and cried out, "We march north! Do not stop unless commanded to do so!"

The soldiers lurched forward; any movement seemed better than standing still. They emerged at a flat portion of grass leading to Gowanus Road. They were safe, for the moment, but could hear the clamber of British troops ransacking their abandoned colonial campsite. It would be only a matter of time until they reached the retreating Maryland lines too.

"Double-time march!" Watkins shouted.

The Marylanders picked up the pace, proceeding onto Gowanus Road. Josh struggled to keep his musket pressed against his chest, as his limbs felt as heavy as lead shot. A patch of grass on the edge of the road looked as inviting as his bed back in Baltimore; he fought every urge to head toward it and tumble down to sleep.

The men in front came to an abrupt halt. Soldiers lifted their weapons and scanned the horizon as they awaited their next order. Watkins' familiar voice suddenly called out, "To your left, men—to your left!"

The patriots swiveled, but they were too late: A complement of redcoats was already advancing from the tree line, their weapons at the ready. The enemy had the advantage of surprise, and there was no way the patriot forces could assemble a firing line in time.

A few westerners fired off some potshots toward the advancing lines, but even their legendary aim wasn't going to be enough to weaken the advancing British attack.

Desperate and frenzied, Watkins pushed and shoved his men forward while hollering, "Run north! Run north! Run north!" Some soldiers had no choice except to dump their heavy rucksacks and sprint down Gowanus Road. No one had a chance to fire back a single shot at the redcoats.

The sounds whizzed past Josh's ear...*pop, pop, pop!*

A few patriot soldiers ahead of him toppled to the ground amidst the commotion. He had to keep going, even if it meant hopping over or sidestepping a fallen patriot. A second's hesitation and his life would be over before his twentieth birthday.

"*Don't stop! Keep going! Don't look back!*" Watkins encouraged them.

Josh pumped his arms as best he could while cradling his musket and maintaining his rucksack. While others had dumped their belongings, he'd held on tight to his, not wanting to give the British the satisfaction of rifling through his meager possessions. He tried to concentrate on the man in front of him, but his head was swimming and his vision was foggy. This was not the vision of battlefield bravery he had imagined…

He heard shouting up ahead and craned his neck to catch a glimpse of what lay in store. His stomach sank when he realized that another contingent of British soldiers was advancing on them from the north.

"We're skewered!" one of the westerners yawped. "Limeys to our front and back! We must stand and fight!"

Josh watched the red uniforms line up another round of musket fire on the left as the soldiers from the north bounded toward them. As if that weren't enough, stocky figures in unrecognizable foreign uniforms were charging from the tree line.

"German mercenaries!" a soldier shrieked.

"We'll be gutted if we stay here!" another followed.

"Head to the pond!" Watkins screamed.

Gunshots popped in all directions. Gowanus Road disappeared behind the choking smoke of burning gunpowder. Josh trailed after the silhouettes of the men in front of him, hoping the next round of British gunfire wouldn't be his last. Before he knew it, Watkins was plunging him and the other soldiers into murky water.

"Keep your weapons over your head—don't stop until you reach the other side!" Watkins directed them.

Soldier after soldier waded through the brown, soupy water, their uniforms soaking through the sludge and debris. The pond became too deep for some men, and they had to swim feebly to shore. A couple of them floundered and choked, sinking underneath the ooze and failing to reappear. No one had time to plunge down for a rescue attempt; any effort would mean certain end from a British firearm.

Josh dragged himself out of the water on all fours, clawing into the mud. He threw down his musket in frustration to retie his rucksack, as his valuables were starting to tip out.

The thunderous crack of gunfire drew even closer. Josh cursed and lifted his musket back up to his shoulder and rose to his feet. He saw Maryland soldiers continuing to emerge from the pond through the fog and smoke. He was pleased to see Ben hobbling toward him.

"Thank God you made it," Josh said to his friend, who was so out of breath, he couldn't speak.

As Josh waited for his friend to recover, Gist and Stirling materialized with their swords drawn. "My men, gather!" Gist roared. *"My men, gather!"*

Gist held his sword up high to serve as a beacon.

Josh recalled how all those weeks ago, in that Philadelphia courtyard, he had vowed to Gist that he would fight alongside him in his special regiment-within-a-regiment if and when the time arose. Now was that time.

Hundreds of Marylanders swarmed by Gist's side—multiples of the small unit he had handpicked.

"What are your orders, sir?" Watkins asked him.

"Sergeant Watkins, you have done commendable work today." Gist saluted him. "The men heading to Brooklyn Heights need you. Accompany them north and keep them safe."

Watkins looked at Gist, incredulous. "Sir—with all due respect, the battle is *here.*"

Gist shook him off. "You will have plenty of battles to fight. Today I need you to keep these men alive. Now go."

Watkins lowered his head and begrudgingly returned to the pond, where the last of the regiment's soldiers were trudging through the muddy water.

Gist turned his attention to the assembled men. "Gentlemen. There is no one left. We are the last guard. We must ensure that our comrades reach safety…"

He looked out to the sea of redcoats preparing to advance toward their position. "…And we must do it now!"

Gist directed his sword straight ahead. He plunged south, straight into the heart of the British army. Josh, Ben, and the four hundred remaining Marylanders charged directly behind him while screaming at the top of their lungs.

FIFTY-TWO

General Washington was known throughout the colonies and far beyond as a calm, cool, and collected leader. Around the army's camps, stories about his steadfastness and determination under fire had become legend. Even when the patriot forces were routinely outnumbered, it was said that Washington never so much as shed a drop of sweat in the heat of battle. It was understood that he refused to leave even a single soldier behind on the battlefield.

This day—August 27, 1776, on the hillside of Brooklyn Heights—was like no other. His aides were witnessing an entirely new side of their previously unflappable leader. For the first time ever, he showed signs of strain. He paced back and forth, feverishly barking out commands and glaring uneasily out toward the water.

Hours had passed since his hastily convened meeting at the Four Chimneys. The evacuation of his patriot forces was only just now beginning. Not once—not in his entire life—had he ever second-guessed a decision. Then again, he had never experienced a situation so dire before.

Have I done the right thing? he wondered. *How could I purposefully sacrifice so many men? Was I wrong siding with Stirling over Putnam? But what other choice do we have?*

"Tell the sailors to send more ships—anything that can float!" Washington yelled at a junior commander, who rushed off to obey the command.

The general rubbed his temples and focused on the groups of soldiers making their excursion from Brooklyn to Manhattan. Meanwhile, at the Brooklyn dock, thousands of patriot soldiers crowded shoulder to shoulder to form a snaking evacuation line. There was already a major logjam, as the cramped fishing boats and barges could transport only so many men at a time. This was particularly problematic since many more men were expected at any moment—Stirling's lines coming from the south.

"This is too damn slow," Washington assessed as he caught sight of the massive black hulls of the British armada, anchored just around the tip of the island. "They'll be on us as soon as the winds shift."

One of Washington's aides rushed toward him bearing news but too winded to speak.

"Come on, man, speak—have you an update on Stirling's progress?"

The aide caught enough air in his lungs to reply, "Our scouts report that…General Stirling has sent half of the Maryland Regiment north to join the evacuation, sir."

"*Half?!*" Washington bellowed. "My God, what of the *other half*?!"

The aide shrugged. "I believe the general is making a last stand against the British forces along Gowanus Road, sir."

"William," he muttered under his breath. "I hope you know what you are doing."

Washington pointed toward the top of Fort Half Moon, which towered in the distance. "If they can't stop the British from advancing on our position here before we've completed the evacuation, we'll end the day underground or in chains," he stated, turning to his aide. "Light a torch and place it at the top of the fortress. Stirling will know that as long as it stays illuminated, he must continue the fight."

The aide saluted and ran toward the fort to raise the signal.

Washington pinched his nose to help alleviate his throbbing headache.

God is with you, William, he thought; *keep up the fight. You are our last hope.*

FIFTY-THREE

Midday, Tuesday, August 27, 1776
Vechte Farm, Gowanus, Brooklyn, New York

Abigail Vechte stared out the front window of her stone farmhouse and gasped, "Nicholas, come quickly!"

She heard her husband's familiar heavy footsteps echoing through the hallway. He joined her a moment later by the window and peered out.

Outside, a group of redcoats had gathered around the front of their home, trampling their modest vegetable plot. Several were leaning against their split-rail wood fence, their muskets slung over their shoulders. One of the men was gnawing on an apple plucked from the Vechtes' orchard; he disdainfully spat the seeds onto the ground. Another soldier was taunting one of the couple's chickens that had been released from the chicken coop.

"I've seen enough," Nicholas Vechte stated as he stormed toward the door.

Like so many other farmers along this rural stretch of Long Island, the Vechtes were descended from the Dutch settlers who had built the first small towns on this swampy ground. They had been a proud founding family of the town when it was known as Breukelen from its earliest days. This farm had been in the Vechtes' family longer than the British had even been in New York, and now they were trampling through his garden without his permission.

He didn't care that the British ships had filled New York's harbor. Or that all morning he had heard the continuous explosions and gunfire pops. Or that neighboring lands all over the island were billowing pillows of charcoal-colored dust. He snatched his trusty old rifle from a wooden shelf near his entranceway, smacked the door open, and burst out into the yard with his weapon flailing.

"Get your asses out of here!" he threatened. He aimed his weapon at the British soldiers, who scrambled into position and raised their muskets.

"This is my property! You'd best leave right now or I'll—"

A cold metal piece pressed against his left temple. Out of the corner of his eye, he saw a man in black holding a pistol to his head.

"That will be enough of that," the man said in a prim British accent. "Why don't we discuss this further inside?"

Vechte lowered the weapon. "All right," he relented. "Please... promise me you won't hurt my wife, Abigail."

The man shoved Vechte toward the front door and all too politely uttered, "Now, sir, that all depends upon you, doesn't it?"

* * * *

Brown watched as Clinton plucked a bottle off a shelf in the Vechtes' cramped kitchen. He uncorked it, taking a deep sniff. He wrinkled his nose in disgust but poured himself a glass anyway, grabbing a rustic mug from the counter. He drank it down and then tossed the mug on the kitchen table with a smack of his lips. "It's certainly not a London vintage...but I admit, it is good to taste port again—as vile as the American wineries may be," Clinton critiqued.

The British soldiers had no difficulty securing the place. The Vechtes were unceremoniously shoved into a back bedroom and locked inside while the soldiers swept the house, making sure no colonial soldiers were lurking about.

"All clear, sir," a soldier reported, trundling back down the stairs.

"Very good," Clinton said. "Take a few men and guard the perimeter. Shoot anyone on sight not wearing a British or Hessian uniform."

His attention turned to the kitchen table, on which an aide had unfurled a battlefield map.

"The battle is nearly won," Clinton surmised, pointing to a narrow sliver of land between the hills and the river. "We have forced Stirling from his position and have broken Sullivan's lines, sending him running back to Brooklyn Heights."

Brown joined him hovering over the map. "There must only be a handful of Stirling's men still left. They'll have no choice but to ford the mill ponds and head north toward their fortress. To do anything else would be folly," Brown said, remembering the Doans' geography lessons.

"I want them all *dead*," Clinton flared. "I want Stirling's forces annihilated before they can scurry to Washington's embrace."

All good generals had a certain amount of bloodlust, Brown supposed, but Clinton seemed to boast an extra few ounces. *No wonder I like him so much*, he realized; *we are quite alike in that regard*. "In that case, I suggest we continue our advance on Stirling's position by the mill ponds—but move your soldiers north to rendezvous with Grant's forces at the hills along Gowanus Road. If they are foolish enough to try to retreat south, they'll run straight into our muskets."

"Very good." Clinton cackled. "I'll inform the men."

Brown pulled up a chair to the kitchen table with the bottle of wine. He savored pouring it into the same mug Clinton had used. He ruminated for a moment and then raised it upward. "Victory," he toasted.

FIFTY-FOUR

Early afternoon, Tuesday, August 27, 1776
Gowanus Road, Brooklyn, New York

Paddy perched along the muddy embankment of Gowanus Road with his massive hunting rifle at the ready. He fired at will, picking off redcoats advancing down the road from the north, though they were barely visible through the shrubbery and constant tufts of smoke. When he struck down an officer in the center of their company, the soldiers around the man scattered, shocked that anyone could have made a shot from such a great distance.

One down—a thousand to go, Paddy thought as he lined up for another blast.

Ben tugged at Paddy's sleeve. "Let's go!" he implored. "If we linger, we'll be dead, and then we won't be any use to anyone!"

Paddy shoved his hand aside and yelled, "You're spoiling my fun, boy!"

Ben folded his arms as if to say, "You've got to be kidding me."

"Fine!" Paddy conceded. "Just one…more!"

Paddy again squeezed the trigger, this time only winging a redcoat in the shoulder. "Ah, you made me rush and miss my first one!" he berated Ben. He shouldered his rifle and said, "All right, all right…I'm coming."

Unable to conceal his pouty expression, Paddy followed Ben's lead and crouched low as they headed along the muddy path as musket balls whistled overhead.

The Maryland line was getting closer now. Ben could begin to make out the telltale mound of Blokje Berg, which the British had ransacked and on which they had planted a regimental flag that fluttered in the afternoon breeze. He imagined what the scene would look like on a map and felt sick to his stomach: They were effectively surrounded from the north, the east, and the south by British soldiers.

Ben and Paddy found the bulk of the remaining Marylanders, who were sheltered in a grove of oak trees towering over Gowanus Road. Stirling acknowledged the two soldiers who rejoined the group, then drew the men in close. His grizzled face shone with sweat, and his graying hair was flecked with mud and debris. The bright white ascot he wore tied at his neck was now a dirty brown, and his uniform hung loosely off his shoulders.

He doesn't look much like a general, Ben considered, *but he is the only one we have.*

* * * *

Stirling surveyed the group and mopped his forehead. His legs ached so much, he had to balance himself against a tree trunk for support.

He knew he had to remain strong for these men. There was no time to collapse, quiver, or show any trace of weakness whatsoever. He was their general and they were his troops—even if his present army was now dramatically reduced.

He was about to speak when something caught his eye to the north: a beacon burning atop the patriot fortress. It could mean only one thing: *Washington needs us to fight on.*

The sign reinvigorated his resolve. "Gentlemen," he rasped, "we must hold the British at bay for another two hours…to allow General Washington to evacuate to Manhattan. Any less than that and our comrades will be captured or killed. Are you all still with me?"

A murmur of agreement bubbled up from the group, although many of them leaned heavily on their weapons or slumped down, unable to stand at all.

Stirling had watched some of his soldiers struggle to traverse the mill pond, burdened by their weapons, rucksacks, and tired limbs. He had left those men behind to fight another day. Now he was left only with the diehards and the core group of soldiers who had pledged their allegiance to Gist. He had not liked the idea at all at first; it was never good to have troops more loyal to a junior commander than to their general. But, as he looked at each one gathered with him beneath the oak trees, he knew he couldn't have selected a finer group of men himself.

Stirling closed his eyes and envisioned the field of battle to come: the British soldiers closing in on their ranks, the ebb and flow of the action. He imagined the patriot soldiers fighting from beneath these trees as the redcoats swarmed them on all sides. He envisioned them tossing their weapons aside and brawling, hand to hand, like they were scrapping in a pub. No matter how many times he replayed it, the outcome continued to be the same—with the British overwhelming their position, bayoneting most of them to death, and carting the rest away in chains to prison ships. He needed another solution: It simply wasn't possible for them to hold out for two hours from their current position in a defensive posture.

He opened his eyes and looked to the east, where he spotted a farmhouse in the distance. He had heard something about a stone house in the vicinity owned by a family—something like Hechte or Vechte. It was the only one around for miles, so it must be the one. But why would this average-looking country house be surrounded by British soldiers? On closer look, he figured there must have been what amounted to at least two companies spread out across the farm grounds.

Ah, Stirling concluded. *Without a doubt the stone house is concealing someone important—perhaps even a British commanding officer.*

Stirling leapt to his feet—his feet, legs, and hips no longer causing him pain. "Colonel Gist!" he hailed. "Do you see that house in the distance?"

"The house surrounded by redcoats?" Gist asked.

"I am convinced there's a general in that house."

"I think you may be right," Gist said with uncharacteristic excitement. "And look—there may be a possible weakness. Notice the left flank?"

Both men observed the gap in the left fence line surrounding the farmstead. The British had left it mostly unguarded.

"Very good," Stirling gushed. "We must take advantage of that."

That was all it took for Stirling to bound toward the men. "Soldiers, attention!"

Fatigued, filthy, and suffering through a variety of wounds, aches, and pains, the men did what they could do to drag themselves to attention. Stirling decided it was good enough under the circumstances and proclaimed, "We have been graced with an opportunity to change our prospects today—but only if we act decisively and aggressively.... Colonel Gist and I are convinced that within the house behind me is General Cornwallis—one of Britain's highest-ranking leaders. We are going to attack the British center and capture him!"

A commotion spread throughout the ranks as the men absorbed Stirling's announcement. Even Gist registered surprise at what had just come out of his commander's mouth.

Stirling knew there was really no telling who was inside that building. On the other hand, it had to be someone senior. If by some divine miracle the men were to break through the British ranks, capture the farmhouse, and find Cornwallis inside, so much the better.

Now, at least, they had something to fight for.

Stirling looked down both ends of Gowanus Road. The sound of marching soldiers was growing louder, but they still remained out of sight. His troops had precious few moments left of peace. "Men—please kneel and pray with me," he said, recalling Washington's prayer when he had taken command of the Continental Army. "Preserve me, Lord, for in Thee I do put my trust."

"Amen," the regiment responded in unison.

Stirling stood back on his feet and looked toward Gist, who shifted forward and ordered the last two lines of men to affix bayonets to their muskets and prepare for a charge. The regiment stirred with activity as the Marylanders readied their rusted blades for combat.

His eyes moistened as he addressed the men. "Men…my brothers in arms, the fate of our army—and indeed our young country—has been entrusted to us…"

The noise level of the battle was drowning out his voice. He coughed, raising his volume so all could hear. "There is no one else. There is no other time. There is only our regiment. If we fail, our revolution may very well soon be over…"

He regarded all of their tired and sallow faces with appreciation as he battled back the tears. "But—if we succeed, we will be remembered forever."

He unsheathed his sword and held it up high. "I, for one, would rather die a free man, as the Lord made us, than die on my knees. I believe with all my heart and soul that God is beside us today!"

His sword-filled arm dropped to its side. Emotionally spent, he stepped back to allow Colonel Gist to begin the soldiers' charge. Gist followed suit, also drawing his sword and raising it above his head. "Sons of Baltimore—let us demonstrate our fire and might to the British! On my mark, advance!"

With a flourish, he charged forward. Stirling stood by to salute the first, second, third, and fourth lines of the Maryland Regiment, who stampeded toward the enemy with screams and cheers, their bayonets glinting in the sun.

When the final soldier made his advance, Stirling again lifted his sword and followed close behind while jeering, "Prepare to die, British dogs!"

FIFTY-FIVE

Early afternoon, Tuesday, August 27, 1776
The Pier, Brooklyn Heights, New York

General Washington stood by the water's edge to observe the evacuation. Concealing his impatience as best as he could, he watched a rickety fishing boat tack and weave as it meandered toward the shore.

Two worn-out sailors prodded it forward until it thudded against the Brooklyn Heights pier. While they tied it down with rope, one of the sailors called for the next twenty soldiers to clamber aboard: That many would be a tight fit, for sure, but they needed to cram as many people into every inch of that vessel as possible.

The other sailor leapt off the boat, splashing through the shallows of the East River to breathlessly pass along his message. "General Washington, sir! The tide is shifting quickly—we have maybe an hour—possibly two—to complete the evacuation before the British ships will be upon us."

"Thank you, sailor," Washington said, turning to an aide nearby. "How many more of our men are awaiting evacuation?"

"Too many, sir," the aide quavered, turning pale. "Almost three thousand. There's simply no way we can move all these men in time."

"We have no other choice. You have two hours," he stated, his icy blue eyes burning into the man's face. "I need every last man to arrive safely in Manhattan—even if they all have to swim there."

The aide hastened to the pier, shouting orders at other incoming boats.

Washington stomped up the hillside, where another aide with a spyglass drew his attention. "Sir, the patriot line is all but gone," he fretted. "I estimate the British forces will be on the march toward our position in less than an hour."

"I would like to see for myself," Washington requested.

The aide presented the spyglass to Washington, who examined the battlefield in the far distance. As far as he could see—redcoats, redcoats, and more redcoats.

But then, just as he was about to return the spyglass, something else caught his attention. He could hardly believe what he was seeing: Stirling and his men, charging through an opening on the edge of a farm field. Unbelievably, the Marylanders were attacking the British position surrounding a farmhouse. *They must know something*, Washington thought.

Washington returned the spyglass to the aide. "I believe you've underestimated our men," Washington said in a tone to reflect that he had expected these results all along.

FIFTY-SIX

Early afternoon, Tuesday, August 27, 1776
Vechte Farm, Gowanus, Brooklyn, New York

The Sons of Baltimore cut through Gowanus Road and barraged Vechte farm. The redcoats nearest the fence were stunned: How was it possible that this paltry band of retreating patriots was *attacking them*?

When the first line of British soldiers fell into a firing line with martial efficiency, Gist shouted for the Marylanders to feint to the left. The subsequent explosion of smoke and gun blasts whistled far off course.

"First line, ready, aim, and fire!" Gist yelled.

The first line of Maryland men dropped to their knees, rammed rounds down their barrels, took aim, and fired off a volley into the British front line. As the smoke cleared, they were able to confirm a number of direct hits. The British soldiers reacted by scrambling toward the gap in the fence line.

The Maryland men were prepared for this move, positioning themselves to face the enemy.

"Second, third lines, charge!" Gist shouted, firing off a round from his own pistol.

With that call, Josh sprang into action alongside his fellow soldiers. He leapt past the kneeling front line of Marylanders and rammed into the front of the British lines, which now extended a hardened perimeter past the fence line to protect the farm from an attack on their flank.

Josh plunged ahead. Sooner than expected, he and the colonials were atop the first line of redcoats. He struck blindly around his own men until he felt his steel tip jab deep into a redcoat's chest.

The hastily assembled British front line crumbled inward as the Marylanders mercilessly slashed and stabbed into the redcoats with their rusty and bent bayonets. The attack came to an abrupt halt when they realized that a mass of British soldiers had pulled back to the safety of the fence, where they amassed a formidable firing line.

"Pull back!" Gist shouted.

Josh and the other charging colonials scrambled back to the safety of the Maryland line, which stalled the British offensive with another thundering blast of musket fire.

Josh spotted Ben loading his weapon behind the Maryland line and crouched next to him. They looked at each other for what they thought might be the last time.

"Your father would be proud," Ben said.

"Lydia will be proud too, when she hears about everything you've done," Josh said. "I promised her I would keep you safe—but you seem to be doing just fine for yourself."

Ben could only muster a crooked half smile as he rammed a round down his musket barrel. "I'm just keeping alive," he said.

Josh placed his hand on Ben's shoulder. "And I need you to stay that way," Josh remarked. "To protect me from the next barmaid spy."

Ben's face widened into a complete smile: It was the look Josh remembered back from the Cat's Eye.

"Soldiers!" Stirling interrupted them. "We've driven a wedge between the force guarding the left flank, where the fence breaks. There's an opening big enough for us to penetrate. I need our best marksmen to volunteer."

Breaking through a cloud of gun smoke, Paddy stepped forward, a contingent of westerners in tow. "Me and my men hunt and skin bears," he declared with his trademark bravado. "We can handle some soldiers in sissy uniforms with bad accents."

Stirling didn't need to be convinced any further: He knew this to be true. He turned to Josh and other soldiers nearby. "You men—accompany the western ranks toward the left gap in the fence line. We've softened them up, but it will be a pitched battle. We'll be right behind you with supporting fire."

Paddy's scruffy, grimy face appeared at the bridge of Josh's nose. "I killed my first bear with this knife," he growled. "It's yours now."

Josh opened his mouth to respond, but Stirling's commands took precedence.

Ben, who had begun readying his own blade, looked up to say farewell and good luck to his closest friends. A wisp of smoke blustered in his face, stinging his eyes. By the time he brushed it away, both men had already gone.

FIFTY-SEVEN

Early afternoon, Tuesday, August 27, 1776
Vechte Farm, Gowanus, Brooklyn, New York

In the upstairs master bedroom of the Vechte house, Brown studied his reflection in the mirror to the accompaniment of stop-and-start musket fire outside. He drew a razor across his face, scraping away the stubble accumulated from days and nights of marching. He toweled himself off and removed his pristine, bright red officer's uniform from his rucksack. He arranged it neatly on the bed and smoothed out a few noticeable wrinkles. As a clandestine officer, he often wore black or something similarly nondescript. But today, as he smoothed his hands over the soft red wool, he imagined the medals and commendations that would festoon his chest after this victory.

This was the same uniform that had been stripped from his father. Many had said that a Brown would never again fight in the service of the Crown. But he was determined to prove them all wrong.

He glanced through the window and squinted through the gun smoke drifting across the farmland. *My moment has come*, he thought:

vindication. I am on the precipice of putting these sniveling and entitled colonists in their rightful place—underground.

He tentatively pulled on his breeches, shirt, and coat, unsure of whether it would all fit and dreading the possibility of any unsightly moth holes. All seemed to be in fine order as he took his time fastening each uniform button. He clipped his sword to his waist, then slid on one polished dress boot after the other. Lastly, he strapped a small leather pouch to his waist and slipped two daggers inside: one in honor of his father and one for himself. If he had the chance, both of these would carve out the heart of the patriot commander.

He descended the stairs into the main wing of the house and entered the dining room, which Clinton had converted into a makeshift war room. Aides bustled about, tossing maps and strategy plans onto the dining table and scouring the house for more colonial wine—putrid as it was, it served its purpose—as well as food, tobacco, silver, and anything else of potential use or value.

Clinton caught a glimpse of Brown and beamed as if he were welcoming his son on his wedding day. "So, the spy becomes a soldier."

Brown brushed past him, in no mood for Clinton's patronizing nonsense.

Clinton decided it was best to let it go and focus on the maps laid out on the table. "What do you make of the colonials' pitiful last gasp?"

Brown feigned disinterest. "Surely, it will be over by dusk."

Deep down, he had not anticipated a final stand. He had fully expected the shoddy colonial remnants to scuttle away like mice.

Then again, this bold counterattack made some sense to him. What else should they do when facing down total annihilation? Why not go out fighting? He would hope he would do the same, if faced with the same circumstances.

Clinton directed his aides to refresh the men on the fence line with new musket balls and gunpowder. As his staff hurried toward the entrance, the door flew open and a contingent of unrecognizable British troops entered, accompanied by a flurry of shouting.

Outraged, Clinton dashed toward the door. "This is the commander's quarters! How dare you barge in here like a bunch of animals!"

The troops poured out into the hallway, oblivious to Clinton's protests. Clinton was about to unleash a firestorm when the soldiers parted in the middle to make way for two emerging figures.

Clinton and Brown instantly recognized one of the officers, a stocky man with a narrow face and large jowls: General Charles Cornwallis, second-in-command to William Howe.

They did not recognize the other man, who was older with a pouchy face and slits for eyes, but they could tell by his standing and green-and-red embroidered uniform that he was someone of great significance.

The men blustered toward the dining room. Cornwallis, not known for his temper, was evidently irate. "Clinton! What the hell is going on here?!"

"Welcome, sir," Clinton soothed him. "We did not expect you—"

"And *this* is what happens when I am not expected? Why is colonial trash outside? Why are they alive at all?"

"General, please," Clinton said. "I assure you, we have everything entirely under control."

"A bayonet charge from a group of ragtag rebels? I hardly consider that having things 'under control!'"

"With all due respect, sir, our men outnumber the colonial forces by a significant margin. Let them dash themselves upon our lines until they are so exhausted, they cannot fight any longer. It only makes them easier to kill in the end."

"My men will be here within the hour," the older man intervened in a heavy German accent. "Then this will be finished."

"General Clinton—this is General Leopold Philip von Heister," Cornwallis introduced him. "He is our Hessian commander. He's won more battles than you've even dreamed of fighting."

Von Heister kicked his heels and bowed appreciatively.

"Effective immediately, I am taking over command of these forces," Cornwallis announced.

He raised his hand to issue an order when a crash echoed throughout the house. The commanders raced into the kitchen to find that a musket ball had smashed through the window and was wedged into the side of the wooden cabinet.

"It's time to rid ourselves of this nuisance," Clinton snarled to Brown. "You want to be a soldier? Now's your time."

Brown didn't hesitate. He snatched a pistol from the war chest near the entrance and gestured for seven of the soldiers stationed by the entrance to follow him outside.

"Stop at once, soldier!" bellowed Cornwallis. "I did not order you to leave!"

Brown flung the door open without a second thought. *This is not a time for military protocol*, he thought. *This is a time to fight.*

Once again a member of the Brown family would take the battlefield.

FIFTY-EIGHT

Early afternoon, Tuesday, August 27, 1776
Vechte Farm, Gowanus, Brooklyn, New York

The Maryland offensive managed to push the redcoats back inside the fence, where the two sides were corralled like angry farm animals—kicking, stabbing, and shooting at each other at random.

Josh looked up and saw the front door of the stone farmhouse for the first time. *If I could only get near it and break inside, whom might I find?* he wondered.

A wave of redcoats surrounded the entrance, which put aside that thought. Josh yanked his pistol out of his satchel and was about to squeeze off a shot, but the chaos of the battlefield was too much and he feared striking one of his own; frustrated, he shoved it back in.

Instead, he reached for Paddy's knife—and not a moment too soon, as a British soldier was coming right at him. He slashed him across the ribs and then shoved him down on the ground, kicking him in the head before the man landed unconscious.

Josh swiveled to his right to meet another oncoming redcoat with a thrust from his knife, but the man dodged it easily and kicked him in

271

the stomach. He crumpled over, wheezing and trying to catch his breath when the British soldier jabbed his musket butt into his chest.

Unable to get back on his feet, Josh furiously kicked at the man's shins, to no avail; the redcoat loomed over his chest with a raised musket. Josh watched him begin to squeeze the trigger when, for no apparent reason, he jerked awkwardly and slumped on the ground next to Josh with a thud. Josh stared at a hatchet buried deep in the back of the man's skull, which oozed blood.

Paddy reached his rough hand to Josh and hauled him upward to his feet. With both hands he tore the hatchet free from the redcoat's head. Wiping the bloody hatchet on his pants leg, he winked at Josh as though he had just brought down a prized deer. Josh watched Paddy saunter off to resume the battle with the other westerners.

Thankful to be alive, he readied his knife yet again. He was about to engage a redcoat sparring with a colonial soldier, but something else caught his attention—an opportunity, perhaps.

As Paddy and the westerners savagely cut into the center of the British forces, the redcoats had begun to drift away from the farmhouse itself, leaving the front door largely unguarded. Josh reasoned that if he could get inside, he could lead a full-scale attack on whoever was being sheltered.

He raced over to Ben, who had just cracked his musket into a red-coat's skull. He pummeled the enemy soldier lying on the ground two more times for good measure.

"You finished with him yet?" Josh asked.

Ben, who was about to drill him again, paused midway to look up at his friend. "Huh?"

"You can only kill a man once," Josh pointed out as Ben regained his senses. "Listen—we've got to get inside that house. You with me?"

"You bet I am," Ben said.

A younger Marylander who had overheard their exchange asked, "Can I join you?"

Josh and Ben exchanged glances as if to ask, "Why not?" and tugged him along.

The three scrambled toward the stone house, their knives drawn. They were within a few footfalls of the front door when it flew open and a mountain of soldiers flooded out.

Ben, instantly surrounded, had to furiously slash himself free so he could retreat back toward the center of the farm field and rejoin the westerners.

Josh and the other soldier found a clear opening. They lunged toward it just as a British officer in a sparkling clean uniform appeared in the doorway. The officer aimed his pistol at the other Maryland soldier and blew a hole through his forehead.

As the Marylander collapsed, Josh brandished his knife at the officer.

The redcoat seemed dumbfounded, as though he could scarcely believe a patriot dog would have such gall as to challenge him to a knife fight.

To Josh's astonishment, the officer seemed to relish the idea. He holstered his pistol and drew out his sword, thrashing out at Josh with a fierce blow against the younger man's blade. Josh felt his footing slip and he tried to parry the blow and strike, but the man was too agile and, from the look of his immaculate uniform and clean-shaven face, hadn't yet expended much energy in battle. The attacker caught Josh's ankle with a sweeping kick, sending him tumbling into the mud.

The British officer loomed over him, drawing his sword with both hands for a death blow. Josh flailed his knife wildly, but the redcoat knocked it out of his hand with one swipe. The redcoat deposited his sword back in his holster and drew his pistol. "Stop struggling," he advised in a patrician voice. "You are only going to make death more painful."

He pinned the pistol against Josh's forehead. "Are you one of those Marylanders I've heard so much about?"

Josh refused to give him any satisfaction with an answer. *If you are going to kill me*, he thought, *just stop the jabbering and do it already*.

"You're brave, I'll admit—with a little more training, you might have amounted to something. But, alas, you've come an awfully long way just to get a bullet in the head on this silly island."

* * * *

David Brown tightened his grip on his pistol, which pressed against the young colonial's temple. The soldier was clumsy and inexperienced, to be sure, but Brown admired his guts and determination. In some small way, he reminded him of himself as a young soldier—eager to prove his value and move up the ranks. *At the end of the day, though*, he judged, *you are nothing but a traitor to the Crown.*

He squared up to take his shot when some movement appeared in the corner of his eye. Before he could react, a burly figure slammed into his left shoulder, sending him sprawling into the mud and his pistol spiraling several feet away.

He was shocked by the realization that his attacker was a Negro—a rarity in both armies. The man was deceptively strong and agile for someone who lacked height, Brown thought. "I daresay," Brown remarked, "you don't belong in this battle. What have the colonials done for you?"

"Freedom," the Negro answered.

"Freedom!" Brown taunted. "Freedom to pick cotton or shine a colonel's boot?"

"No," he countered. "Freedom to *kill you*."

He struck Brown squarely across the jaw. Another blow landed in Brown's right eye, which went dark. The colonel felt warm blood ooze from his mouth.

This is not how I am going to die, he thought, *not at the hand of some self-righteous Negro*. He fumbled around for his pistol, which was nowhere in sight. He withdrew one of his knives and plunged it into the Negro's shoulder, directly next to his collarbone. The sensation of the blade digging into his enemy's flesh made his entire body tingle. Re-energized, he scrambled to his feet and plucked the dagger from the man's shoulder. He kicked him in the ribs, enjoying the Negro's agonizing screams of pain before desperately rummaging on the ground in search of his pistol.

I'll be damned if I am going to waste my time in combat against some fledgling Marylander and a slave boy, he thought. *I must find my pistol so I can finish them off and move on to much worthier opponents.*

"Stop struggling," a voice said. He turned and saw the Marylander—that *damned kid again*—aiming his own pistol at his chest. "You are only going to make your death more painful."

Brown couldn't take his eyes off his pistol. *How could I have been so careless?*

"Did you lose something?" the boy mocked him, targeting the gun even closer to his heart.

"Don't be stupid," Brown said. "Surrender before you're killed. You colonial dogs will lose—and suffer terribly. For what? You don't know how to govern. You aren't worthy of this land. You think taxes were high before? You just wait until we conquer you, claim all of your properties, rape all your women, and leave you with *nothing...*"

The kid's grip on the pistol wavered; Brown's intimidation tactics seemed to be having an effect. *This kid is no soldier*, he thought. *Probably a farmer or dockworker.*

"Your taunts don't mean a thing to me," the Marylander sneered. "You think you are so much better than me. You probably would rather die than be captured by someone so young and of such low rank. How about we test that out, hmm? I can shoot you dead right now, or you can surrender yourself over to me. Perhaps the British will be willing to ransom you back—if they'll have you, that is."

"Never!" Brown exclaimed in disgust as he raised his sword. Now it was time to teach this boy a lesson. He would show this kid how the Brown family fought. He would chop him apart limb by limb, make him beg for mercy, slice off an ear perhaps, and who knows what else prior to gutting him. Then—and only then—would he separate his head just before his final breath.

Brown flailed his sword in a wide arc, missing the kid's gun hand by a fraction of an inch. He reared back for another swipe when he heard an explosion. He dropped to his knees as he felt a searing pain in his chest. His sword plunked down from his drooping arm.

One moment he was on the smoke-ridden battlefield looking across at the Maryland kid who had pulled the trigger; the next he saw himself in a mysterious room with his disgraced father.

Then he was in darkness.

* * * *

Josh was mesmerized by the sight of the life abandoning the British officer who seemed to have taken such pleasure in toying with him. Strange—he didn't know him at all but felt a vague connection to him, though he couldn't fathom how or why. Either way, he was glad the man was dead. *Good riddance*, he thought, spitting on his corpse.

Josh bent down to assist his friend, who was sweating profusely and writhing in pain. He tore at Ben's uniform to expose the jagged stab wound. He ripped off Ben's loose tunic underneath and pressed the torn cloth against the wound to slow the bleeding.

"Ben—can you hear me?" Josh shouted. "Stay with me..."

Ben's eyes fluttered open. "My shoulder...hurts like hell," he wailed. "But...I can still see your ugly face...so I must be all right." After discharging a few painful coughs, he croaked, "Did we get him, mate?"

"Yes, we got him," Josh said. "But your day of fighting is done.... We have to get you to the Maryland lines. Can you stand?"

Ben groaned at the prospect but managed to retort, "I can stand better than you after you've had a couple of pints at the Cat's Eye."

"Let me help you up," Josh said, grabbing Ben by his good shoulder. They struggled together to get him on his feet.

"I feel...dizzy," Ben murmured, nearly toppling back down.

"Stay awake, soldier!" Josh yelled, dragging him back up. "You've lost some blood...and you probably need water..."

Josh looked at the chaos all around as the Marylanders brawled and scrapped with the redcoats, holding them at bay within the farm fences— for now. Josh knew he had to move at lightning speed if he hoped to save his friend. With Ben leaning his weight against him, he reached into his rucksack for his canteen. He opened it with his teeth and poured it over Ben's lips. Ben's mouth opened and he dutifully swallowed.

Josh saw British soldiers advancing in his direction and pulled the canteen away from Ben as he gargled the water. "Sorry," Josh said, stuffing it back in his rucksack. "We have to go—*now*…. Come on, Ben. You can do this. Walk together with me…one leg at a time…"

The splash of liquid gave Ben just enough energy to focus on moving forward with Josh.

Still, he had to lean heavily on Josh to steady himself as they began walking.

The pair reached the fence when Josh spotted a familiar face coming toward them: It was Gist, leading a secondary charge of Marylanders with bayonets fixed.

"He's badly wounded—pierced through the shoulder," Josh explained as he passed Ben on to two Maryland soldiers.

"There's no help we can offer him now," Gist said. "Bring him to Stirling's position. The best we can do is keep him away from the British."

Josh watched as the two soldiers helped lead Ben away from the farm. "Please…take good care of him," Josh called to them. The men were unresponsive, concentrating on the task at hand. In a few moments, they vanished into the field.

Josh's attention returned to the battlefield. Gist's charge had effectively slammed into the British soldiers along the fence, but the momentum was beginning to shift as more redcoats materialized in droves.

"The tide is turning against us," Gist admitted. "We can't keep this up much longer…"

Josh was prepared to rejoin the fray one last time when he and Gist heard the mournful call of the regimental trumpet from Stirling's ranks.

"Pull back, men, pull back—to the Maryland lines!" Gist barked in desperation.

Josh joined the remaining colonial soldiers as they hurried back to their entrenched position on the edge of the farm fields. He took one final glimpse back at the farmhouse—which he had been so tantalizingly close to entering—receding in the distance. Before his head turned back, he saw a mass of Hessians marching into the fenced-in yard.

Another second at that farm and we would all have been butchered, Josh realized. *But how much time do we have left?*

FIFTY-NINE

After testifying at the court-martial, William Smallwood sailed to Brooklyn Heights to help the effort in any way he could, although he knew he had already missed a great deal. He found Washington standing alone atop a hill that sloped downward from Brooklyn Heights, just outside the gates of Fort Half Moon.

Smallwood saw Washington staring at something and decided to join him and find out what had claimed his attention. Smallwood squinted in the same direction into the sunlight toward the drifting gray smoke below.

At first he couldn't make out anything, but then his mouth involuntarily went agape at what he saw. The men were witnessing the last stand of the Maryland Regiment.

Washington lifted a spyglass to his right eye for a closer look. He then shared it with Smallwood.

"Astounding," he marveled, choking with emotion. *"Simply astounding."*

It was like watching waves crash onto a shore, Smallwood thought, as the miniscule group of Marylanders thrust themselves forward into the British lines. Every time they were thrown back, they redoubled their efforts and charged again, pushing the British farther and farther back toward their farmhouse fortress. Many soldiers fell and yet they still charged…again…again…and again.

"My God, what brave men I am losing today!" Washington exclaimed.

The two continued to soak in the battle below, praying for a miracle that would spare the Marylanders. After Washington was handed back the spyglass, he noticed something beyond anything he could have imagined. "My word—he's done it! Stirling has reached the heart of their command!"

The regiment had fallen back into an entrenched position on the edge of the farm, propelled back by the surging number of British soldiers. Still, the Marylanders lit up the afternoon sky with a fusillade of gunfire and held their own like no other group of soldiers that had ever fought before.

Smallwood glanced over at the bay, where the British ships still lay at anchor. Behind them, in the brief stretch of the East River that flowed between Brooklyn and Manhattan, patriot soldiers were scrambling into barks, barges, and skiffs and paddling furiously to the opposite shore.

The painstaking evacuation was far from a success. Thousands of troops remained on the long line at the Brooklyn Heights pier, waiting for their opportunity to escape.

Stirling would somehow have to hold them off even longer, Smallwood recognized, as he turned back to Washington. But the general was already gone, hastening down the hillside toward the Brooklyn Heights piers.

* * * *

Washington arrived at the Brooklyn shore to personally inspect what, if anything, could be done to speed up the exodus. For most of the early morning, he had overseen the herding of some five thousand troops at a snail's pace to the Manhattan shore. They hadn't made nearly enough progress since then.

Stirling's advance not only inspired Washington, it convinced him the evacuation could be accelerated—at least to ensure that the Marylanders' herculean efforts hadn't gone for naught. He was well aware that once the British broke free and headed north, the patriot forces would be pinned against the shoreline and massacred.

A sentry on the edge of the shoreline peered nervously into the horizon, gauging when the British armada on the other side of the island would prey upon their boats. He visualized activity on the decks of the massive British ships—sails being unfurled and anchors being weighed. After several hours of tidal flows restricting their movements, the British navy was nearly free and clear to sweep across the water and target their positions.

"General! The ships!" the sentry shouted.

Washington had already observed the enemy's progress; his head sank. "Not enough time…"

The sentry cocked his head. "Excuse me, sir?"

Washington tried to retain his composure as he explained, "The tides will shift any moment now, and the British will once again have the upper hand. Our army will be split and trapped."

Even with several large barges now arriving from Kings Landing, they would still need at least two, maybe three, hours more to get the remaining men across. This was ample time for the British ships to take advantage of the veering tide.

It was also only a matter of time before the British crossed Gowanus Road and marched toward Brooklyn Heights, easily reaching the now empty Fort Half Moon. From there, they would hop over to the water's edge, where Washington's army were sitting ducks: outmanned and outgunned.

Try as he might, he couldn't find another way to speed up the evacuation. It seemed as if he—and the Continental Army—had run out of options. He contemplated—if for a fleeting second—what the terms of a surrender might look like. Would the British be willing to spare his men?

The thought was erased from his mind when he saw something completely unexpected: Smoke was billowing on the Manhattan shoreline and flowing down the harbor and along the island's southern tip.

Washington roused his aide. "Look over there. Are cannons firing upon Manhattan?!"

The aide shook his head in confusion.

"Look at that gray cloud." Washington pointed. "And yet…I hear nothing. Not a single cannon shot. How is that possible?"

As the smoke enveloped the river and cascaded toward Brooklyn, Washington had an epiphany. "Divine providence has indeed blessed our army!" he exclaimed as tears formed in his eyes. "It is *fog*—a beautiful, thick fog! Only the Lord himself could have granted us such miraculous good fortune!"

Washington stormed back and forth across the docks, spewing out commands as he had never done before. "Make haste, men! Triple time! Summon every last ounce of strength! God has blessed us! We must take advantage of the fog!"

The boats careened into the harbor as the oarsmen paddled until their blisters opened and bled. They threw safety to the wind, squeezing more men in than the vessels could support. Rucksacks filled with possessions were tossed overboard; the soldiers retained only their serviceable weapons. The boats tipped and swayed, nearly capsizing as more and more soldiers were guided onto the boats.

Somehow, the boats departed and remained afloat as they made the crossing.

Washington watched in awe as the fog billowed throughout the hills and across the water, as if sheathing the chosen people, ensuring their safety.

"Thank you," Washington whispered, peering up at the sky.

SIXTY

Midafternoon, Tuesday, August 27, 1776
Vechte Farm, Gowanus, Brooklyn, New York

The British had fully regained their footing by the time Mordecai Gist reached the main line of Maryland troops in the fields outside the farmhouse.

Whereas they had previously allowed a telltale gap in their ranks near the break in the fence, the British soldiers now massed together like a red wall. They were unrelenting as they barraged the Maryland lines with firepower.

We embarrassed them, Gist thought, *but, like a hornet's nest shaken too many times, they're now out for vengeance.*

Gist hurried behind the front line of Maryland soldiers, who were valiantly firing back against the renewed British forces, even as they ran low on shot and their weapons jammed.

The battlefield had become a haze of pops, screams, smoke, and confusion. Whatever element of surprise the Marylanders had employed earlier was now long gone.

Gist hunkered down with the third line of Maryland troops as they primed their muskets. Stirling found him a moment later, his uniform soaked through with sweat.

"Colonel Gist!" Stirling shouted above the musket fire. "Where have they concentrated their troops?"

Gist pointed toward the break in the fence line on their left flank. "They are getting reinforcements by the minute, sir," he reported. "They've filled in any gaps in their left flank where we broke through their lines."

Stirling's voice went up an octave with sudden excitement. "Where are the reinforcements marching from?"

Crouching down low, Gist moved forward a few yards and pin-pointed a gap in the trees.

Stirling untied his necktie, tossing it on the ground. He pointed to the fabric and demonstrated as he spoke. "If this is the farmhouse…and the reinforcements are arriving from here…then we should cut them off as they leave the tree line. At the same time, we move to the rear of the farmhouse and strike while they are off-balance."

"Yes," Gist agreed. "We can slow them down with our sharpshooters long enough to allow us to break their lines from behind."

"Exactly," Stirling said, his body surging with adrenaline. "Send the westerners to the right with two dozen of our best weapons."

"Sir, we can't spare any more weapons," Gist informed him. "So many have jammed that we barely have enough to supply our front line."

Stirling didn't seem to hear Gist or, at the very least, didn't care. "Let them use whatever they can get," he said, springing to his feet while leaving his necktie behind.

Gist sprinted off to find Paddy and share the news. *When there is a plan*, he thought, *there is always hope.*

* * * *

The acorns snapped and popped underfoot as Paddy, his ten westerners, and Josh headed into an oak grove on the edge of the farm field.

Josh could hear the sounds of the battle echoing through the trees as the Maryland front line fought a war of attrition with the British forces on the perimeter of the farmhouse.

It was a virtual stalemate: The patriots had fewer men and were running low on shot, but they had forced the British to stay bottled up inside the farmhouse grounds. Yet the redcoat army was growing larger with every passing moment. Eventually, it was inevitable that the British ranks would simply overwhelm the Maryland forces and win the day.

But the Sons of Baltimore refused to go down without a fight. Paddy held up a leathery hand as the group reached a clearing in the grove. He marked the place where they would stop and set up their position, and then pointed to his right, where several figures were making their way through the undergrowth.

The newcomers' greenish uniforms, size, stature, and superior marching skills conveyed only one thing to Paddy, which he blurted out as if it were a swear word: "*Hessians.*"

Paddy didn't hesitate to aim his hunting rifle and fire off a shot. The round whistled through the forest past several oak trees before striking one of the Hessian soldiers in the neck. As he fell, the twenty-odd Hessians pivoted with their muskets in unison, their sights set on Paddy.

"Head west!" Paddy shouted as the Hessians fired off a volley.

Paddy and the colonial soldiers took off through the forest as shots exploded all around them. The musket shots thunked into the trees surrounding Josh, and he barely managed to duck behind a thick oak in time. He started to peer out with his musket when several branches overhead burst into a shower of splinters from a series of shots.

He dashed for the safety of another trunk, where three westerners were crouched down, waiting for the right moment to strike. While the enemy reloaded their weapons, ten westerners spun out from behind several trees and unleashed a cacophony of rifle fire; half of the Hessian contingent dropped to the ground.

Inspired by the display of marksmanship, Josh shifted to the side of the tree trunk to line up a shot. He was disappointed to find that the remaining Hessians had already scattered, fanning out into the grove to take defensive positions.

Josh cinched up his grip on the musket and took a tentative half step into the forest clearing. He was lost and there was no one in sight. He had a bad feeling that men from both sides—who seemed to have comparable hunting skills—were stalking each other, prey upon prey. His eyes darted from one tree to the next, desperate to spot anyone—friendly or otherwise—so he could regain his bearings.

Damn those westerners and their silent footsteps, Josh thought, sliding his bayonet onto the musket barrel. He was distracted by a flash of movement; his instincts took over and he gave chase. The blurry figure scampered behind a tree just as Josh heard gunfire echo through the forest.

Josh lunged toward the shadowy figure on the other side of the tree. Before he knew what was happening, he was yanked to the side, a hunting knife tipped within a hair of his jugular. Quivering, Josh turned just enough to see the weapon was being gripped by one of the westerners. The man rolled his eyes. "Jesus, boy, you'll get us both killed."

"You mind…ah…pointing this thing at them?" Josh asked, waving the knife away from his throat.

The westerner wiped his blade against his jacket and stared out into the forest. "These fuckers are well trained, boy," he said. "No more stupid mistakes, you hear?"

Josh acquiesced as the westerner tiptoed past the edge of the trunk; his head darted back and forth as he eyed the darkened forest clearing. A popping noise sounded too close for comfort. Josh asked the westerner, "Do you see them?" as he watched him slump into the dirt with a gaping hole in his chest.

Josh peeked out from behind the tree and spotted a Hessian soldier stepping into the clearing through a cloud of his own musket smoke. The Hessian paused to glower at Josh with slate-gray eyes. Josh let loose an uncontrollable wail from deep in his throat and charged toward the man with his bayonet. Before the Hessian could escape, Josh rammed him through his sternum, pinning him to an oak tree. The soldier struggled to escape, but Josh dug the blade in deeper until the resistance stopped and his eyes went blank.

Josh tugged the bayonet free from the man's chest, and his body slid down to the ground. Josh looked down at his hands, which had collected some of the man's blood; he dropped the weapon to his feet in disgust and said, "This wasn't even your war…" As soon as the musket clattered to the dirt, Josh realized what he had done and knelt down to retrieve it.

A hand thumped his shoulder. Josh froze in panic.

"We need to get back to the front—*now*," Paddy warned him.

Josh stood back up with his musket, wiping his bloody hands on his uniform. "I don't understand—we still have men left to fight."

"Look," Paddy said, pointing into the distance. Where there had originally been twenty Hessians with at least half of them having been killed, there were now at least three times that amount storming in their direction.

"Shit…"

Paddy seized Josh's shoulder, dragging him out of the forest as five of his fellow westerners fired behind them in an effort to slow down the Hessian advance.

The colonists scrambled over crooked tree roots, branches, rocks, and clusters of crushed acorns, driving themselves as hard as they could toward the daylight at the edge of the forest.

Upon reaching the edge of the clearing, they plunged back into the war zone, rejoining the rapidly depleting Maryland line, which had been propelled even farther away from the farmhouse fence.

"The Hessians…are right behind us…heading this way!" Josh beckoned the Marylanders, while regaining his breath. "We must…launch another attack!"

"But…they've already begun their charge," one of the soldiers informed him.

That's when it occurred to Josh that half the regiment was missing.

* * * *

287

Stirling had instructed his mini-contingent to form a wide circle around the perimeter of the farmhouse. Occasionally, a redcoat on the outer edge of the farmhouse detected them and opened fire, but their musket balls fell several yards short. The group skidded to a halt at the lower corner of the farm's fence, on the opposite side of where the Maryland lines were engaged in a pitched battle.

In spite of his bandaged injuries, Ben was able to keep up with the others even though he was unable to even hold a weapon. He made out the forms of Hessians soldiers pouring into the grounds from the trees on the far side, but the rear corner was only lightly guarded.

"Men, rally right here," Stirling shouted, raising his sword. "On my order, move forward with me!"

Stirling gave the signal, and the men followed him into battle. He positioned himself next to Gist, while the men lined up on both sides, forming a lengthy column of bedraggled, unyielding soldiers.

"On my mark, march!" Stirling shouted, decisively anchoring his sword downward. With every ounce of their remaining energy, the colonials rolled forward while screaming, "Revolution!"

The British showered them with musket shots, but they remained vigilant and continued to press forward while holding their own fire until they were within better range. Gist fought right alongside them, his sword drawn and his shouts nearly as ear-piercing as those of the younger men.

As their feet moved from dry farm soil to grass near the house, the British shots started to take their toll. A Marylander on Gist's left spun backward as a musket ball sliced through his shoulder; another colonial was struck in the eye; and another was felled by a bullet in the hip.

Stirling knew he could wait no longer: He screamed the order to fire, and the remaining Marylanders let loose a massive volley against the British.

"Prepare for a second volley!" Gist called as gun smoke filtered throughout the farm. His thinking that they could reload faster than the British retaliation was misplaced; the shots sailed toward them at a furious pace.

But still the men continued forward, leaving their wounded, dying, and dead behind. There was no time to mourn or even think about their losses. This was a fight to the finish.

"Men—move forward with me!" Stirling squawked. "We've got them backing up!"

Gist knew that Stirling had no idea whether the British were backing up or if their men were prancing toward their doom. Either way, he believed in him and their cause, even if it meant fighting to his remaining breath. If he were to go down here and now, it would be a noble death for his country.

Yard by yard, the patriots scratched closer to the British lines—even as the bombardment thinned their numbers. They were within a yard of the fence line when Stirling ordered the men to halt but continue firing, no matter what. He motioned for Gist to join him behind the ranks.

When Gist reached the general, Stirling's face was twisted in concentration. Gist was about to speak, but Stirling overlapped him while raising his fist toward the Brooklyn Heights fortress in the far distance, where faint signal torches illuminated the sky.

"The evacuation is not yet complete," Stirling said. "But I have just enough men standing for one last charge. Take the rest of your men and head to Brooklyn Heights, where you can still escape. Your men have fought too long and too hard to die here."

"Absolutely not, sir," Gist resisted. "If you charge, we all charge with you."

"That's an order, Colonel," Stirling commanded. He reached into his interior jacket pocket and handed Gist an envelope sealed with wax. "If I do not return, give this to my family," he requested. "Please."

Gist tucked the envelope safely into his own jacket pocket. They both had so much to say to each other, but neither leader had ever been one for small talk—even as the end neared.

"Good luck. It's been an honor, sir," Gist mustered, shaking Stirling's hand and rounding up his men to depart.

Stirling said nothing as his eyes burned with tears.

* * * *

Stirling's half of the remaining Maryland men stood a few yards back from the fence. "Gentlemen," he called to them, "on my order, we charge the fence."

He held his sword aloft, its fine steel glinting in the afternoon sunlight. He took a deep breath and exhaled. "*Charge!*"

The men sprinted toward their objective, their bayonets surging ahead of them. The instant they reached the fence line, the Maryland men slashed into the redcoats on the perimeter. Stirling and four of his men cleared the fence in a furious leap; on the other side, they hacked and stabbed their way through the herd of soldiers.

His blade plowed desperately into a sea of red uniforms, but it was no use: There were simply too many of them. They surrounded and overtook Stirling and his men, clubbing them with their musket butts until they were driven to their knees.

Stirling looked up into the sky and saw the horde of redcoats around him. He slashed outward with his sword, but his efforts were futile. He felt their hands on his shoulders, gripping him by the back of the neck and wrenching him onto his feet.

A hush fell over the battle scene: It was over.

Stirling felt a strange presence nearby, though he couldn't explain it. He had taken quite a beating and figured his senses were no longer to be trusted.

Then he heard an erudite English voice that had an unusually chipper tone: "Ah—*Lord* Stirling, I presume?"

He deduced the identity of the speaker, even though he was still not visible.

The sea of soldiers parted, making room for General Charles Cornwallis to strut toward his newest prize.

"Allow me to introduce myself, *Lord*, I am—"

Stirling loathed the mocking emphasis on the word "Lord." He would rather be bayoneted that moment than suffer humiliation at the hands of this arrogant bastard. "I know who you are," Stirling spat.

"Good." Cornwallis grinned, pacing in front of him with hands behind his back. "Then we may skip the introductions and proceed right to our immediate business: It is with great pleasure that I hereby accept your surrender, *Lord* Stirling."

He held his hands out for Stirling's sword—the gentleman's sign of the end of battle.

Stirling slung his shoulder downward, breaking the grip of one of his captors. He slammed the base of his sword into the groin of another soldier. He jerked free and catapulted himself forward. A dozen redcoats pointed their muskets at his nose, and he froze in position.

"Hold your fire!" Cornwallis exclaimed, waving his handkerchief in the air.

Stirling strode past Cornwallis and approached von Heister, the wizened old Hessian commander. He placed his sword in the Hessian's hand. "I hereby surrender," he said to the surprised German.

Von Heister was speechless. He turned to Cornwallis for direction on how to handle the awkwardness of the enemy's action, but the general didn't pay him any mind. He flicked his hand toward his aide, who stepped forward and clamped iron manacles onto Stirling's wrists.

As they shoved him toward the stone farmhouse, Stirling turned his head back one last time to Gowanus Road and the New York Harbor beyond. He made one final earnest prayer that he had fulfilled his commitment to General Washington.

SIXTY-ONE

Late afternoon, Tuesday, August 27, 1776
Gowanus Road, Brooklyn, New York

Gist caught a glimpse of Stirling plunging headlong into the British lines and hopping the fence. He turned around and saw the redcoat lines stirring and beginning to break free of the fence line. He gnashed his teeth together and uttered, "Curse them all."

He had only a handful of men left at his side. In a few moments the British soldiers would be atop their position.

Gist, determined to follow through on Stirling's mission, made a split-second decision as his sword ascended. "Marylanders! Reunite with the main force!"

There weren't many of the Maryland lines left who were healthy enough to follow him back, but those who could retrieved their muskets and sprinted behind him, the British hot in pursuit.

Another round of musket shots blasted around him. Gist jerked his head around to see that two of his Maryland men had been struck down, their heads flung backward from the impact of the musket balls into their backs.

He urged the remaining men forward until they reached the Maryland lines. They dropped to their knees behind the front line of soldiers. Gist, well aware that he had left a trail of fallen patriot soldiers behind him, gathered his wits. He was the commander now and was entrusted with the responsibility of leading as many men as possible back to safety through a gauntlet of British fire.

He ordered the men to send one last volley against the redcoats. After they fired, he commanded them to head back toward Gowanus Road. "Make haste and don't look back!" he shouted. "And don't stop until you reach the mill ponds!"

The men hugged their muskets and leapt to their feet, running toward the roadside.

As they fled, Gist glanced over at Paddy and his small group of weathered western Marylanders. They remained crouched down with their rifles, intent on picking off British soldiers one by one.

He caught Paddy's eye and said, "It's time for you and your friends to go. That's an order, soldier."

Frowning over his rifle barrel, Paddy stubbornly fired off a shot into the fence line. "Sir, that's one order I can't follow."

Gist swung his arm in desperation. "If you don't go right now, you will all die!"

Paddy came within inches of Gist's face before he roughly shoved his loaded hunting rifle into his arms. "Take this," he offered. "It will help get you and your men back home safely. As for us, we came here under our own free will, and we'll leave under it, too."

The westerner drew his hatchet in one hand and his long hunting knife in the other. Without looking at Gist he said, "When we charge, run as fast as you can toward the road. We'll hold them off as long as we can."

All of the westerners slung their long rifles over their shoulders and drew their blades. Paddy shouted out a command and they sprang into action, rushing at breakneck speed toward the fence line while hollering war cries and hitting the British with everything they had.

Gist did a double take at what he was witnessing: The British soldiers' line was so shaken by the animalistic attack that several of the men dropped their weapons in terror and fled toward the farmhouse.

Thank God for our wild men, Gist thought. *They've bought us the time we need to survive.*

* * * *

Gowanus Road was surprisingly still as the surviving Marylanders regrouped.

"We caught 'em by surprise…that's for certain," Ben said, coughing, as he staggered forward while cradling his injured shoulder.

Josh wrapped his arm around his friend's good shoulder for support. "Lean on me—and stop talking."

"When have I ever done that?" Ben remarked.

The pair continued to trudge down the road with nearly twenty other survivors. Gist brought up the rear, a hunting rifle cocked in his arm. It was an eerie sensation, Josh felt, to be marching away from the heart of the battle rather than into it. But as he looked at the faces and bloody injuries of the men around him, he could see they had no fight left in them.

After this unending day of charging and retreating, torturous gunfights and hand-to-hand combat, Josh wondered how any of them were able to continue onward. The heat and humidity were becoming unbearable. Josh felt his heavy uniform begin to chafe, and his feet throbbed in his boots.

Josh tried not to consider what might happen if the British were to show up now: Many of his fellow soldiers would probably raise their arms and surrender without a fight. They had to keep going at all costs. He longed to get home. His father was gone, and Tessa was becoming a faded memory—but there was his mother and Lydia, both of whom he would give anything to see again.

They were only yards away from the mill pond where the bulk of the regiment had retreated earlier.

Several Marylanders reached the pond and stepped in up to their knees, eager to escape.

Josh and Ben were lured to the edge of the stagnant brown water. Josh was about to follow the others when Gist's voice boomed, "Fall back, men! Do not get into the water!"

Josh knocked Ben to the ground and instinctively positioned himself on top of his friend's bad shoulder. He swung his musket up in the air.

But it was too late for the soldiers immersed in the water. Four redcoats perched on the opposite bank had a clear angle at them. The redcoats fired indiscriminately. Musket balls riddled the bodies of a few of the men right away, their bodies drifting down into the murky water.

Others tossed their weapons aside and tried to paddle toward the shore for their lives. The redcoats easily picked them off one at a time.

Josh shoved a round into his musket's muzzle, tamping it down with the ramrod. Despite having done this hundreds of times since the morning's first light, his hands trembled and his vision was dizzy.

He lifted the musket to his eye, aimed for one of the four soldiers on the other bank, and squeezed the trigger. The weapon clanked, producing nothing whatsoever.

Jammed.

Cursing, Josh tossed the musket aside.

Ben looked up at Josh. "Leave me here…. Make a run for those trees."

A shot soared just over Josh's head and plunked into the pond.

"Please…go!" Ben begged him.

Ignoring his friend, Josh reached for the pistol he carried around his waist. He loaded it and prepared to fire. He squeezed off a shot, which struck the cheek of one of the snipers. The other three steered away from the bank toward the cover of trees.

"I'm not going anywhere," Josh declared. He reached for his powder horn to refill the pistol. He shook it into the muzzle, but only a fine dust emerged. It was empty—drained from the day of incessant fighting.

Throwing the horn aside in frustration, he peered around and saw only five remaining Marylanders—plus Gist, who was sheltered within a grove of trees.

Gist caught Josh's eye as he held up the hunting rifle. Josh stared at the weapon and knew right away who had bequeathed it to the officer.

"Bolton—you're the only one in position to get them," Gist shouted. "On the count of three, I'm going to throw this to you! You'll need to rush over and grab it. One…two…three!"

Gist heaved the rifle as far as he could. It spun in the air and landed on its stock with a thud, ten feet short of Josh.

"Shit," Josh cursed. There was no way to snag the rifle without leaving his wounded friend alone in the mud, directly in the redcoats' line of fire. But he also recognized there was no way to escape across the mill pond without putting down three soldiers.

"I have to go get the rifle," he hissed in his friend's ear. "Don't move a muscle—you'll just make yourself a bigger target."

"Don't be so dramatic—just go already," Ben said, flattening his body into the mud.

Josh glanced at the redcoats on the other shore. They were nearly done reloading and would have an easy shot on the two of them if he hesitated any further.

Josh lifted himself up and bolted toward the rifle. He snatched it up before the redcoats could react.

As he ran back, one of the redcoats fired on Ben. He flinched as the musket ball landed inches from his leg.

"Hold on, Ben—I'm coming!"

Another shot exploded into the mud—this time near Ben's arm. Josh knew they weren't going to miss a third time. He had to act now.

Josh managed to reach Ben's prone body just as one of the redcoats was about to fire off another shot. In one deft motion, he raised the rifle to his eye, sized up the soldier, and squeezed the trigger. The rifle recoiled in his shoulder; for a moment he worried that his shot would be off course. A split second later he watched the soldier clutch his chest in a torrent of blood and fall over.

That was the opening Gist and his men needed. They charged from behind the trees, their muskets firing across the pond. One British soldier toppled over and another was winged in the shoulder. He and the other remaining redcoat scampered back toward their lines.

Josh leaned over Ben and wiped the sweat off his forehead. "Someone up there must be looking out for us," Ben wisecracked, holding his shoulder in pain.

A blanket of fog appeared over the pond. Gist extended his sword toward the other end and ordered, "We only have a few moments to take advantage of this cover—let's go now!"

Josh assisted Ben to his feet. They stumbled into the shallow water through the haze. Josh thought, *Almost there. We can do this.*

SIXTY-TWO

Late afternoon, Tuesday, August 27, 1776
Brooklyn Heights, New York

All around Washington, patriot soldiers poured into the oncoming boats. This seemingly God-given fog was their best—and perhaps only—chance to make it across to Manhattan.

After this grueling all-day evacuation, Washington watched as the final two boatloads sailed across the river toward safety and an aide was given the go-ahead to extinguish the flame atop Fort Half Moon.

"General Washington—that's the last of them," another aide informed him. "All the men are out. Shouldn't we leave as well?"

Washington looked forlornly at the hilltop above him as it disappeared behind the fog.

Even though he knew it was foolish, he still clung to the hope that at least some of Stirling's regiment would appear at the docks.

The Marylanders had already done the impossible: They had held back the bulk of the British army long enough to allow the Continental Army to escape and continue the fight for independence.

The British would find Brooklyn abandoned.

"No," Washington replied. "Not yet. We can't leave without the men of the Maryland Regiment."

The aide turned to the general. "But sir, forgive me.... They are already gone. You saw it for yourself. There is no way anyone could have survived that charge on the British center."

Washington held firm. "We will wait."

As the fog swirled around him, Washington listened intently for the telltale sounds of soldiers approaching. But everything remained silent, except for the cry of the gulls and the breaking of the waves on the shore.

His aide spoke up again as the last fishing boat arrived at the dock. "General, *please*," he pleaded. "We must go now!"

Washington hung his head in defeat. Resigned, he slumped toward the boat as it bobbed in the water. He and the aide stepped aboard as a sailor tossed off the docking lines.

As the boat pushed off from the dock and drifted into the current, Washington's eye caught something. Just a mirage, he thought at first. But then he saw them...ghostly apparitions fading out of the blowing wisps of fog.

"Wait!" he exclaimed, rising in the boat.

First one...then two...then four...then *eight* staggering figures materialized out of the fog.

The boat captain and every available hand feverishly paddled back to shore. When they were within shallow distance, Washington leapt from the bow and into the water, racing toward the men.

They were a sight to behold: smeared in mud and soaking wet, their uniforms torn and almost falling off. Many were badly bruised and bleeding.

Somehow Washington recognized one man from among the withered group: *Gist*.

"General Washington, sir," he croaked with a feeble salute. "The Maryland Regiment, reporting for duty."

With that, Gist reached into his jacket and pulled out the soiled and tattered Maryland regimental flag. He laid it gently in Washington's hands.

Washington's eyes became transfixed on the flag. "Colonel...how..." he somehow managed to say as his throat became filled with emotion. Then, composing himself, he took Gist's hand. "A grateful nation thanks you and your men for your honorable and faithful service. It is my privilege to serve with you."

He wrapped his powerful arm around an exhausted Gist and helped him and the other soldiers into the boat.

* * * *

Josh rested his head against his shoulder as the boat sailed deeper into the fog bank. He closed his eyes and allowed the salt spray of the river to cool his face.

He stared at the eight men and General Washington around him. They had been the only Marylanders able to escape after Stirling's charge. It was only at Gist's insistence that they'd made it out alive.

Now Gist, whose face was streaked with mud, leaned heavily, completely spent, against the side of the boat, lost in thought. Ben cradled his arm in a makeshift sling and splashed water onto his face. The other five men fixated on the gray nothingness, seemingly without any life left in them.

Josh opened the leather satchel at his waist and felt around for his father's brass seal. He wrapped his fist around it and squeezed tightly as he closed his battle-worn eyes.

Soon the clanging of halyards was heard, and then, through the fog, the hectic shouting of men. Finally, the imposing Manhattan buildings came into view as the boat clattered to a halt at the Battery docks and soldiers scrambled to secure its mooring.

Washington, the first to stand, clutched the Maryland Regiment's flag. "Let us go now, patriots," he stated with a renewed swell of pride. "We have a war to win."

AUTHOR'S NOTE

Saving Washington is a fictional novel, based on the scant historic facts surrounding the bravery of the Maryland 400 at the Battle of Brooklyn on August 27, 1776. Until recently, there was little written about the actual event that took place, other than Thomas Field's "Battle of Long Island" written in 1869. My intention was to create a novel that not only brought the event to life in a vivid way, but also explored why teenagers would enlist and sacrifice themselves for the ideal of freedom. I chose to write the novel in a cinematic and contemporary style, with historical markers that avid history readers would appreciate, as well as a story line and dialogue that young adults could relate to and take pride in.

While Josh and his parents, Ben and his mother, Tessa and Paddy were fictional characters, the rest of the characters in the book were real people. The locations are real. The battle scenes are real. The divine fog was real.

I apologize for taking some liberty in condensing, simplifying, and resequencing events that occurred over the course of a number of days, down to thirty-six hours, in an effort to accelerate the pace of the story. I also adapted some of the actual events (e.g. Stirling's presence at Four Chimneys, when the fog occurred, etc.) to help explain why decisions were made and to draw out the thin line between escape and disaster. In some cases, I used modern location names (Federal Hill) to describe a location.

ACKNOWLEDGMENTS

There are a host of people who have helped me craft and bring the incredible story of the brave men from Baltimore to life.

First and foremost, I have to thank Matt Hansen, Gary Krebs, and Mike Perry, who helped me find the right words and the proper historical context. Most importantly, helped me recreate the emotion of the time that drove naïve teenagers to become hardened patriots. You were tireless and exceptional.

Thanks to my publishers, Maddie Sturgeon and Michael Wilson of Permuted Press/Post Hill Press for their trust and support.

To Meryl Moss for her creative promotional efforts and sense of the market.

To Gregg Fienberg of HBO, for his ongoing advice and belief in "America's 400 Spartans" as a story that needed to be told at this moment in history.

To my agent, John Willig, who fell in love with the story when I first proposed it to him and never gave up until we had it right. John, I can't thank you enough. It also helped a bit that your sons are named Josh and Ben!

Lastly, to Cindy for her continual support and incessant encouragement every day.